CRAIG W. FISHER

Baker Street Irregular

GODWINSON
PRESS

First published by Godwinson Press 2022

First edition

ISBN: 978-1-7397807-0-8

This book was professionally typeset on Reedsy.
Find out more at reedsy.com

Contents

The Baker Street Irregulars

Originating as a fictional gang in Arthur Conan Doyle's *Sherlock Holmes* novels. It was one of many nicknames given to the World War Two British spy networks of the Special Operations Executive due to their unconventional tactics and location of their main headquarters on Baker Street in Central London.

Introduction

Thank you for reading my debut novel. It was started as a distraction from world events during the early stages of the Covid-19 pandemic. I hope you enjoy the story and meeting the characters.

Most acronyms, military terms, slang and foreign phrases used are either further explored in the story or are self-explanatory, but I have added a glossary to the back of the novel for extra convenience. I have occasionally opted to use some American-English words instead of their more usual English counterparts but have retained standard English spelling throughout. Also, I have used *whiskey* when American or Irish, and w*hisky* for Scottish.

I have included information in the historical notes at the end that contains some spoilers, so you should avoid it until after finishing the story. Please feel free to ignore it if you don't wish to know more about the real-life places and people who inspired some of the novel's characters and events.

To contact me or join the email mailing list for news about special offers and other releases, please see my website at **CraigWFisher.com** or follow me on Twitter @craigwfisher.

Adult Content

This publication contains various subject matter and language that may disturb and is unsuitable for young readers or those who may be easily offended.

Due to the historical setting and genre, the story includes, but is not limited to, misogyny, racism, graphic violence and death, as well as briefly addressing issues such as sex, torture, suicide, rape, and the Holocaust.

This novel is a work of fiction, inspired partially by actual events. All offensive opinions are imagined, and outdated language is intentional but used fictitiously in the historical setting.

In memory of the 91 male and 13 female members of the Special Operations Executive (F Section) who gave their lives for France's freedom.

* * *

This is no war of chieftains or of princes, of dynasties or national ambition; it is a war of peoples and of causes. There are vast numbers, not only in this island but in every land, who will render faithful service in this war but whose names will never be known, whose deeds will never be recorded. This is a war of the Unknown Warriors; but let all strive without failing in faith or in duty, and the dark curse of Hitler will be lifted from our age.

Winston Churchill - BBC Broadcast, London - 14th July 1940

Occupied Berlin 1947

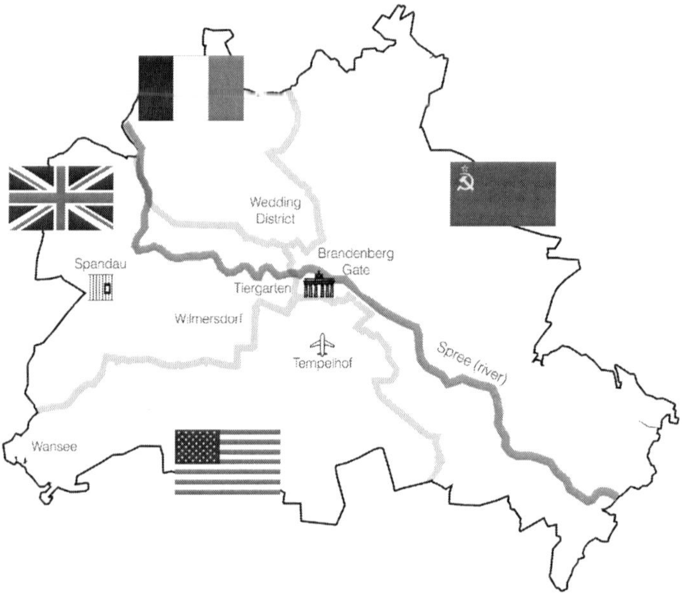

1

Out of the Frying Pan

Berlin, Early Hours of 27th February 1947

One last check of his watch and a reassuring pat on the knife he kept in his jacket pocket, and he disappeared into the all-consuming darkness of the Berlin night. He had no way of knowing who had made the connections yet.

Bill knew he wouldn't last long alone. He needed help, and he needed information. Above all else, he needed to get the investigation back on track and prove his innocence. But unfortunately, this would have to wait. He had a more pressing issue right now; he needed somewhere safe to get his thoughts together and work out his best course of action. It was only a matter of time before *they* came to the conclusion that it was him who had killed Irene.

He headed towards the dim light at the end of the street and the unmistakable odour of stale beer and tobacco smoke.

Here he could stop and gather his thoughts. Pausing to lean on the wall outside, he pulled his pipe from his overcoat and absent-mindedly stuffed it full. He didn't want to enter the bar and add witnesses to the growing list of evidence against him.

Three hours ago, he was a decorated war hero and trusted servant of His Majesty's government in good standing. Now, even he wasn't sure. Fumbling a match from the little silver vesta case, he lit the bowl and sucked hard to get the embers going. He'd packed it too tight.

Strictly speaking, the bars were not meant to be open this late. However, apart from a few of the rougher areas of the Russian sector where no one, apart from the incredibly brave or terminally stupid, dared to venture, there were a few places that tended to stay open later than others. That was a courtesy of the Berlin Police and their penchant for cigarettes, good bourbon and brown envelopes stuffed with US dollars.

He had to assume they would soon have plenty of evidence in their hands. Eyewitnesses would place him at the murder scene. Perhaps he even left some clothing behind. He couldn't recall for sure. The inexplicably absent concierge certainly knew he was a frequent visitor. What would they think? They knew his father was German, of course. No doubt they also had everyone's dirty secrets in a big manila file.

He used his finger to carefully tamp down the tobacco and relit. It was certainly feasible that a man with Bill's background might be persuaded to flip. But to murder a fellow agent?

He sipped thoughtfully and paused to watch the smoke dance in the dull glow spilling out from the beer hall. What should he do now? It's not like he would ever switch sides.

Even a British bullet would be better than a Soviet jackboot.

How could he find out who Irene's real killer was? Whoever it was had caught her by surprise. Was it someone she knew? A double agent? Was the bullet meant for him? Bill started to run the suspects through his throbbing mind. The questions seemed endless.

"Do you have a light?" A confident, almost cocky, young kid with a dirty cap had appeared in front of him.

"Here," Bill replied in perfect German and passed him a battered old matchbox he kept in his other pocket. Even this long after the war, a silver vesta case might be a nice trinket that would earn him a punch in the mouth, and Bill decided there had been quite enough killing for one day.

"Thanks, mister."

He was all of about eighteen. Bill supposed from his accent he was a Berliner. Most of the Germans here these days were from elsewhere, either by luck or circumstance. In 1945 the Berliners had been a dying breed. Bill chuckled to himself at the sick joke.

Almost two years on, the city still showed all the scars of war. The rubble had been mostly cleared, and the theatres, pubs and bars were reopening where possible, but the numerous empty yawning gaps betrayed the area's recent history. Even the brothels had started popping up again, some attracting even the most prestigious of foreign visitors.

Dirty cap wandered off down the street with the sort of swagger that gave Bill the impression he was probably in a uniform not long ago. In the war's final days, the Germans had sent anybody who still had use of some limbs to die at the altar of National Socialism. Most were either baby-faced Hitler youth or the so-called *Volkssturm*, which from what Bill understood, consisted mainly of men with little desire or ability to fight, and had even fewer teeth. The actual fighting force of the so-called Fatherland were mostly dead or captured, which, if they happened to be caught by the Ivans, was much the same thing.

The truth was that, despite his family connection, Bill had never felt anything that could be mistaken for patriotism for Germany. On the contrary, it was a country that had first intrigued him and later surprised him, but now he felt nothing but disgust.

The war had taken Bill all over Europe. He had seen atrocities committed by all sides, including his own. He tried to tell himself that it was simply war. He was no politician or psychologist, but he had seen that, in some men, the war had removed all pretence of any civilisation they had left. All that was left was the beast we all were deep down in some primaeval self.

Most men, he concluded, though, were good. They kept their moral standards and their love for their fellow man. He had seen little of that in Germany. Germany had left him angry. It appeared to Bill that the past fifteen years had sucked all the good from the place, leaving nothing but a shrivelled shell, almost devoid of humanity, with few exceptions. Perhaps all the moral men had died amongst the others?

The Eastern Front, in particular, hadn't chosen prudently who would starve or freeze to death. For all the good the Russians had done in demolishing the German army, they had survived and brought their own brand of terror to the streets.

He remembered a quote from his past life: *Hell is empty, and all the devils are here.*

Who had said it? Bill couldn't remember. Shakespeare? Byron? It didn't matter anymore. Not much did. Bill couldn't imagine many poets or the great bard himself rushing into places like the Bergen-Belsen concentration camp, where even the angels had neglected to tread. Again, Bill sniggered to himself at his half-joke. He had once been told he had gallows humour. Whatever it was, it was all he knew now.

Through the glass, Bill could see men sitting and playing cards, others at the bar. Most of them out this late would be military men on their downtime or the better-off locals. Many of the more upwardly mobile Berliners were black marketeers. Everyone in Berlin would look the other way for a price.

There was no strict curfew here in the Berlin-Wedding district, and in any case, the French patrols didn't care to get too involved in enforcing closing times. They would much rather stop in for a quick nip of schnapps during their shift than close the places down early. As a result, some of the grubbier places a little out of town stayed open most of the night.

Bill relit his pipe. The stale ash taste gave way again to the thick, nutty smoke. He was glad he had kept his pipe pouch, even if the tobacco on the floor at the scene would lead them back to him, assuming the bullet lodged in her skull didn't.

Most of the contacts he had in the city smoked cigarettes. Bill could never stand the taste of cigarettes, and he avoided them wherever possible. The stuff they seemed to smoke in Germany made Bill imagine it could be ground-up horse shit and bus tickets. It probably was.

Thankfully, Berlin was awash with American cigarettes

and those from other allied nations, which were somewhat more tolerable. The only thing worse than the cheap German smokes were the Russian ones.

He thought again about the twisted anguish and blood over Irene's otherwise perfect, beautiful face and the pain he felt in his heart.

He slipped his pipe back into his pocket and looked up to spot a wide-eyed kid in a dirty cap quickly disappearing around the corner.

Then he heard the unmistakable sound of approaching footsteps.

2

Into the Fire

Somewhere Near Paris, Occupied France, 9th June 1944

Green light. Time to jump.

Before he knew it, Bill was out and away. He always hated a night jump. He had never trusted the Air Force to know what the hell they were doing. The cold blast of air hit him, and he waited for the inevitable jolt as his chute deployed fully. He would never get used to the alien feeling of abandoning a perfectly good aircraft. But, at least this time, unlike other times before, they were travelling light. The bulk of the drop was money, weapons, radio sets and ammunition, all neatly packed to fall of their own accord. Being a low-level drop in very little wind, it should fall roughly where they were heading. That was the theory, at least.

They were to meet the French Resistance on the ground. If the worst happened, they had enough food to get through a few nights to stash the goodies in the undergrowth and arrange contact. Bill hoped it didn't come to that. He certainly didn't relish the thought of even one damp night in a spiky French hedgerow. At least he had plenty to keep him occupied.

Contrary to training and all good survival planning, he had dedicated an entire pocket of his smock to two pounds of his favourite St. Bruno Flake tobacco and five chocolate bars he'd swiped during their last supper. The last time he was in Northern France, there was a noticeable shortage of decent tobacco, and he wouldn't make the same mistake twice. There was also no better currency when trying to win the favour of a difficult local than fine tobacco and decent chocolate.

The gentle descent allowed him to take a good look at where he might land. The Liberator's dull hum faded into the distance somewhere, but with no moonlight, he couldn't make it out anymore. Without visible reference points, he couldn't tell how fast he was falling, and before he knew it, the ground was racing up fast. Dangling from the deployed canopy like the last chicken in a butcher's window, he braced himself and was pleasantly surprised by the soft landing.

He quickly gathered his chute, removed his helmet, and unslung his Thompson. That had been a bitter argument at the stores. New policy dictated that they were to take Stens, but Bill had almost come to blows with the jobsworth quartermaster when he had refused his. There was no way he was taking a glorified plumbing pipe, with a spring weaker than a wristwatch winding, into France. It was well known the Sten could be a formidable weapon with a high rate of fire, but it was also cheap to manufacture and seemed to jam at the worst possible moments. Many an agent had been killed or captured when their Sten jammed.

Bill preferred to put his trust in the American-made Thompson. Its chunky .45 round was also far more likely to cause the enemy to have a very bad day than the 9mm of the Sten. Also, if it came down to it, Bill figured he could probably kill a man by throwing it at him, it weighed so much. They may have to leave them at the drop zone anyway, as travelling around with loaded sub-machine guns while masquerading as locals wasn't advisable in the heavily occupied region of Paris only a few days after D-Day.

Back in the early days, of course, they were lucky to be armed with much more than a sharpened pencil. In '41, the idea was purely infiltration. To blend in and observe. All transmissions were by dead drop and messages sent through to a wireless, as the radio operators were referred to. Now, with the invasion coming, they were trying to get the resistance better armed and had brought their own radio set. With the increased risk of a confrontation, the agents were also much better equipped to deal with the enemy.

He heard the others land almost silently, followed by the thudding sounds of the heavy canvas supply drop bags. Predictably, there was no sign of their French counterparts. Great, thought Bill. Now they would be dragging the heavy loads on their own. There were no worse timekeepers than the French.

Without a word, Jack and Lena came jogging out of the dark and squatted, still panting, next to him.

"We ditch the chutes, helmets and smocks in this hedgerow for now and start to gather up the supply bags," Bill instructed. "Go."

With no further discussion, they were up and moving. No

sooner had they stashed their parachute gear, they were back out in the dew-soaked grass hunting out the bags. It was like looking for a piece of hay in a massive stack of needles. They carried torches but didn't dare use them in such an occupied area. The Germans could be patrolling the lanes nearby and had no doubt heard the US Army Air Force B-24 that had dropped them. The RAF had arranged to bomb a nearby empty woodland to cover their sortie, and hopefully, the Germans would assume it was just a stray bomber from their mission.

The first bags came into view. They had been packed to allow one man to move the bag short distances, so Bill swung two up onto his shoulders and walked the entire one hundred yards briskly back to the hedgerow. On his second run out, he heard the distinct *crump, crump, crump* of the nearby bombing run. In the dull flashes that lit the sky, he spotted the other bags and made a mental note of their locations. Every bag seemed heavier than the last.

An hour later, they had all the bags together and well camouflaged. The cold sweat started to cause them chills, so they put their windproof smocks back on. They would also provide at least some concealment if they had to wait out the following day. Next, they had to ascertain their location. If the worst had happened, they, not the French, were at the wrong rendezvous point. It was decision time. Venture out from the safety of their warm nest, or sit tight until the following night? Bill checked his wristwatch. There were still two hours until first light.

"I'll head out towards that lane and try to work out where we are," he said. "You two sit tight. If anything happens or I'm not back by twenty hundred hours tomorrow, proceed with plan B."

Bill knew no further discussion was necessary. He had known his colleagues long enough. Bill was a far better soldier than he was a spy. He had been constantly reprimanded over how long he took to decode messages and was crap with a radio, but one thing he could do was blend into any environment. His French and German were flawless, and his ability to fight and shoot quickly became legendary back at headquarters.

Bill darted across the field, using the hedgerow and trees as cover to hide his silhouette. He ducked under a low-hanging branch and vaulted a small wooden gate. He even surprised himself with his agility. Maybe he was wasted in the army, and his true calling was as a gymnast. Finally, he was at the lane. He peered into the gloom in both directions and listened carefully.

Crossing the lane and heading right, he moved as quietly as possible, avoiding twigs and branches and trying to stick to the dirty edges of the track. Bending down, he noticed a handful of cigarette ends and some burnt matches. Locals? Unlikely. Probably a patrol. The trail seemed cold, but he was no Navajo tracker.

Further down the lane, he could see a farmhouse and some kind of orchard. Now he was getting somewhere. All he needed was a couple more points of interest to pinpoint where he was. He hopped the farmhouse gate and moved like a shadow into the log store lean-to on the side of the house.

Squinting into the darkness toward the fruit trees, he spotted a sight that stopped his heart. A half-concealed German 88 mm flak gun. He waited but couldn't see any movement. How had the crew of this monstrous weapon not heard or seen their aircraft? If they had, Bill figured, at the height they came in at, one well-aimed round could have left them in a crumpled wreck in that field.

He risked a look into the window at the rear of the farmhouse and saw three German soldiers asleep in chairs, with numerous bottles and detritus at their feet. In the dim glow from a lamp, he could see they were breathing but couldn't make out their uniforms.

He moved through the trees towards the gun and waited. No movement. He dropped onto his front and crawled the last few yards. Ignoring the shell boxes, he grabbed a few bits of paperwork from an empty ammo box, then changed his mind and replaced it when he saw five German 'potato masher' grenades neatly stood in a row. He checked they had their primers and dropped them into the ammo box with the papers, then made good his escape back to the lane.

He pushed through the hedgerow, this time preferring to travel on the field side of the foliage. He stopped, pulled his smock over his head, and checked his linen map with his torch. Then, orienting it with his little button compass, he sought out the little farmhouse and the lane past the orchard in the red glow.

He had a few of these linen maps, one showing the drop zone and surrounding area, another overview of the area around Paris, and the final one of the city centre itself.

"There!" He had spotted it. Even the gun emplacement was annotated with a question mark. The intelligence was good, but the sodding Air Force had done it again! They were a clear mile from the proper drop zone.

"Useless bastards," Bill muttered, clicking off his torch.

He hoped the French would stick to the plan and wait until

the following evening before moving off.

After dropping the ammo box with Jack, Bill and Lena had checked their weapons and begun working their way cross-country towards the drop zone rendezvous. The ground was wet but reasonably firm underfoot. They covered the mile carefully in just under half an hour. Bill checked on Lena, who was on her first proper operation, to ensure nerves weren't getting the better of her.

"How are you holding up?"

"Fine, do you think the French will have waited?" replied Lena, focussed only on the task at hand.

"They'd better had."

* * *

He had to be sure the French hadn't been captured, and it wasn't an ambush they were about to stroll into. After circling the area and doubling back, Bill spotted the Resistance fighters waiting near the field's corner. He removed the red filter from his torch and, with a short double flash, received a reply, and they made their way to the huddled group.

After the customary nervous exchange of passwords and confirmations of identity, they all shook hands.

"We will make acquaintance properly at home, yes?" said the group's leader in clearly-strained English. He was a handsome man, stout and tall, and about the same height and build as Jack, with a neat moustache. Stick him in a brown suit with brogues, and he would have looked like the spivs Bill had often seen near the market in Spitalfields. It was one of the few places where you could still get most things, for a price, of course. Like the rest of them, including Bill, he was dressed in circa 1930 French peasant couture, with a moth-eaten jacket and old, poorly repaired boots.

It was important to blend in, and SOE even had a department that produced European-weave fabrics and artificially aged them. The Gestapo had taken to inspecting the fabrics of those arrested to check for British fabrics. By 1944, everything was flawless, from the false ID papers to the ration coupons. They could have convincingly passed off the king himself as a French peasant girl.

"Please, my friend, we can converse in French." Bill wanted everything to be as clear as possible, thus avoiding any mistakes in the plan.

"Very well, comrade." Bill couldn't help but note the French word *camarade* here. It could be used to mean friend, but as with much of the Resistance, they were probably communists or at least left-wing socialists too. Bill had never cared for politics. He didn't care who was in charge, as long as he was left alone. He drew the line, however, when governments decide they want to round up an entire race of people and enslave them, or worse. The way Bill saw it, if the government's boot is on your throat, it doesn't matter if it is the left or the right one. "We will split here," the leader said. "You take Andre with you in the truck. The rest of us will return to town on the bicycles."

"Sounds like a good plan. Are you certain the truck won't draw too much attention?" inquired Bill.

"No, that is all covered. Good luck."

* * *

"This truck is well known in this area," said Andre, grinning, his teeth showing through his thin lips. With his pale skin and pointy features, he looked in the glow of the truck's dash, not entirely unlike Nosferatu. It almost made Bill feel uneasy. Hurtling along country lanes, bouncing up and down at every pothole like a sadistic roller coaster, didn't make him feel any better. "The Boche all know we collect from the farms and take supplies back into the city. There are many orchards and farms, so we collect fruit, cider, meat, and run it back to the city. Here."

Bill inspected the papers Andre handed him. They were like a gold-plated, get-out-of-jail-free card. It was clearance to run supplies, food and alcohol for La Coupole Brasserie on the Boulevard du Montparnasse, signed by General von Stülpnagel himself.

The average German soldier liked nothing more than to drink, rut like a hog and get himself well-fattened whenever humanly possible, not necessarily in that order. Bill recalled La Coupole from one of the brochures he'd seen before, during intelligence briefings. They were given out to German soldiers on leave in the city, listing all the German-friendly cabarets, cinemas, bookshops, bars and restaurants.

It was widely known how well the businesses of Paris were prospering under the occupation. Before France was annexed entirely, the Vichy French Government had originally paid three francs per seat to cinema owners to close them off permanently to all but their German masters. There was even a list of *bordelles* for use by the Germans, amusingly to Bill, right next to a list for sexual health clinics.

The collaboration with the invaders was staggering, and Bill knew they would have to be extra cautious in the city. He had worked with the French and among the Germans before, and they were off to a good start. For now, with their flawless identity papers, a pass to give them access into the city with a vehicle, a small arsenal of weapons, and his pocketful of tobacco, he was filled with confidence.

3

Home, Bitter, Home

Paris, early hours of 10th June 1944

Once they had emptied the truck, Bill made his way upstairs to see where he'd be calling home. The building had certainly seen better days. The once-grand cornice and coving work was hanging off, cracked and peeling. Around the room were various make-shift beds, books and bundles of clothes. It looked like a transit depot for the last train to nowhere. He wondered about his new colleagues. How long had they had to live like this? Could they honestly trust each other? Do their families know they are in the Resistance?

He pulled out a couple of the waxy flakes from his smock pocket and started to rub them in his hands nonchalantly. He hoped Lena would be here soon. Jack had gone to brief the French and give them an inventory of the weapons they had brought with them. They were poorly armed, from what

Andre had said on their journey to the city. The Resistance had been reaching out to their trusted contacts in the French Police in the hope of securing more weapons, but the Germans now had their wiry fingers in every French flan.

The police were even expected to account for every bullet, but Bill assumed the same wasn't true for the Germans. He doubted the average Gestapo officer would be expected to list each shot expended into the back of every suspected partisan's head. Although, with their reputation for efficiency, Bill wouldn't be surprised if he saw some Nazi goon digging out the lead from an old Jewish woman's skull just to balance the books. Shaking his head, Bill started packing the rubbed tobacco into his pipe.

The Gestapo, the state secret police, and their sister unit, the SD, were among the most feared in all the occupied areas. They differed mainly in peculiarities of their uniform and came under the same umbrella of psychotic maniacs, otherwise known as the RSHA or Reich Main Security Office. The SD was the official intelligence service of the SS and the broader Nazi state. They wore the same uniforms as the SS but with a diamond SD patch on their left arm. They could clear entire cafes, and people suddenly fell into silence at their mere presence, such was their reputation. They also specialised in catching spies.

If the Resistance thought they could re-take Paris, Bill hoped they had more than the handful of Stens and revolvers they had brought along. Unfortunately, bravery and a handful of grenades weren't likely to stop a Panzer division with its tanks and artillery.

The young girl they'd briefly met earlier walked in and sat opposite Bill with a grin playing on her lips.

"That's some present you've brought for us. You sure know the way to a girl's heart." She opened a small canvas roll, laying down a German MP-40 onto it, and began to disassemble it with the efficiency of a well-practised gunsmith.

"Are you quite sure you wouldn't prefer chocolates or roses?" Bill smiled.

"I'm sure, *monsieur*," she replied, "you can't kill Germans with flowers."

"Quite so, and you certainly wouldn't soften their hearts," joked Bill as he finally got his pipe to stay lit.

"My only aim is to stop their black hearts. I hate them. They arrived here and treated us like we are second-class citizens in our own country." Nicole was now carefully cleaning each part with a lightly oiled rag.

She may have been young, but he also sensed there might be more to her hatred of the Germans than just words. He had a feeling she may have already seen action. "How old are you, Nicole?"

"I'm eighteen. Why?" she said with more than a little defiance. Bill assumed she had been asked this question before, probably with the implication she is young and naive, which Bill had been careful to avoid.

"I am just curious." Bill tried to calm her and lighten the mood. He blew out a stream of smoke.

"Will you be staying until the liberation? We are going to push those Boche bastards out of Paris soon."

"I expect I will be somewhere around, keeping myself busy," Bill answered vaguely.

"Have you met Lieutenant Roland yet? He is our main strategist. He has been in contact with the allies. We will be taking Paris back when the Americans arrive."

"Then I hope you have more than a few sub-machine guns." Bill was concerned the Resistance was biting off a lot more than they might be able to chew.

"The Parisians are a tough bunch. This won't be the first revolution where the French have overthrown their oppressors."

"True enough," Bill mused, "you certainly have a good head on your shoulders. So try to keep it there."

"They won't get me," Nicole defiantly exclaimed. "I owe them one."

Andre suddenly entered the room like a cockroach escaping a flooding cellar. The dim lightbulb caught his chiselled features. He seemed to have a head full of angles. He moved almost as strangely as he looked.

"Ah, Willy! Stay away from that one! She is dangerous! The last man who chatted her up ended up with Roland's boot in his balls!"

"Shut up, Andre! We were discussing the war!" Nicole said through a stifled giggle.

"But don't worry, Willy, when the time comes, she is just as dangerous with that *Schmeisser*!" he exclaimed as he gestured towards the now re-assembled MP-40.

The MP-40 was the submachine gun that many Resistance fighters tended to favour. These were the captured weapons they were well-versed in using over the British and American weapons, like the ones Bill's team had brought. It was reliable as long as it was kept meticulously clean. The only flaw was how the magazine fed the rounds. If it was incorrectly held by the magazine with the supporting hand, it could jam. It was better to hold rifle-style behind the magazine or by the magazine housing, but, Bill thought, like people, nobody's perfect.

"There is food ready downstairs, Willy." Andre gestured, then lit a cigarette, lounging back in his bed.

"What about you, Andre? What do you think are the chances of taking Paris back?" asked Bill.

"I don't know, Willy, but I know we will surely die trying if that's what it comes to," replied Andre.

"None of us get out of this life alive. So I guess we all have to die for something."

"I'm going to kill that bastard Misselwitz," Andre swore. "Do you know what happened to my friend Jean?" Bill politely shook his head. Andre continued, "We met during the last war. Leo and I ..." Interrupting himself, he explained, "He is the handsome chap who you briefly met earlier." Ah, the spiv, Bill thought. "Anyway, after the poison gas at Verdun, we were both transferred to a labour battalion to help with digging and general labouring. That's where we met Jean. We all became close friends. In our downtime, we would all have a drink and play cards. Sometimes Leo would sneak a nice bottle of eau-de-vie out of the officers' mess, and we would share it."

Bill listened intently as Andre smiled at the memory.

"Jean loved to draw. He used to sketch animals and scenes from his childhood and the world around him. He was passionate about politics and was keen to hear the news about how the Russians were doing after overthrowing their aristocracy. Truth be told, he was a bit of a Bolshevik himself, I think. The armistice was signed, and the war ended before we could get sent back to the front," Andre continued. "After the war, we all kind of lost touch. I didn't hear anything of Jean until I joined the Resistance. It seemed to me almost everyone was happy with the Germans being here, and those that weren't simply turned a blind eye to the horrors they brought with them, so I asked around, and here I am. Last year Jean had risen to be the leader of the Resistance, and that's how we got reacquainted. He was different though, more serious somehow."

Bill now realised who Andre was talking about. Jean Moulin had been the president of the Council of the Resistance. SOE had even smuggled him back to England to meet and make plans with de Gaulle and drop him back into France. He had been captured the previous year and never seen again.

Andre stared blankly and stopped speaking. Tears were starting to well in his eyes. Bill thought he looked like a gargoyle on an old Gothic church as the water flowed down his angular cheek.

"They tortured him, Willy." Andre wiped his face and continued, "Misselwitz, and the man they call the Spy Hunter, Klaus Barbie. They butchered him. I saw him when he was moved to the railway station. He was like a dead man walking. His face looked like a bruised-up rotten apple and was covered in open wounds. No one saw or heard from him again. Even our contacts at the concentration camps said he never showed up. So, we know he is probably dead. When his sister went to Misselwitz a few weeks back to ask for his ashes, he simply laughed at her and told her that they had fed him to pigs." Andre drifted off again into a stunned trance.

"Best to leave him, I think. I'll take you down and introduce you to the others," Nicole said as she propped her MP-40 against a small table.

As they reached the bottom of the stairs, out through the glass door, coming across the courtyard, he spotted Lena. As she approached the door, she spotted Bill and flung open the door to hug him.

"I'm so glad you are safe, Bill!" she squealed, then kissed him full on the lips. "We got stopped and questioned by some German Military Police, and I was sure they'd see through my cover story, but they let us on our way. God, it's so stressful. Training can't prepare you for staring down a German while they check your ID for real, while you hope your story stacks up. How have you done this so many times and stayed sane?"

"To be honest, Lena, I'm not so sure I have. Every time I've had to lie, it seems a little bit of me dies and never returns. The trick is to try to truly believe what you are telling them. Remember; if we stick to the plan, the hardest is over. They are careful about who is entering the city, but with the allied advance, Jerry's on the back foot, and the word is that moving around Paris is getting easier."

"I hope you're right. I'm not sure I'm cut out for this after all. I'm glad I'm here with you, Bill."

"If we all do our job, we'll be fine. Let's get something to eat and a good night's sleep, and we'll start the planning in the morning."

The kitchen was full of beautiful smells and one hell of a mess. Bill found a clear bit of the table and carefully set down his pipe on its side. Leo-the-spiv was chatting, in French, to Jack. Jack noticed Bill's presence and gave him a grin, raising his small glass to him. Bill nodded back.

"Pleased to meet you, Willy," a slightly skinny man called out as he grabbed Bill's hand to shake it. "We have been told you are Britain's finest."

"I don't know about that. There's this plump bloke who wears a hat, lives in London and smokes a lot of cigars. He's pretty good too."

Bill realised who he was talking to. This was Roland Boursier. He was not what Bill had expected. He was tall but gaunt, with a prominent forehead and a large Adam's apple protruding from a sinewy neck. He looked almost Slavic rather than French. Since the Dunkirk evacuation, he had set up numerous resistance groups across Northern France. If the Gestapo could extract what he had in his head, it could bring a lot of the network tumbling down.

"Ha ha! You are an amusing chap, Willy! I am Roland. I think you may have been told about me, no?" He laughed as he poured out three glasses of cognac from a fine looking decanter. "You must be Lena. Pleased to meet you, *mademoiselle*."

Nicole smiled at Roland and hugged him warmly, then realising they wanted to talk business, went off in search of food.

Bill first sipped the brown liquid carefully, and to his surprise, it wasn't the cheap fake brandy-coloured schnapps he was expecting but the real deal. He let the nectar run down his throat and smiled at Roland before knocking back the rest. "Pretty good stuff you have here, Boursier."

"Call me Roland, please. So many things fall from lorries here in France, Willy. You just have to be standing in the right place at the right time to catch them." He turned around and clattered some pans. "You must be hungry. Please sit down."

Clearing a space at the table, Bill and Lena sat down. The kitchen was almost as badly damaged as upstairs. Bill imagined this is what Pompeii must have looked like after the volcano, but probably here had fewer orgies. Roland set down two bowls of steaming chicken stew. It smelled delicious.

"*Coq au vin*, my mother's recipe," he proudly announced, switching into French.

The garlic fragrance filled Bill's nose as he waited for Roland to hand out the spoons. He also set down two cups and a bottle of wine. Roland noticed Bill looking at the cracked plaster.

In perfect English again now, Roland explained, "This place was owned by a Jewish family. Since they were taken away, it has been used as a safe house. Officially housing dancers from the nearby cabarets and employees of Brasserie La Coupole. The police leave us alone, as the building's owners are known as collaborators, and personal friends with General von Stülpnagel, the military commander of Occupied France. In actual fact, the owners help our organisation, but don't worry, no one outside this building knows you are here. Even the local Resistance commanders have not been informed of your mission."

"And what of the previous occupants?" inquired Bill. Of course, he knew all about the roundups but wondered how well-informed Roland was.

"The Jews? The French Police called them up in '42 during the *Rafle du Vel' d'Hiv'*. The roundup of all the Jews of Paris, to confine them in the *Vélodrome d'Hiver*. Of course, I wasn't in the city at the time, but it was a very open secret. The French Police went house-to-house with a list of so-called undesirables. Families with children were dragged from their beds by Frenchmen. Can you believe such a thing, Willy? They were told to pack one bag each and that they would not be returning; that their homes were needed for good, Aryan families. The story went that they were collecting them to relocate them to the east for work, but the French politicians and police chiefs all knew what was really happening. The bastards. The year before, they had sent out green tickets to all the foreign Jews, telling them they needed to attend a status review, which was just cover for a trap. Anyone who showed up was arrested and immediately put on trains and sent to concentration camps in the Loire Valley. I can tell you, Bill, the stories coming back from those camps are not pleasant. According to my sources, the camps were closed last year, and every one of them was sent on trains to the east, to places in rural Poland."

Bill ate his stew and hung on every word. He knew well of the places Roland was referring to. Some SOE ex-partisan fighters had told him about factories of death in German-occupied Poland. The Germans had buildings connected to truck exhausts. Execution chambers where they could murder hundreds at a time; men, women and children alike.

"Anyway, the velodrome has a sealed glass roof. All the toilets were boarded up as they were potential escape routes. There were around seven thousand people in there, all shitting wherever they could. They had to share one tap. Apart from the Red Cross and a few local churches bringing whatever food they could, they were starved for five days. Anyone trying to escape was shot. Many chose suicide, however they could manage it. Mothers even suffocated their babies so they wouldn't have to face what they knew was still to come. Eventually, most of the French Jews were sealed into the ghetto in Drancy, just out of the centre of Paris, guarded by the French Gendarmes. Since then, most have been sent to the east. Sent to the east is what the Boche say when they mean sent to be murdered, Willy."

"The Germans love a euphemism. It hides their actions even from themselves," Bill replied.

"When they eventually cleared the last of the Jews from Vichy France, the children were initially held back, split from their parents, who went straight to their deaths. The little kids arrived in Drancy alone, some only two, barely big enough to carry their little cases. After a while, they were collected and sent to meet their maker too, Willy. How could a Frenchman do such heinous things? I ask myself all the time. We have managed to get at some of them to re-pay what they did, but when the Germans found out, they took retribution on the camp at Drancy. One of the Gestapo men who arranged all this and made it possible is sitting eating sausage and drinking beer just a short way from here. The ring leader of death, Ernst Misselwitz. Don't forget who it is we are dealing with, Willy."

"I am only too aware of who we are dealing with, Roland." Misselwitz was the new head of the Gestapo in Paris, having replaced his old boss, a clever man by the name of Josef Kieffer. Kieffer was a model Nazi. His intelligence was only matched by his cruelty. Misselwitz had clearly learned the ways of his old master.

They back at Baker Street knew many of the SOE operatives that had gone missing in action had last been seen in the custody of Misselwitz. Bill had studied the intelligence file. The photo had been taken early in the war when he was in one of the Eastern Front murder squads in Ukraine.

"No one keeps their secrets long with those demons asking the questions. They are pure evil, Willy."

Bill could feel the anger course through his veins. Then, composing his thoughts, Bill asked, "Are you sure we are safe here?"

"Yes, sir, we have been in this building for over a year. We never get raided, as the cabarets have made it clear there will be no shows if their girls or security staff are harassed. Of course, there are none of their girls here, but with Nicole and a few others coming and going, it keeps up appearances."

"Our target resides at the Gestapo headquarters. Have you got some good information about it?"

"We are not amateurs, Willy. I will have the photos and plans ready for you in the morning. Eat as much as you like and help yourself to whatever you require. Our home is your home. Good night—bonne nuit."

Leo, who had been chatting to Jack, got up and followed Roland out with a courteous nod towards Bill and Lena. Jack rose unsteadily from his chair, picked up what was left of a bottle of clear schnapps, and joined the other two who were hiding their laughter as he stumbled into the seat opposite them. He relit the cigarette dangling from his lips. As if reminded, Bill checked for his pipe and collected it from the table. He always thought best when he was smoking. He carefully removed the ash and bits from the bowl with his small penknife and started rubbing a couple of more flakes from his pocket.

"So, tomorrow Jack and I will look around and see if there is anywhere suitable for an observation post near the Gestapo headquarters," Bill said. "Lena, you will need to drop a coded note to let the section know we have arrived safely in the city. In the morning, we will set out the emergency protocols with our new companions in case we get split, or something happens. It's too dangerous to use the radio set in the safe house, so we will rely only on the dead-drop for now." Bill packed his pipe as if in some kind of trance. He always meticulously filled the bowl loosely, pressed it down, repeated, then a final small pinch more on top with a last gentle press. He used a match for an initial charring light and then a second.

"We will meet tomorrow evening after our reconnoitre for a full briefing," Bill added. He tamped the charred top layer down, as he often did with his finger, and relit. "We are in no mad rush. The allies won't make it to Paris for a few weeks, at least. Get a good few hours' sleep, Jack. Be ready to go for midday." They both nodded and trudged out. Bill was starting to feel tired, too, so he poured himself a small glass of whatever the clear noxious liquid was and made his way upstairs.

4

Vera

64 Baker Street, London, 2nd June 1944

The week prior to their departure to France

"Look after my girls, please."

"Of course, Vera, could you imagine two more perfect gentlemen?" replied Bill, with more than a hint of sarcasm.

Vera was in her late thirties, a good ten years older than Bill. Outwardly, she brimmed with confidence and had a commanding air about her. But she always looked on edge in a way Bill could never quite place, almost world-weary.

"Actions speak louder than words. If I get either of my girls or the staff car back in anything other than perfect condition, I'll have your guts for garters!"

"Understood. Thanks for letting us use the motor."

"That car had better be back here by oh nine hundred hours

and no later. If the colonel realises it's gone, you'll be losing both your pips and your head. Seriously, though, Bill, look after them, especially Lena. Violette has been to France once already, she's a tough cookie, but Lena is still just a girl and doesn't need the likes of you scaring her off before she's even started," Vera replied, rummaging through the drawer full of various keys.

Vera was Romanian, and the word around F-Section was that she was not to be trusted. Bill assumed this was in no small part because of the other popular rumour that she was a Jew. Some were even convinced that she was a double agent. Bill never trusted rumours. He'd far rather judge people as good or bad with his own two eyes.

"Going anywhere nice?" she asked.

Bill watched her sorting through the metallic jumble of keys. Then, finding the correct one, she placed it gently into Bill's hand and tried to hide her smile.

"Probably the picture house and maybe a row on the lake."

"Very romantic, I'm sure," she remarked, grinning. "Pop the key back into the drawer when you get back. And, Bill ..."

"What is it, ma'am?" Bill always pronounced it to rhyme with arm, not like ham.

"Don't ma'am me, Bill. It makes me sound like an old lady, and I'm only a civilian, remember? Not *clubbable* enough for the bastards to commission me, still."

"A couple of pips on your shoulder doesn't change what you are doing to win this war, and it's more than most, Vera."

"Thanks, Bill. I appreciate it." She bit her bottom lip as she fought to find the courage, then perched herself on her desk and fumbled for her pack of Senior Service.

Vera only ever smoked Senior Service. Bill instinctively

pulled a match from his case as she dragged one out and placed it carefully between her lips. He had resisted and resigned not to learn a great deal from his time at boarding school, but manners had been drummed into him early on.

"Look, in case I don't see you before you leave, if you get the opportunity, ask around what's happened to my girls, would you? We've lost contact with so many over the years. I still live in the hope that some evaded capture and are in hiding with the Resistance."

"... And we all know how disorganised they can be," Bill added.

Vera exhaled a cloud of smoke and looked to the floor for inspiration. "One more thing. Lena still thinks you are all going over together. I felt it would be better for Lena to tough it out alone. Plus, they were a man down on another team and need someone with experience in the field, so I have reassigned Violette elsewhere. She knows, but Lena doesn't yet. So best keep it that way for now. Besides, she has you two idiots to look after her."

Bill, a little stunned, didn't reply but smiled at her joking insult.

"I know you are surprised, but it's how it is."

"Yes, of course," Bill said, regaining his composure, "I understand. I think Jack will be a little disappointed."

"Yes. Just ... you know ..."

"I will."

"Good luck, Bill," she said, smiling kindly.

5

House of Horrors

Paris, 10th June 1944

Barely noticing the commotion downstairs, Bill stayed in his semi-conscious state as long as he could. That middle ground between awake and asleep, where you are aware of things going on but cannot make sense of it all, like some strange, semi-conscious, waking coma. He fought off this odd heavy straitjacket and wondered if that was what dying felt like. He immediately shook the image and peered out of his uncooperative pupils to see Jack snoring in the far corner of the room.

The others, including Lena, were gone. He could now clearly hear the coming and going downstairs and stood up to see what was happening. He was still dressed. He had no intention of being woken in the night by the Gestapo in nothing but his underpants. He picked up his smock and started emptying the pockets. He put everything into an old canvas sandbag he had brought for the purpose. He kept hold of his pipe in its little green drawstring bag, a small packet of French tobacco and his ID card.

"Wake up, you lazy bastard," Bill said as he booted Jack and laughed at his pal's reaction.

"Leave me alone and wake me when the war is over," Jack grunted.

"No problem, brother, I'll just pop along to Berlin and stick a round in Hitler's dome so we can all go home."

"That'd be great. A bullet in the Führer's head and a big cup of coffee, what else could a man ask for?"

"A bacon sandwich?"

"Christ, I remember those."

* * *

The Gestapo building looked like many other grand buildings in the neighbourhood if you ignored the twenty-four-hour guards. It was a large building with thick, solid walls and many oversized windows. It was of typical Parisian construction. Each floor had a black iron balustrade in a mock-balcony design across the lower part of the windows. Bill imagined at least one of the rooms would be sound proof for the Gestapo to carry out their own particular kind of interrogation; probably the basement, thought Bill, which would be fitting for the types of demons who inhabited the field grey uniforms who made this house of horrors their home. The Gestapo cynically referred to their torture rooms as kitchens. The kitchens often needed good drainage, he had heard.

The top floor was where the prisoners were kept. There was no traffic on the broad avenue, mainly due to the fuel shortages, and somewhat eerily, minimal sound. The Germans had also commandeered the houses on either side. Bill watched Jack stroll past, a newspaper in hand, and surreptitiously glance up at the top floor windows, then back down to give the guard by the front black iron railings the slightest of nods. Most Parisians gave the house a wide berth for a good reason. Much like the greatest of illusionists, the men in this building could make anyone disappear.

Bill sat opposite on a small bench. Sometimes the best hiding places are in plain sight. What sort of spy or Resistance operative, except a complete lunatic, would sit in front of, much less walk past, the Gestapo headquarters in Paris? He watched as the SS guards stood around in the small front courtyard. Without observing for a few days, it would be impossible to ascertain the handover times and procedures. He could not sit on this bench for more than half an hour without being approached and questioned. Bill watched Jack cross the street and wait near a lamppost, behind the trunk of one of the avenue's trees, almost out of sight.

Bill could now see that entering the fortress would be almost impossible. Although the building was joined on both sides, the roof line was much higher and dropping down would require ropes. Besides, Numbers 82 and 86 were also occupied by the Germans. Bill was no stranger to open-field combat, but those tactics would not work here. There were too many look-out points from high vantage points. They'd just get picked off.

Their target would have to come out sooner or later. Bill had thought about snatching him, tying him up and rushing him towards the allies and being done with it, but knew it was a fanciful idea that would raise too many alarms. It would jeopardise too many other operations in the city, and how would he get through the German front line to reach the British? Moreover, there would undoubtedly be other SOE agents with different targets in Paris. Maybe they would just shoot him and run.

Number 84 on Avenue Foch was a vast building with six floors. Since the SS counter-intelligence service, the SD, and the Gestapo were basically one and the same in the occupied territories, they shared workspace and often even uniforms. Bill recalled the intelligence briefing; their man worked on one of the upper floors. Ernst Misselwitz had risen to commander of the Gestapo in Paris. His primary job was the capture, interrogation and imprisonment of spies. This included French Resistance and SOE agents. He, along with his assistants, had been responsible for the disappearance of dozens of agents.

The building also housed a counter-espionage radio unit that, using the codes found in possession of agents or extracted using interrogation, had been used to draw out others into revealing themselves. Bill knew there would be other SOE teams targetting leaders at the nearby Fresnes Prison, where most of the captured SOE agents were thought to have been imprisoned, but this was not their mission. Instead, they would be focussing on what the French had dubbed *The Street of Horrors*.

Back in March, the French Resistance leader, Pierre Brossolette, was found in a crumpled heap at the foot of 84 Avenue Foch, having thrown himself from the window of his cell on the top floor. Rumour had it that most of the bruises and cuts on his body had been inflicted prior to his suicide. Locals had heard his screaming for several days.

Bill drew deeply on his pipe. He suppressed the wince as the taste of the local tobacco hit his taste buds. It was only a small thing, but getting caught with British tobacco was a one-way ticket to the basement opposite him. He wasn't used to such a fine cut, and he regretted drawing so hard as the tongue-bite hit.

If they couldn't get a better, safer view of the headquarters, they would have to gather some Resistance fighters to help contain the building when the time comes and hope to flush out the rats. He made a mental image of the house and surroundings. Jack passed behind Bill's bench, making his way back towards town. Bill waited a few minutes, then stood up, brushed off the odd tobacco flakes, and started to follow him.

A few minutes later, Bill caught up with Jack, and the two men continued the almost flat gradient toward *l'Arc de Triomphe*.

"I almost feel sorry for the thing," Bill muttered.

Jack looked up at the monument, which appeared a light tan colour in the light.

"Why's that, Bill?"

"Well, it's stood there over a hundred years, a solid embodiment of French accomplishment and victory, right? And now the bloody Germans stomp about under it and parade their army in front of it while France bows its collective head. After everything they have achieved in the past, they have nothing to show for it but the shame of capitulation. I can't imagine England would have gone the same way."

"I wouldn't be so sure, Bill. Remember that Poland, Czechoslovakia and others are having to suffer them too. They just have to hope the Russians can push through on their side."

"I'm not so sure life under the Russkis will be much better for them. Certainly, the aristocrats will be packing their bags as we speak."

"It's just modernisation, Bill. The workers' power will eventually overthrow their old masters unless the master is a little Charlie Chaplin lookalike who has successfully brainwashed the people into being afraid of even their neighbours."

Bill thought about how many spies and saboteurs working against the Germans were communists or sympathisers. Even the Polish Resistance were hoping for a sweeping Russian victory. Bill knew the government had sided with Uncle Joe as a means to an end but couldn't help wonder if it would one day come back to bite them.

* * *

"It's impossible, pal." Jack pushed back in his chair and blew out a plume of blue smoke.

"If we have learned anything, isn't it at least that anyone can be got at?" replied Bill as he carefully stirred his espresso. Only in Paris could you find proper coffee like this. They were right in the heart of the lion's den. They had carefully chosen the most downmarket and quiet of all the cafes along the *Champs Elysees*. Most proudly displayed signs stating they were for *Germans Only*.

The blonde waitress smiled at Bill from behind a stack of glasses. He had barely noticed her when she brought the coffees, he was so deep in thought. She was around thirty, with bright red lipstick, short-bobbed hair and a small silver crucifix around her neck. The way her cotton dress moved with her hips made Bill thankful he was not a Catholic, or he would need to go to confession to cleanse the thoughts he was having.

The room had cheap prints of classical art on the yellowing walls. Mostly they seemed to depict soul-stirring battles of the Napoleonic era. The cafes were all relatively quiet, perhaps due to the overcast weather. Maybe the Germans were all busy packing their loot, ready for their inevitable retreat like rats from a sinking ship. The media would, as usual, have very few of the facts, choosing instead to mention only the splendid acts of bravery by the glorious German Wehrmacht. Still, Bill had no doubt the allies would have secured at least one port by now, and with most of the German divisions on the Eastern Front, it wouldn't take long for them to be pushed back into Germany.

"It will be like getting into a can of beans without any tools." Jack swirled his cup and necked his coffee. "We will have to get a squad together to surround the place. Roland reckons he can get at least some of the police onside. We'd better have a vehicle ready, too."

"I can't imagine when the time comes that many Parisians will do much to assist the Germans. Even the collaborators are going to start covering their tracks. Maybe we can get all of them onside? Maybe the collaborators will see it as some sort of redemption for their treason?"

"I will make some subtle enquiries in the coming days." Jack started to fumble some coins out of his pocket.

"Good man."

The blonde waitress strutted up to their table like she was a model in a fashion show. She was too short for the likes of Maison Chanel, probably around five-foot-two, but everything was right where it should be. She collected the coins and winked at Bill as she picked up the empty cups.

As he watched her shimmy away, he silently thanked God he was an atheist.

6

Only Once

Paris, 17th June 1944

"The papers you found at that eighty-eight battery near where we met the Resistance turned out to have every gun position east of Normandy on them." Lena smiled at him. "The section has put you in for a mention in dispatches."

"Great," Bill feigned, "more trinkets. I'll see if I can swap it for a pay rise."

Lena laughed, shook her head, picked up her little satchel and left the room.

One thing they can't train you for is the monotony and boredom. Bill had kept himself busy going over the drawings he had made of the Gestapo HQ and compared them to the plans the Resistance had obtained. He wanted to be sure he hadn't missed anything. He couldn't go down Avenue Foch too often, as he would start to be recognised. They had agents watching the street and taking notes for all he knew. Life in Paris seemed to continue. There were, however, the regular power outages and the evening curfews to contend with. Despite the swastikas and German uniforms everywhere, you'd hardly know there was a war on or that Germany looked like they were starting to lose it. Coffee and liquor were plentiful, here at least, which was half the battle of keeping the civilian population compliant. Bill knew the rural populace was far less fond of their new masters.

Jack spent most of his time getting the various Resistance groups in the area ready for the coming liberation. Lena was in touch with Baker Street most days, feeding back the varied intelligence they had requested. She had started to embrace her role. Bill had seen her leave that morning with new confidence in her step. If it were possible, she suddenly seemed even more attractive to him.

Bill contented himself helping with the cooking and generally felt like a spare part. To Bill, though, this was supremely more welcome than some of his previous experience of operations in France, hiding in damp basements. He worked his way steadily through his tobacco and planned out various scenarios that would expedite their mission. Each time he came back to the same conclusion. They would have to wait for the day of the uprising. The Resistance had already started to make armbands to identify themselves. The last thing anyone wanted after four years in hiding was to get shot by their own side.

SOE had initially been reluctant to send an agent as experienced and knowledgeable as Bill back to France. They thought he knew too much, should he be captured. Bill knew, however, by this point in the war, with all the department had learned, they would not risk other operatives if a team went missing. They would already have a file of all the other operations they knew about, change the various plans, and get the possible compromised agents to a new safe house. It didn't matter much to Bill anyway. He'd already decided if he was arrested, he'd hide one of his issued glass vials under his lip and would bite down on it long before the SD got a chance to get to work on him. It wasn't a thought he relished, and he quickly shook it away.

The various plans for the attack on the Gestapo HQ ranged from the almost ludicrous, storming the building with grenades and pistols, getting the target to a field, and asking for a Lysander airlift out of France, to the benign: camp outside and starve them out. In the end, Bill had applied Occam's razor. The simplest solution is usually the best. First, they would have a van ready and surround the building with as many guns as they could muster. Then, if possible, they would take all the officers inside as prisoners.

The staff at number 84 seemed to vary. On top of torturing Bill's colleagues, the dark shadows inside were also instrumental in the evacuations, mistreatment and reprisals against the Jews in Drancy. They knowingly sent women and children to their deaths. What was this? Was there a word for it? Evil didn't seem strong enough somehow. Could it simply be put down to war? This was certainty more than war. As if the Germans didn't have enough on their hands with the Russians, Bill could barely imagine the logistics needed to kill vast swathes of the non-combatant civilian population in their occupied territories. They say that evil triumphs when good men do nothing. Bill was determined, despite his increasingly cynical attitude to all about him, to do whatever he could to bring the puppet masters of these obscene crimes to some justice. Justice to Bill would have meant he'd happily plaster their brains up the nearest wall, courtesy of 230 grains of Colt .45 ACP. But unfortunately, Westminster seemed to have other ideas, and they were meant to capture their target alive.

"Missing home, boss?" Lena had just walked back in.

"Miles away, sorry, Lena."

"You look like you were pondering your existence."

"Something like that. Any news from our divine masters?"

She pulled a small piece of paper from her pocket. It was a shopping list of gibberish.

"Look, Lena. I'll parachute into the most dangerous place in Europe, I'll pick up a rifle and run towards my certain death, I'll even drink the strange noxious substances that masquerade as schnapps in some of the local cafes here, but I refuse to learn this weird black magic you call deciphering."

SOE had tried to teach him every time he'd returned to England. They had some of the best instructors in the art the country could find, but it remained a complete mystery to him. Even the F-Section boss, Buckmaster, had urged him to learn the new double-transposition cyphers, which involved inventing and learning a short poem and using words from it to encode and later decode the messages. Sometimes the codes were encrypted five times over, and a short message could take half an hour. For Bill, it was too much like the maths he had hated at school. Buckmaster had wanted to move him onto the training staff to assist the combat instructors, and Bill thought this was probably partly due to his reluctance to learn and constantly failing the cypher course. In the end, the staff gave up and resigned to sending him into action with appropriate support operatives. Lena took to it like a fish to water. She could decode the messages in a matter of minutes.

Lena flipped it over and double-checked the message. "The word is the liberation of Paris is to be a French operation. de Gaulle has convinced Ike at SHAEF to allow the French forces to roll in alone and take all the credit."

"Eisenhower seems to have a soft spot for the French. Maybe he wants to make sure they give the Americans the best hotels in the city. It is a long way from Paris to Berlin, and there aren't many cities worth staying in before then unless you like rubble and ersatz coffee," sniped Bill.

"There's more," she continued. "Buckmaster himself intends to come to Paris after the liberation." She looked up from the paper. "It would seem he wants to start to wrap up the operations personally. I guess they won't need many spies in France once it's only the French here to worry about."

"More like de Gaulle doesn't want anyone else around to claim any credit for saving the country he has abandoned for four years. It must stick in his craw just how many of his glorious countrymen switched sides and helped the Boche."

"We know what we are achieving here, and they can't take away our accomplishments," Lena replied proudly. "I have distributed the money we brought with us, which has already helped arm and feed ten Resistance groups in the city. That's probably a hundred combat-effective troops to help when the time comes if they can secure enough weapons."

"Your healthy optimism is really making a difference to this mission. I'm getting nothing done here surrounded by tobacco, maps and drawings."

"Your time is still to come. Jack and I know why you are

here, and neither of us would feel as safe as knowing you will lead the final stages. We know they don't give out Military Crosses for just anything. The staff said you are a real soldier. I was heartbroken when they sent Violette off on her own mission without me. I have never made friends easily, and Violette gave me the confidence to leave my abusive boyfriend, angry I had joined up. He thought I would be a nurse, of course, but he got violent with me the night before I travelled to the finishing school. I met Violette after the interviews. She had just returned from France and inspired me to stand on my own two feet. She was also the one who encouraged me to go along on that double date."

"I guess I owe Violette a lot, being lucky enough to be seen with you, the most beautiful agent at Baker Street."

"I think Jack was the real lucky one, being out with Violette. Anyway, I'm trying to say that I know the spying part comes harder for you, but that is why we are a team. It was your confidence that helped me, including on the day we arrived here."

"You have come a long way in a short time. It's not so easy being the prey in a field full of predators. No one is here for medals, and I'm no soldier. Not really. I became an officer because I thought it would be an easy life. I wanted to escape after the strange theme park of academia at Cambridge, and the army seemed a good skive. Once the war broke out, though, I knew I needed to do more. If I could use my knowledge of languages to help the effort, I would. Combat and weapons training seemed easy, like with you and the cyphering."

"Well, you are a warrior to me, Bill, and I don't think we can fail. I'm proud to serve with you." She had lowered her voice to just above a whisper and sat down beside him, putting her hand on his thigh.

"A warrior doesn't mean you never fail. It just means you will always fight. But I'm glad you are here too."

She threw her leg over him and, now straddling him, planted her lips on his. He felt the inevitable rush of testosterone and held her there tightly.

"Sorry to intrude, boss," Jack said from the doorway. "I'd happily leave you to it, but I've just heard something is happening at the target location."

Lena quickly stood, clearly embarrassed, her cheeks flushed, and she looked at the floor.

"What is it, Jack?" Bill asked without betraying any emotion.

"Another unit has spotted vehicles being readied at the prison, and the SS have bolstered their numbers at 84. So, I think we ought to take a look. Roland, Leo and Nicole are currently looking at the police precinct across town, but Andre is here, and he has the delivery truck ready for us."

"We'll be down in one minute. Make sure there are no weapons on board, and get a few boxes of supplies, so it looks like we are out on deliveries if we get a tug."

Jack disappeared from the doorway, and Lena looked up into a half-glance at Bill and laughed.

"I guess we had better continue this later when we have some free time," Bill said, grinning.

"If you play your cards right."

Bill never was much good at timing … or cards, now he thought about it.

* * *

"Pass as slowly as you can, Andre," Bill advised from the passenger seat, casually leaning on the open window. Jack and Lena were in the back, sitting on crates, looking through the gaps in the canvas panels.

Bill could see some black Citroëns and an armed motorcycle with a sidecar parked outside number 84. Just past them was a Pan-Pan painted up in patchy camouflage, with a German cross on the side. The baby, four-man armoured vehicle looked like a car drawn by a child, with a menacing 20mm gun poking out. It was an armed convoy. They were clearly worried about an attack from the Resistance.

They slowed to a walking pace, and as Bill looked on, two French *gendarmes* waved them on and shouted something about there being nothing to see. But there was something to see. Something that made Bill's blood run cold.

He felt a stifling feeling from somewhere in his lungs. He heard himself try to shout out, but adrenaline had incapacitated him. The last time he remembered feeling this way was a few seconds before he had some out-of-body experience, and something took over his movements like he was a marionette. That time he had fought the paralysis to stand to run towards a machine gunner and two riflemen with a primed hand grenade in his hand. This time was very different. Any action he took would jeopardise the whole mission. For the good of the entire team, his subconscious had taken over and incapacitated him. It was all he could achieve to sit very still and stare in disbelief. Their truck sped up again and hurried down the Avenue.

Andre spoke. Bill let the words enter his consciousness, but he didn't really listen. They bounced around his head, not landing. They drove for some time, but Bill didn't know for how long, or for that matter, where the route had taken them.

They pulled up outside a fairly well-kept cafe with polished brass lanterns on either side of a large glass double-door entrance. Inside, the tables were all immaculately arranged, and each chair identically not-quite pushed in. Bill walked around to the back of the truck with legs like jelly. He was about to ask if the others had seen what he had. He got his answer. Lena was curled up on the truck floor, hugging her knees and gently sobbing. Jack had one hand on her and was staring back at Bill with eyes as wide as dinner plates.

Bill paused for a few seconds. Then, he re-gathered himself mentally and said as tenderly as he could, "Stay here, Lena, but try to stay quiet," then, "Jack, Andre says this cafe is sympathetic to the cause. Let's take a look."

Jack vaulted out of the truck. "What happens now, boss?"

"Honestly, I really don't know. Maybe this will force our hand. We'll have to think hard if we actually need this bloke alive. Perhaps it will be easier just to risk it and slot him?"

They walked into the cafe, and a sizeable balding man wearing an apron appeared from behind a mirrored wall. His eyes had a strange squint that made it look like he was checking a bus timetable behind while one eye was looking straight through you. It looked like he'd just climbed down from the famous Paris cathedral of Notre Dame. What with his odd oversized build, he indeed reminded Bill of Quasimodo. He nervously looked to Andre, who answered the silent question with an imperceptible nod.

"Liberte!" he exclaimed. A phrase that, when used appropriately, could be answered likewise or with a hail of bullets in the wrong company.

"Liberte!" Andre replied. "Cognac for my two friends and

me, please, Rene."

They sat at a window table with a good view of the street and the truck.

"So, who was that, Willy?" asked Andre.

"An agent and friend of ours." Bill felt like he was in a circus with their new friend Quasimodo and Andre with his own set of bizarre facial features. Even when he was being friendly, he looked like a rodent with his odd inset eyes. "She is also Lena's best friend."

"That is not good. She won't last long in there, Willy. Not many do."

Bill knew he was right. He couldn't shake the image. The agent they were dragging in for questioning was Violette. Scratches covered her face, and one of her eyes was shiny, purple and fully closed, like a boxer after ten rounds with two angry bears. Bill wondered if she had been in Paris the whole time. If there was one thing Bill had, it was an almost photographic memory. When those memories and sights are bad, they could come back and haunt him at times.

Just as they had passed by 84, an officer in a grey uniform, who looked like a pin-up boy for the Nazis with his blue eyes, blonde hair and strong chin, had hit Violette in the back of the head with the butt of his pistol. He looked to be perhaps twenty-five. In the brief seconds afterwards, he had a maniacal grin on his blood-speckled face. With a bit of help from his photographic memory of faces from the briefing at Baker Street, Bill knew his name to be Ernst Misselwitz. Bill had the image of the monster's claret-daubed face seared on his retinas. He couldn't shake it.

7

Defendu

Arisaig, Scotland, August 1940

"Seven inches. Just the right length to get through a thick overcoat and uniform underneath and still have enough left to penetrate the chest between the ribs."

Boy, what a charmer, Bill thought.

Bill had already been in the army for six years. He had no real love for shooting or combat, for that matter. He'd even been given an old air rifle when he was young but never really understood the fascination. At school, shooting with a rifle as a cadet in the Officer Training Corps had come naturally to him. He soon learned he could also take the right wing off a gnat with a pistol. He should have had his shooting assessment annually, but Bill knew the assessor from his days at Bloxham School, and a couple of ounces of tobacco was enough to see him pass with flying colours and get the morning to himself.

Such was army life for Bill. Any excuse to do nothing and

head into the nearest pub. He was glad to have chosen a desk job in the General Service Corps when he first joined up. He was well educated enough to know he didn't fancy his career prospects being shouted at in the infantry for the next however-many years. Bill didn't take kindly to being led by fools too keen to get a bullet in the belly, so he considered life as a junior intelligence officer most fitting to his keenness towards self-preservation. But, unfortunately, it wouldn't last. A clandestine war behind enemy lines was a shock to his well-planned, uncomplicated life.

"Do you have somewhere better to be, Number Fourteen?" scowled the instructor.

It had been whispered among the other recruits that Mr Fairburn was recruited from the Shanghai Police and that he was the deadliest man in the free world with a blade. His eyes had the look of an alpha predator. Hungry for its next kill. He wasn't young by any means. He must have been well into his fifties, but his movements seemed to defy nature. He held a rank of some sort but preferred Mr Fairburn or simply sir. He was well versed in the art of ending lives, so he'd probably served in the last war or somewhere else overseas.

Unlike the rest of the army, most of the staff here, other than the few you saw in uniform, seemed keen to drop any recognition of rank, including their own. As Bill would learn, this organisation functioned on information and trust, not egos. Among the recruits were civilians, civil servants, soldiers, officers, and even the odd member of the peerage. They were known throughout, including to each other, as numbers and nothing more. They were told lives may depend on not knowing each other, for now at least. The staff were generally just sir or ma'am.

They all knew it was something different. Untried. All they knew when they signed up for training was the name of this new organisation and that they would be expected to learn all the things required to survive, fight and kill behind enemy lines. It was apparent why ranks were irrelevant here. Some of the staff encountered on the course were civilians, who Bill and some other recruits on the course technically outranked. They were all small cogs in a faceless engine.

"No, sir. Sorry, sir," replied Bill with a new, more obvious keenness.

"Good. Next, we shall move on to techniques. Remember, there are no rules. This is gutter fighting. Kill or be killed. No time for mercy. Once your target is identified, you must, at all costs, kill them. There is no time or place for risk. Incapacitating or rendering the enemy unconscious leaves you with the risk he may still be able to raise the alarm should he recover."

Yup, thought Bill. A real charmer.

"You can forget all those Yank westerns where the hero creeps up, lifts the enemy's chin and easily slits his throat. Apart from the shock, they will still be able to scream out and certainly still have time to flick off a safety catch and pull a trigger, compromising your position to a now vigilant enemy. If you are working silently, there is no finer weapon than the one you will handle today. This is the F-S knife. It will become the best friend you could wish for in the field."

Bill looked grimly at the polished steel stiletto dagger being shown.

Christ, how the hell had he got himself into this?

* * *

"Now you try, up and in pairs, one from each pair take a training knife."

Bill was determined to find someone weak. As he scanned the room, Fairburn appeared in front of him.

"Ah, Number Fourteen, there is an odd number, so you can help me demonstrate."

Bill reluctantly took his position as the weak antelope while the lion stalked away to hide in the savanna behind him. He glanced into the box of blunt rubber training knives, then chanced a look at Fairburn to see him still clutching his own knife, just with its brass-tipped leather sheath on.

"Face the front, Fourteen!"

"Yessir, sorrysir," Bill stammered.

"Now, remember, you want to get in as close as possible. Thrust the knife into the side of the neck. This is only the practice, so don't try to hurt each other! Then you punch forward, taking out the whole throat. It's messy but very effective."

Bill felt the cold brass hit him in the neck. At that split second, it felt like a hammer blow, and he felt his vision dim like someone was dropping the theatre curtain for good.

Then everything went black.

* * *

"Ha ha, come on, son, wake up. It wasn't that hard!"

Bill blinked at the spinning colours in front of his eyes. He had no idea how long he'd been out, but it seemed long enough for the others to have stopped and crowded around him.

"Right! Back to it, you lot! Your turn now, Fourteen!"

And that was how the rest of the day went on. Drilling with

the knife and practising sticking it into various body parts like some obscene voodoo doll or a diviner testing for various fluids. At one point, Fairburn brought out some pig carcasses to practice on. The aim was to let the knife do the work. Very little pressure was necessary to get the blade in deep. The thin, prismatic shape of the long, pointed knife and its razor-sharp point and edges meant it went into flesh like butter.

* * *

Since arriving in Scotland, they had spent the past couple of weeks on various skills training. The first week had been dedicated to endurance, physical training, and escape and evasion techniques. Running up and down the multiple peaks of Inverness-shire in old, poorly fitted boots was not quite Bill's idea of a fun time, but he had, so far, done well. From the beginning, he had planned not to come first or last at anything. Wherever he was in danger of winning the runs, he pulled up when out of sight to allow the rest to catch up, then tucked himself into the lead pack, allowing someone else the glory of coming first. He figured to join an organisation training people to blend in behind enemy lines, it was best to become 'the grey man'. Inconspicuous was the aim of the game.

The staff had thrown in a few obstacle courses involving crawling on your belly and elbows through thorns and brambles under an old fishing net. It had led to an interesting night pulling thorns out of each other by candlelight. In his group, there had initially been thirty recruits. However, after the week in London taking psychological, intelligence and mental tests, the group had been reduced to twenty-two. They then boarded buses to head to Scotland, which the staff told them was phase two. By the end of the first week there, only thirteen remained.

There was still much more to come in Scotland; unarmed combat, demolitions, Morse code, weapons training and radio operations. Various specialists joined them to teach each set of skills, including an old Scottish captain, in full uniform, kilt and all, to introduce 'ghillie' techniques on how to blend into the environment. There was also an American known to Bill as Major Smith to teach how to strip and clean the various weapons that would be issued. The Colt 1911, a couple of revolvers, and the Thompson submachine gun.

Bill thought that Americans must make the best or the cheapest guns. Then he hoped it was the former.

Only five of the original thirty recruits remained at the end of phase two. Bill had been careful to not chat too much to his fellow recruits, but he was nevertheless sad to see some of them go. They would perhaps get supporting roles in the organisation or employment elsewhere in the services, he comforted himself.

The final phase of this initial training was parachuting at RAF Ringway in Cheshire. The recruits were housed in a stately home on the outskirts of the airfield. There was one thing, at least, that the Special Operations Executive did well: requisitioning the best buildings. Moreover, they had political clout because Bill was sure this would have been the base commander's quarters during peacetime.

Another good thing about SOE was the breakfasts. Bacon, butter and sugar were supposed to be on the ration, but it seemed they had failed to mention this to their cook. On the second day, they had learned to control their gluttony after most of them had seen their breakfast come back up again the previous morning during the practice jumps from the tower. All the recruits passed the parachute phase, but Bill would never see them again. He never even knew their names.

Finishing school in Hampshire would be the culmination of training, where he would be thrown in with yet more strangers, all of whom had completed the other stages of training separately.

8

Half Crowns

Beaulieu, Hampshire, England, September 1940

"What is *Fritz* doing here?" he demanded to no one in particular.

Jack's accent had caught the attention of an oil-slick-haired Military Police officer who had been making himself at home for several hours before their arrival. He had a pretentious pencil-thin moustache that he probably thought made him look like Clark Gable, but actually, it looked like he had been supping milk stout. As was recommended, Bill had not worn his uniform, whilst Jack was still a civilian anyway, pending his commission as an officer.

Jack ignored him and continued to wait at the bar for the two beers that would shortly be heading his way. Bill placed his hat on the table, lit his pre-filled pipe and assessed the room through the smoke. Aside from anything else, smoking helped to give enough time to observe, evaluate and plan while remaining largely unnoticed. How could a casual observer possibly realise that this bloke at the corner table had already pinpointed both possible rear exits, worked out all the routes to the chair beside the officer, and taken in the locations of the various empty bottles and glasses to use as weapons on the way? This same inconspicuous pipe-toker had also appraised the other patrons and clocked the two most apparent threats: a gorilla-looking sergeant who was playing dominoes with an equally ugly but slightly smaller corporal. Both had their red berets on the table in front of them, and they were clearly accompanying the belligerent officer at the bar.

The only other customer was an older gent ignoring the others and doing a crossword with an untouched half of ale in front of him. Bill now knew he had the advantage. He had assessed the danger. Jack threw an almost imperceptible look about him, and Bill was now sure his friend had just done the same.

"I asked you a question, Fritz!" the officer barked, this time directly at Jack.

Without a word, Jack smirked, lit a cigarette, paid the pretty, blonde barmaid and strutted toward Bill's table with the drinks in hand. But, by now, the thuggish-looking domino lovers were paying full attention to them.

"I am an officer in the British Army, and in the name of the King, I wish to know your names!" The officer was drunk, and now his demands sounded more like pleas. He swayed on his stool as he spun around and steadied himself on the bar.

"I think you ought to answer 'im," grunted the gorilla.

"And I think you gentlemen should return to your game and let the adults deal with this," retorted Bill in a calm but firm voice. Bill was probably the same age as Sergeant Gorilla and weighed around three stone less, which only riled him further.

"You mouthy ..."

Just as the sergeant got out of his chair, Jack, who had settled in the spot to Bill's left and had a good view of the room, stood and turned slightly right, keeping his left shoulder toward the threat. Bill watched the officer and checked he had remained perched on his stool.

The gorilla thrust a giant fist toward Jack. His big mistake was the force he put behind it. It was a boxer's punch, with the power from his whole upper body. If it had landed, which it probably had on other less suspecting targets in the past, his opponent would be asleep before he hit the deck. But, instead, Jack moved barely six inches to the left and back. The gorilla lost his balance as his fist met nothing but fresh air, and Jack snapped an open palm up into the gorilla's jaw, whipping his head back, and simultaneously thrust a knee into the side of his, sending him falling to the floor like felling a mighty Scotch fir.

The thud had lifted all the tables in the pub, and Bill rescued his pint. The corporal had already started his way towards Jack. Bill had already seen that Jack knew this, as he shifted his weight to the right and allowed the corporal's clenched left hand to pass him harmlessly. Jack responded with a headbutt to his face that landed with a sickening crunch. The corporal dropped to the ground and started sobbing, his hands trying to stem the blood flow from his nose.

"You bastard, you could have saved my beer!" exclaimed Jack when he noticed his empty glass rolling away. "And you could have helped, Bill!"

"You were doing just fine. I was waiting in reserve." Bill grinned, stood up and moved towards the now pale-faced officer. "There is no Fritz in here, sir. My father was German, and my friend here is Polish by birth, and the pair of us will drink wherever we damn well choose."

The dumb-struck MP lieutenant said nothing and sat silently. Bill assured the barmaid the two apes would be fine and ordered another beer. He left three half-crown coins on the bar and apologised for the mess. The two lumps of gristle had removed themselves from the floor and returned to their table. The corporal was holding a blood-soaked rag to his face and looking at the officer with pleading, puppy-dog eyes. Bill returned to his friend, and they drank their pints swiftly but casually and headed for the exit.

The older chap doing his crossword stood and blocked their way. "Good work, gentlemen. I see my colleague has taught you well. You forgot one important thing, though! Always give them a kick in the testicles at the end, just to make sure!"

He had the excited enthusiasm of youth in his eyes.

"Er, thank you … sir?" Jack ventured.

"Well done, lads. Cracking work. My name is Sykes. Eric Sykes. I believe you already know my partner, Mr Fairburn?"

"Of course, sir, it's a pleasure to meet you," said Bill, shaking the man by the hand. He had a solid, firm handshake. It wasn't the desperate grip of a man trying to look strong, more like the grip of a working man that had real strength without even trying. The man was a legend. He and Fairburn were becoming well known among the other recruits as probably the finest street fighters in the world.

"I'll have the staff deal with these other three. I believe they have been vetted to be posted up the road on a security detail near the commando training depot, but I'll see that they are returned to their units with a flea in their ear."

9

Cabaret

Paris, 1st August 1944

Bill watched the young scantily-clad girls work the room through the dingy fug. Sometimes the life of a spy was such a burden to him. The various field grey uniforms in the club seemed to attract female company like moths to a flame. Bill couldn't really blame them. The Germans threw their francs around like confetti. It was hardly surprising, considering how little they would need them in the coming weeks. How the girls brought themselves to lower their standards to a sufficient level actually to sleep with them was another matter entirely.

The cabaret over, the girls were going about the business of making some proper money. Bill looked over and saw Delphine walk over to Misselwitz's table. She leaned over as she seemed to be speaking to him, and Bill got one hell of a view of her pert derrière. Yes, he thought. It appeared risking life, limb and liberty did, indeed, have its perks. Bill adjusted his bow tie as he looked on. It suddenly felt very hot.

"Can I get you another, sir?" the Southern-sounding waiter inquired. His peculiar accent sounded out of place in Paris. Bill knew French well and could tell by his inflection that he probably grew up speaking Gascon, or another of the odd regional dialects down near the Pyrénées.

Bill was surprised to see him. He had materialised out of the smokey haze that hung in the air like a cloying veil. So cloying that Bill had not even bothered with smoking his pipe, as it would just be a waste of tobacco with all the cheap blue smoke from the numerous German cigarettes that surrounded him. In any case, he only had French tobacco on him.

"Yes, please."

The waiter disappeared back into the thick haze beyond. Bill risked a glance to Leo and Andre's table. They were ignoring him, fully absorbed in their conversation. Their job was solely backup in case Bill was compromised, and it all kicked off in the club. Leo and Andre were known here, like many places in Paris, as the well-liked delivery men. Working delivering liquor for fake collaborators certainly had its perks, Bill thought, as one of the half-naked sirens shimmied towards their table. The handsome Leo looked up with a delighted grin and pushed a banknote into the girl's garter. Andre looked up at her, cigarette-in-mouth, with the kind of smile that could turn milk sour from ten paces.

Bill looked across just as Misselwitz grabbed Delphine and yanked her down hard onto his lap. Bill was going to enjoy killing him. He watched as Misselwitz grinned, grabbing her all over and roughly pulling at her breasts. Poor girl. Bill suddenly felt guilt wash over him for involving her.

Too many girls had been dragged into this beastly war. Bill had, at least, managed to send a message to Vera, through Lena, with news of Violette's capture and imprisonment at the hands of these grey-uniformed beasts.

The waiter appeared with Bill's brandy on a little silver platter. As he set down the glass on the table, Bill placed the money for the drinks, plus a healthy tip, onto the miniature tray. The waiter bowed his head politely and disappeared again. In a nest of German vipers, it doesn't pay to get too noticed if you are a helpless French mouse.

Bill sipped carefully at his drink and watched as Misselwitz shoved Delphine off him and stood up. He looked to be unsteady on his feet. Perfect.

All he needed now was for the intelligence passed through Roland to be correct. Every Friday night, Misselwitz crossed the Seine and headed to his private apartment in the Latin Quarter with one of the showgirls. With his standing and rank in the Gestapo, the girls had little choice, and with a breathtaking level of arrogance, he would lead them to his lair alone.

Even though two years earlier, Heydrich, the overall head of the Nazi State Police, had been killed by partisans in Prague, Misselwitz considered himself untouchable. He thought the numerous reprisals upon the French for killing their occupiers in the proceeding years made him invincible. Even with the allies almost within striking distance of Paris and the war going very badly for the Germans, this clown was still going about the business of illicit and highly immoral encounters with the locals even by the standards of the Nazi Party.

Bill sank his Brandy. He needed the French courage. As

Misselwitz gathered up his greatcoat and hat from the lobby, Bill rose and moved towards the exit too. The petite middle-aged maitre d' looked like a china doll. His tiny hands were covered by white cotton gloves that appeared to have been stolen from a child's bear. Bill collected his hat, long coat and gloves and hastily dressed. He tipped the miniature toy man and headed out into the city.

Bill would have preferred darkness, but the curfew was getting stricter. Moreover, the daily power outages aside, the Germans were becoming increasingly concerned about reprisal killings or allied bombing. Unofficially, most of the soldiers were now stationed on the outskirts of the city, and the officers left in the centre gave very little credence to the pliant populace turning on them. In any case, they knew getting shot in Paris with a hard-on or a belly full of wine was, whilst undesirable, none-the-less preferable to being reassigned to the Eastern Front.

Bill headed straight down towards the river. The northern side of the city was far too open and obvious for either a secret liaison or a successful assassination. Misselwitz and his latest victim were just in sight ahead of him. Bill stopped to light his pipe at the end of a narrow alleyway. With a gentle tug, a revolver was dropped into his right coat pocket, and Jack walked to the opposite side of the street, feigning a slight meander that might appear the man was drunk to a casual observer. Bill checked his pipe was correctly lit and continued on his afternoon walk. It was close to curfew, and the streets were quiet apart from a few people heading home. Most people knew to stay indoors for fear of a random attack by a drunk Nazi with nothing to lose.

Bill and Jack were pretty safe in their fine clothing and false

ID papers showing they were French-German businessmen. They would hold up to a random stop, but they had no way of knowing how they might look with closer scrutiny. They hadn't had long to concoct a cover story, but hopefully, it wouldn't come to that. Bill forced it out of his head with a cloud of awful stale-tasting French tobacco.

Rounding the bend and heading towards the famous Île de la Cité, the island in the Seine that formed the old town of Paris in ancient times. An old Roman fortress used to stand here, followed by the fortifications of the medieval era. It stood like a mountain to resist the Viking attackers from the river below. Bill imagined how the river must have run red with the dead Danes and French. Today a German officer would be quenching the blood lust of the river once more.

He closed down the distance to the staggering figure ahead. Bill took a casual glance around as they approached the Notre Dame cathedral in all its Gothic splendour. The area was deserted. No witnesses. The hit was a go. Bill had intended to shoot him and run, but he decided at the moment that a quieter method might be best and far, far more satisfying. Killing rarely filled Bill with such gleeful anticipation, but this one he was genuinely looking forward to. He tapped out his pipe onto the floor and put it in his pocket.

Misselwitz suddenly stopped. Shit, Bill thought, he'd heard him. After a few raised words with Delphine, he struck her hard with the back of his gloved hand across the jaw. She squealed and then did her level best not to look back at Bill. She failed as her eyes just caught his with a silent pleading prayer for rescue.

Bill reached into his left inside pocket and drew out his commando knife. Invoking both the training of his instructors and the spirits of the dead warriors of old, he ran the final few yards towards the bastard. The red mist suddenly rose through his eyeballs like lava, and his veins pumped pure adrenaline. He gripped the stippled handle of this steel implement of death and prepared himself in the final few seconds for the impact. He focused on the exposed neck of his target and held the knife out to his side as he moved in. In barely another second, Misselwitz, this psychopathic facilitator of mass murder, would be dead. Time seemed to slow to a crawl as Bill felt the ghosts of his pagan forefathers at his shoulders. Clear sight now, he felt his mind flooded with nothing but clarity. One aim, one strike. He couldn't miss.

Then a sledgehammer blow to his left calf buckled his leg under him. A warm feeling trickled down to his ankle as the cobbled road rose up to strike him a second time on the opposite knee, and he crumpled into a pile. The cold stones met hard with his head, swimming now with confusion. His knife bounced harmlessly out of reach as he went for his gun. Drawing it out, it suddenly went on a flighty retreat into a nearby hedge as a jackbooted foot connected with it. He heard a female scream in the confusion and watched as Delphine tried to run. Two steps were as far as she got. A dull thud, followed by a deafening ringing as his ears refused to let him hear anymore. Delphine slumped, her right leg sickeningly twisted back behind her, onto the hard ground, and a tide of blood spilled from the gaping exit hole in her face. It ran down and off her lips like a pulsing waterfall. One of her black shoes bounced away to find his lost blade. Then more black.

All black.

Nothing but black.

* * *

He risked opening his eyes for a moment to find himself on another cold, stone floor. This time the cobblestones were replaced by some kind of tiles. He sat up. His wounded leg had been carefully bandaged. He was almost naked, except for some grubby white shorts which were not his own. He attempted to work out where he was in the dim light emanating from under the door. The room was quite large and empty. He squinted into the cavernous immensity.

Bill risked a quiet "Hello?" in French. No reply. Bill tried to invoke those pagan gods again, but they remained silent. Hopefully, that meant he was, indeed, alone. He didn't need the silent, brooding anger of the gods on his back, as well as everything else.

He felt queasy and suppressed the urge to vomit, risking losing whatever fluids he had inside him. He doubted he would be getting any water anytime soon. He was suddenly very thirsty.

Carefully supporting his lower leg, he managed to get up onto his knees and shuffle across the wet floor. It was cold and slippery, but not enough to cup any to drink. In the centre of the room was an iron grill. A drain, Bill thought. It began to dawn on him where he might be.

The door swung open with a blinding flash of candlelight. Silhouetted by it was what Bill assumed was Death himself. Wearing a long black cloak, he was coming for Bill. In place of a hood sat a peaked cap, which, as Bill began to focus, he noticed had a grinning metallic skull staring back at him, appearing to move in the spilling candlelight. This grim reaper had no scythe, though. Instead, this one held a Luger.

"If you are looking for a drink, I'm afraid the bar is closed," Bill snapped. The best form of defence is attack, he hoped.

Death flipped a clunky switch in dire need of oil on the wall somewhere. The screech signalled the ceiling fairies to begin their peculiar dance, and in a mass of flickering, the bulbs started to glow with an ominous amber light.

Looking around the strange room confirmed to Bill what he already knew. The floor and walls had been recently washed down and gave the tiles a wet sheen that reflected light up onto the face of the Nazi officer that dwarfed him. His over-emphasised mouth lines looked like he had on a permanent smirk. He looked like he had been the kind of kid who used to pull the wings off flies. His eyes looked like those of a wolf. Pure predator. His cap was on a tilt and pulled down slightly too far. As Bill surveyed his face, the shit-eating grin widened, sitting above an angular jaw and weak-looking chin, which could be made of glass. One punch could shatter it like Waterford Crystal, he thought.

"You are hardly in a position to be making jokes, dog," the spindly lips spat out.

"I'm not in much of a position to be doing a lot else." Bill shrugged. As his heart rate increased, so did the throbbing pain in his leg.

Death had noticed his slight wince. "I'd be happy to give you more balance by adding a matching hole in the other leg."

"You are in a lot of trouble," Bill tried in his most convincing voice. "I am a German citizen from Alsace and a businessman with a great many connections. My people will realise I am missing and contact your superiors."

"Superiors?" he scoffed. "And you are going to stick to that story, are you? You see, we know you are a spy. The sooner you admit it, the sooner we can move you to a far more comfortable accommodation."

This wasn't good. They couldn't know he was a spy for sure already, could they? One thing *was* for sure; this chisel-faced devil would find out the truth, or at least some of it. Despite what they tell you in training about resistance to interrogation, it would be only that. Resistance. This wasn't some movie where the hero sticks out his chest and shouts, *Never!* This was real life, where fingers get snapped, and teeth get pulled. Everyone has a breaking point. At least they couldn't make him pregnant, Bill comforted himself with his usual sardonic humour.

"I don't know what you are talking about," Bill replied, resigning to his fate.

"That is a shame. Luckily though, I quite enjoy my work. You are just doing your job, dog, and now you must understand that we must do ours."

Misselwitz walked through the doorway. In his left hand was a small leather doctor's case. In his right was a heavy wooden police baton, which he handed to his friend. Both of them grinned maniacally as they approached.

The gods turned away.

10

The Kitchen

Paris, 6th August 1944

Bill lay as still as he could manage. It was all he could do to stop the pain. Of course, he'd prefer not to be lying on the floor, but needs must when the devil drives the butt of a Luger into your mouth.

His leg was in agony. Bill knew enough about wounds to know he needed treatment and antibiotics soon, or he risked it going septic. Thankfully, it was a pretty clean hole. The bullet had gone straight through without deforming. However, Bill had seen enough men shot to know it could have been far worse. He felt inside his mouth with a grubby finger and found two of his teeth were broken. The lacerations inside his cheek were still weeping blood, and he turned and spat the dark froth away.

He tried to get his mind to focus and attempt to remember how long he'd been here. Three days, maybe? Four? His unconvincing cover story had not held up for long, and he'd resorted to simply staying silent. In the last interrogation, the Devil had beaten his back with some kind of club. At least one of his ribs felt broken. Misselwitz had promised his fingers were going to be next. Could Bill withstand that? He had never felt so thirsty in his entire life. If the torture didn't kill him, the thirst surely would.

The iron door rattled open, and Bill instinctively flinched, recoiled and then curled into a ball. He waited for the inevitable shoeing, but it never came. There wasn't even a guard at the door. Was it a trick? Maybe someone was helping him? Should he attempt to get up and run?

Most of his questions were answered with a resounding *no* as two SS dogsbodies dragged a bloodied figure in the shape of a man and slumped it on the ground in front of the open doorway, and disappeared from sight. It was certainly human in form, but the blood, bruises, snot and dirt that covered the face made it very hard to recognise what used to be his best friend, Jack. He opened one eyelid, but the eye rolled aimlessly around in the socket. The SS guards returned, picked up Jack and continued dragging him along the corridor. Finally, the iron door slammed shut with an alarming bang.

Bill had spun them a lie, stayed silent and done his duty. Lena would have alerted HQ, and any current planning to which Bill had prior knowledge would have been changed. Of course, by now, their Resistance friends would have moved to another safe house, too.

They had given Jack a proper going-over, and if he looked like that, he hadn't yet given in either. But, he wouldn't last another session. He hadn't seen Violette for weeks, but he had heard one of the guards talking about her. She was still here.

They obviously assumed he couldn't understand German.

His two friends were in this building somewhere, suffering. King and country? That's bullshit. They had done their duty to operational security and bought Baker Street time to re-plan. Now it was time to do their duty to each other.

* * *

"So, you're sticking to your story? You know your friend? He won't last much longer. He isn't quite as strong as you." Misselwitz was, it seemed, cast as the good cop in today's chapter of *tell us what we want to know, or we'll hurt you.*

Bill knew they were working him over. Jack was twice the man Bill was, so he knew they must have been giving him a far worse time of it. The Devil was sitting next to Misselwitz on the other side of the filthy, blood-stained table staring through his soul with a surgeon's scalpel in his hand. Bad cop, Bill thought. Definitely the bad cop.

"We can help, you know. We have a dentist in the building. He practised in Vienna before the war. One of the best. Are you still having trouble with your teeth?"

"They are broken." Bill struggled to form the words. Misselwitz nodded like a concerned parent, his boyish features forced into a look of concern as his head bounced up and down. Bill would have liked nothing more than to bounce his head up and down off the cold stone floor.

"We have more of you, by the way. Even a girl. Violette, is it? Yes, she is a feisty one. Maybe I will let Klaus have some more fun with her." Misselwitz flinched as he realised he'd let the Devil's name slip. The Devil shot him a stern look. It clicked in Bill's now fragile mind. The Devil was Klaus Barbie, the man they called the spy hunter. Head of the Gestapo in Lyon.

Bill sat in stoic silence.

"I see we still have our work cut out for us," Misselwitz said politely, then smacked Bill across the face with a gloved hand.

Barbie sat and waited. Bill continued to say nothing. The floor was covered in blood that was not Bill's. Maybe it was Jack's, Bill wondered, as a cold wash of guilt ran down his spine. He could only hope it was not Violette's. He had no idea who he should pray to, even if he'd wanted to. No gods ever visited number 84, Avenue Foch.

"This is the last chance you have to save your friends." Misselwitz kicked Bill hard in the shin under the table. A rush of pain shot up, and Bill stifled a scream through broken, gritted teeth.

"Guard!" Barbie suddenly demanded.

A young SS guard entered the room. He was barely an adult, with a helmet that looked too big for him. He was so pale that Bill imagined you could hold him up to a lamp and see all his internal organs, like a newborn fish. Hardly a prime example of their so-called Aryan race.

"Take this," Barbie said as he handed the SS child the scalpel, keeping his eyes locked on Bill's. "Go with the other guards up to that spy bitch. Do whatever you like with her, then cut her throat and let her bleed out."

The child nodded and turned to leave.

"Wait!" Bill shouted. He had never felt so ashamed in his whole life. They had broken him. He just could not let Violette be punished, raped, and killed for the sake of his pride. They would find out what they wanted to know anyway, so why let them kill Violette?

Barbie reclaimed the scalpel, said something quietly to the youthful guard, and then dismissed him. He carefully placed the scalpel back in the little leather bag and then pulled out a notebook and pencil.

"So, what is your name, and who do you work for?"

To the surprise of his two captors, Bill ceased to speak French and switched to German.

"My name is William Hoffmann, and I am an intelligence officer in the British Army."

"So, a spy?"

"No, I am an intelligence officer."

They say potato; Bill says p*omme de terre*. They were going to get just enough information to keep him and the others alive, but he would not make it too easy for them.

"So, where is your uniform? The Reich will not recognise you as an enemy combatant."

"The Reich can kiss my arse," Bill retorted, earning him another hard slap from Misselwitz.

"Not very clever to annoy us further, Mr Hoffmann. What was your mission? To kill Ernst here?" Barbie continued, using Misselwitz's name in retaliation for revealing his own, not even lifting his eyes from his pad.

"Something like that. We were to observe and report activities at the Gestapo headquarters."

"Good, good. You see? Now we are getting somewhere. There is no need for all this hostility."

Throughout the next half an hour or so, Bill went on to tell them about how they arrived and to whom they reported. He just left out the part about hiding with the Resistance and words like *spy* and *SOE*. He denied knowing Violette but confirmed Jack was his fellow operative and that he had persuaded Delphine to help but that she was not part of the Resistance. He assured them no one else in Paris was involved. But, of course, it was all relatively useless to them now. The allies were closing in, and the Germans would soon be out of France for good anyway.

"Good, Mr Hoffmann, good," Barbie said, reclining back into his chair and pretentiously steepling his fingers like a philosophy professor contemplating existence.

Bill contemplated leaping the desk and biting his throat out. He figured he was dead anyway, so why not try and take one of them with him. The knowledge they would surely kill the others in revenge afterwards was all that stopped him.

SS kid returned from locations unknown with an enamel bowl full of cold broth and a piece of stale bread.

"For now, you will eat. You may return to your cell, and then we will talk again about the lies you are still telling us. We will want to know who else is helping you in Paris." Misselwitz smiled as awkwardly as a lizard trying to dance the tango.

* * *

They had left him alone for a couple of days now, presumably just working on Jack and Violette. They had stuck to their word so far, and he had been fed a little each day, plus the odd cup of water, every once in a while.

Bill's cell was on one of the upper floors. He had a view of the wide, tree-lined avenue through the large, barred windows. In other circumstances, it might have been a pretty view. Whoever designed Paris sure knew how to make a statement. The little garden in front of the building opened up to the avenue proper and looked to be maybe a hundred yards wide. You could fit an entire company of men standing shoulder-to-shoulder across it.

He hadn't spotted Lena or the others. That was good. It meant they knew to stay away. Bill hoped it wasn't anywhere he knew about, wherever they had gone. Anything his interrogators might get out of him would put his friends at risk.

There was some shouting coming from downstairs. Bill strained to listen but couldn't make out what they were saying. Some doors slammed, and some odd swear words were uttered, but still, Bill had no idea what was going on.

Some more time passed in relative peace, perhaps twenty minutes, and then Bill heard the sound of engines. Peering from the window, he saw a drab-painted motorbike and sidecar ridden by a German dispatch rider. He wore a long green greatcoat and the usual German piss-pot helmet, with ludicrous oversized riding goggles that made him look like a kind of squat praying mantis. The large metal gorget around his neck on a thick chain indicated he was from the *Feldgendarmerie*.

He pulled up and got off the motorcycle, which the large man made look child-sized. He removed his goggles, and Bill could see he was at least sixty with a square, strong face and a large nose. He looked like a seasoned fighter. Going by his age, he had probably served in the last war. The giant man pulled out a pack of cigarettes and dragged one out with his mouth. Misselwitz, who had now emerged from the building, greeted him with a *Heil Hitler!* salute, which was summarily ignored by the veteran *Feldgendarmerie* NCO, who merely pulled out a lighter and lit his cigarette. A visibly perturbed Misselwitz stopped for a moment, obviously thought better of saying anything, then walked up to the green giant, who gave him a friendly nod and offered him a smoke.

A military field ambulance, followed by a *Kubelwagen,* pulled up alongside, and two men hopped out of the little armoured car. They, too, were military police but junior in rank to the old stalwart, who remained talking to Misselwitz, almost oblivious to their presence. The two ambulance crew opened the rear door and patiently waited by it.

The commotion downstairs restarted, and Bill watched as they wrestled a prisoner out of the building and towards the waiting ambulance. The prisoner wore a black felt bag over the head, wrists bound behind, and appeared extremely unsteady. The young SS guard was dragging the prisoner along on unwilling legs. The prisoner suddenly bucked, throwing the guard off-balance. The bag had come off in the movement, and Bill could see it was Violette. She was still sporting a black eye, but it was definitely her.

As she stormed closer to Misselwitz, she spat a big gob of saliva at him, hitting him square in his face. Misselwitz instinctively went for his pistol in the holster at his hip. The large NCO grabbed him by the wrist to prevent this with one hand, as the other took a handful of Violette's hair, almost lifting her off the ground. As she dangled on tip-toes, Misselwitz shot the NCO a look, and they exchanged words, but Bill couldn't hear what. The young guard had picked himself off the ground, re-took control of Violette, more roughly this time, and bundled her into the waiting ambulance.

Good girl, Bill thought as he grinned at the little victory she'd scored. The young guard disappeared back into the building. Misselwitz pulled out a small white handkerchief and wiped his face. His usual calm demeanour had morphed into a seething rage. His face was flushed, and he was breathing through gritted teeth. The big NCO continued to smoke and sauntered away to chat with the ambulance crew.

The young SS guard reappeared, this time with another guard to help drag a second prisoner. This one was clearly a man. He was slumped over, and the guards were dragging him along. The bagged head of the figure tried to look up. Even from this height, he appeared to be relatively tall and well-built. Jack, Bill surmised, it had to be Jack.

As the guards manoeuvred him towards the ambulance, Misselwitz, almost incandescent with rage now, shouted, in German, "Hold him up straight, at once!"

The two guards immediately stood up the prisoner. He wore a loose-fitting blue shirt and cheap trousers, elasticated at the waist, with black plimsolls. Even in his malnourished state, Bill was sure that this must be Jack. Misselwitz drew his Luger and aimed at his head.

"Nooooo!" Bill screamed as loud as he could. His broken ribs sent a sharp, stabbing pain through his left lung.

It was one thing to yell into the abyss. It was quite another when the abyss seemed to scream back.

Misselwitz looked up at Bill in the barred window, forced a sideways grin, and then returned his gaze down at the prisoner. The military police NCO and his two colleagues looked on, saying nothing.

Doing nothing.

The moment seemed frozen in time. Bill's heart ceased to beat and turned to ice inside his chest as Misselwitz fired three shots at the bedraggled shape, which slumped to the ground when the guards released their grip. A large pool of blood spilled across the paving slabs.

Bill slid to the ground and stared at one of the plain walls of his cell in utter disbelief.

11

Liberation

Paris, 18th August 1944

This was the worst time for Bill. Why had they kept him here, except to kill him? It had been a week since they had whisked away Violette and shot Jack. Bill had never felt so utterly alone. The surly guards had fed him, and he had regular visits by an SS physician who had treated his leg but had categorically refused to speak to him. It suited Bill just fine. Anything he did want to say to the miserable old sod would probably have earned him a punch in the throat anyway, perhaps by proxy via one of the guards.

It had all stopped about two days ago. When he was last taken to have his dressing changed, for most of the day, Bill could smell burning, and from within the depths of the building, he had been able to hear slamming doors and the distant sound of vehicles.

The noise had already subsided when he was dragged back

up to his cell. He had then watched from his barred window the SS doctor leave the building on foot, wearing his greatcoat, with his case in hand. He had waited a few minutes, long enough to smoke a cigarette, for a smart black staff car to collect him. The purring engine changed pitch to an ominous growl as it disappeared from view along the avenue.

Now he sat in peace, alone in his cell. He suspected his firing squad was being assembled. His final release from this hell would soon be arranged, courtesy of the most sadistic organisation to trample the earth since Genghis Khan's Mongol hoards.

He licked his lips to find there was no moisture left. He desperately needed water. He hadn't taken on fluids for a couple of days. As he sat staring at the blank walls, he wondered if he should drink his urine. Try as he might, he couldn't remember if that was the right thing to do or not. In any case, he had no cup, and any other way he could think of getting any into his mouth didn't bear thinking about. Finally, Bill decided he'd instead try to sleep and not overthink it. If the Nazis didn't kill him soon, they'd find him dead already.

* * *

He woke with a start and pulled the wiry blanket off, rubbing his itchy, dry eyes. He felt thirst like he'd never known before. A crippling thirst.

There was another dull, distant thud. He hadn't imagined it. The dark sky flashed like sheet lightning. The gods were angry. Bill had no idea how long he'd been drifting in and out of consciousness. His head felt like a giant football, only half-inflated.

The rumbling and flashing took Bill back to the long autumns when he was young. Returning to school for the autumn term had always hit Bill hard. He always felt despondent standing at the entrance to the open car park, waving off his mother and aunt.

Without fail, Bill's mother had collected him from school to spend the six free weeks at home every summer holiday. Bill had always felt sorry for the boys in his dorm who had been left to while away the break at school. Whilst trips and games had been planned for them, homework and additional studies were never far out of sight. Looking back now, Bill wondered if some parents had left their kids there for the summer hoping for some academic advancement.

His mother and aunt had taken up the reins following his father's untimely death. At home, his nanny, Hannah, had also helped with the more menial tasks during his early formative years. She had also brought him up speaking his late father's mother tongue, much to the dismay of his Aunt Nelly, a staunch nationalist. She had tolerated Bill's father in her sister's life and was friendly enough to Hannah but had never truly forgiven Germany for the war. Her sweetheart had died at the Battle of Mons in 1914, and she held a bitter resentment toward the country and most of its people ever since.

The autumn term, though, for Bill, held another adventure. Bonfire night was always a date to look forward to. Whilst the school organised a bonfire and fireworks celebration, it was nothing compared to the covert version of the event he and his friends planned in the fields beyond the cricket green. Invariably, one of the boys would have stolen some whisky or brandy from home during the holidays. Perhaps another would have some woodbines. They would trudge to the far side of the field, dragging various bits of dry firewood behind them.

They had managed to get away with it every year until Bill was twelve. One of the boys had stolen some fireworks from the groundskeeper's shed near the cricket nets that year. After a few tentative attempts, they finally got one lit. But unfortunately, none of them had any idea what they were supposed to do with it, and the rocket had launched off sideways, bouncing harmlessly into a nearby hedgerow. A few moments later, they were trying to light a second one. This time stuck in the soft ground when suddenly the first rocket exploded with an almighty *BOOM*! A shower of sparks spat into every direction, and the boys flinched, then fell about, laughing.

They then spent half an hour drinking, smoking and talking about whatever you talked about before you discovered girls. Some of the others were still lighting fireworks. One particular stray rocket had fizzed off in the direction of Yew Tree Farm and been quickly forgotten.

Bill was passing a bottle of brandy around the circle as one of the boys shouted, "Shit, the barn's on fire! Leg it!"

Dropping their bottles and cigarettes, they spun on their heels and took off back towards the school as fast as a herd of gazelles making off from a pursuing lioness. Their bonfire was still burning brightly behind them, and its glow was now joined by that of the dry barn, which was now a blazing inferno.

They vaulted the gate and sprinted towards the cricket green, only to be met by four angry prefects in the near darkness. This in itself would not have been a significant issue but for the fact that their headmaster, Mr Armitage, had recently extended the ability to carry out corporal punishment to the senior prefects.

Bill squinted out of his window again. Now the sky was flashing white, over and over. All he could think of was the fireworks on that night at Bloxham. They had taken a beating from the prefects. The following day's assembly was a lengthy reprimand to the gathered schoolboys en-masse from the headmaster about citizenship, respecting the community and the sins of stealing. Bill had somehow forgotten most of that and fondly recalled only the night of fireworks, drinking and merriment.

Now here, on this cold dark cell floor masquerading as his uncomfortable death bed, he smiled as he listened to the advancing French forces. Death for him, he decided, would now be inevitable. Be it from a German bullet, thirst or, in the ultimate irony, a French artillery shell. This was his end.

He smiled to himself, happy he had at least managed to pass word back to Vera, through Lena, that Violette had been here in Paris. If nothing else, he clung to that thought. The thought that there might be a chance to rescue her, now that the war seemed to be coming towards an end. He then pictured Vera in his mind's eye, nervously fussing over every detail of the changes in operations that were necessitated by his capture. Almost able to smell the distinct odour of the Senior Service cigarette trembling between her lips as she cursed him for being so negligent.

He closed his eyes as the crippling thirst kicked at him from inside his skull and his kidneys silently screamed. He didn't care where he was going next. He knew it probably wouldn't be heaven, and he had just spent the past week in hell. Still, eternal nothingness might, at the very least, be a blessed relief from the pain he was now feeling. Through it all, he felt a small amount of satisfaction that he had done his bit for the liberation of France, then slipped into unconsciousness. Sleep was immediate. The type of sleep from which you expect never to wake.

* * *

"Bill?" a disembodied, angelic voice spoke to him.

He was startled and almost fell from the winged horse he had been riding in his dream. But then, the clouds of his mind cleared, and standing in the shadow of his own Valley of Death, there indeed was no evil, just an angel.

Lena stood over him, tears in her eyes. "You're alive!"

"The amount of pain I'm in would suggest so," he barely managed through his parched, cracked lips.

Lena handed him a bottle of the sweetest water he'd ever tasted. Better than any whisky. He let the life-giving fluid flow through every fibre in his body. Then, finishing the bottle, he slumped back against the wall.

His brain was still throbbing, and his insides felt like they had been passed through a housewife's laundry mangle. He gazed up at his saviour and beamed. Lena flashed back a relieved grin.

"They shot Jack," he ventured.

"Who told you that?" she said as Jack, helped by Andre, limped around the doorway.

"You can't get rid of me that easily, you bastard," Jack grunted.

12

Retribution

Paris, 18th August 1944

The city was in chaos. There were shops and restaurants with shutters down, fearful of both the Germans and Resistance reprisals as well as various armed groups marauding the avenues looking for victims.

Bill saw a small band of fighters in tricolour armbands aiming their guns at a line of men in front of a red brick wall. He looked away as the shots rang out. This was brutal, antediluvian mob justice, and Bill nodded to himself approvingly.

He returned his gaze as the Parisian streets absorbed the crimson fluids. The ground beneath them was like an island floating on a corrupt sea of blood stretching back through time. The city had been built on the deaths of thousands right back to the Viking siege in 845. Bill gripped the butt of his sub-machine gun and hoped he could get through this particular one. He didn't have the mythical horns on his helmet, but he still felt every bit the stranger in this peculiar place.

Glancing over at Jack, he could see that Lena was helping him put his armband on. No one wanted to get shot by their own side this late in the game. Jack was grimacing in pain and cursing the world. Bill took another long swig of water.

The truck continued to rumble down the Champs-Élysées. All around, there were resistance liberators on the march. Most were civilians. Some wore French Police uniforms. Bill spotted a man in his fifties dressed in full Great War French infantry uniform, medals and all, carrying an old bolt-action Lebel rifle. The grey-haired man waved at their painted truck with a giant hand as they passed. Bill smiled and nodded back. This was their day.

Most of the Germans had cleared out, but along their route, they had seen a few dead who had been stripped of their boots and rifles and, Bill was in no doubt, their valuables and gold teeth too.

The army had not yet arrived this far into the city. Distant shots rang out, and Bill instinctively ducked, much to Jack's amusement.

"A little nervous there, Bill?" He chuckled, then stopped and grunted in pain.

Bill just frowned back at him.

The truck veered precariously around some abandoned vehicles. The city was being cleansed of its demons. Bill checked the breach of his Thompson one last time to check the full metal-jacketed holy water was ready to go, should it be required.

Bill sat on the truck floor as the movement got too much. His leg was stinging with the rumbling of the truck's progress through the city. As they swerved side-to-side, he peered above the olive drab tailgate and saw burnt-out tanks and smouldering vehicles all over the street behind them.

They pulled up outside their old safe house. All the windows were smashed, and the door was hanging loosely from its one remaining hinge. Two Resistance fighters were standing out front. Roland slowed the truck, said something inaudible to them from the driver's side window, and then carried on along the street. A short while later, they halted at Rene's cafe.

The extensive glass frontage had somehow remained intact. There were the smouldering remains of two *Kubelwagons* on the opposite side of the street. Around twenty armed men were gathered around the burnt-out twisted steel carcasses. They stood around, laughed and chatted as the blackened skeletal remains of the cars' occupants looked on and smoked from every opening.

"You two need to rest up here while we try to find a medic," Andre told them as he lifted Jack by his arm to his feet.

"What happened to Misselwitz and Barbie?" Bill asked.

"We don't know for sure, but another group saw staff cars leaving the building a few days ago," Andre replied, dragging a moaning Jack towards the rear of the truck.

Bill hopped out and then turned to assist Andre. Lena vaulted out, a Sten in her hands, and disappeared into the still-gleaming cafe.

Andre, passing Jack down to Bill, continued, "We attacked the place at the first opportunity, once the uprising started, and found it empty and unguarded. There had been a large fire at the back, where they had been burning files."

They took Jack, one under each arm, through the glass door. They found Lena had dragged a mattress down the stairs and placed it on the ground near the counter. The cafe was a hive of activity. In the far corner, maps were spread out, and two men placed small coins on various points of interest. Near them, another two attempted to coerce an old radio set into life. Men talked to each other at different tables, completely ignoring Bill and Andre dragging a limping Jack into the cafe and onto the mattress. Everywhere were glasses and bottles. The liberation wasn't complete, but already the drinking had commenced.

Brandy and comfortable chairs, that's how a war ought to be fought, Bill thought.

They carefully laid Jack down, and Lena started to check him over. His chest was covered in open wounds. Bill winced as he saw that long, thin strips of skin had been carefully removed, probably using a surgeon's scalpel. The dried blood was mixed with dirt and pieces of material. Jack had really suffered at the House of Horrors, and Misselwitz and Barbie were facilitators of this fanatical sadism.

Having switched off the truck's engine, Roland now wandered in, MP-40 slung on a sling casually over his shoulder.

"Here you go, lads." He placed a wooden crate down. Inside were some apples, a small bottle of clear alcohol, some medical gauze and a loaf of bread.

"You are truly a lifesaver, my friend," Bill said.

Lena got up, then walked off and disappeared through a door at the back of the cafe.

"It's not a problem. We need all the men we can gather! We'll find you a medic and get him back here. Take a day or two to get well. We are working our way through the city, clearing it out house-by-house. Be sure to keep your armbands on at all times. It looks like Jack is in pain, but he should recover. He should rest up. When you feel better, you can come and join us in clearing out the neighbourhoods. These boys in here are all officers of the Resistance. Lena knows most of them. You can trust them, Willy. Just be careful; there's already been enough death without losing good men now."

"I'll need to get clean and make contact with headquarters."

"No rush, my friend. I need to head back with Andre and hook up with Nicole and the others. She's going to be famous. An American reporter has been following us and writing a story about her, photographs and everything!"

Lena reappeared with the now refilled water bottles. She left a full one in the wooden crate and helped Jack drink from another. Andre gathered up the others. Rene, the cafe's hunchbacked owner, followed closely behind. He had an old sword-bayonet in one hand and a crested, grey, tin helmet from the last war in the other. Under his sweaty armpit was a picture frame of some sort.

"Ah! Hello! You look like you have been fighting the Boche already!" he exclaimed, looking at Bill with his one good eye. The other was drifting off down the boulevard somewhere else.

"You should see the other guy."

"I bet! Time to get them out of Paris completely. Good times ahead, good times," he muttered to himself as he shuffled around the counter. He placed his war mementoes back on the empty spaces on a glass shelf where they had proudly stood, presumably since the opening day of the cafe, until the Nazis had arrived in the summer of 1940. He carefully placed the picture frame onto an empty picture hook. It was a photograph of a very muddy artillery piece, with three even grubbier soldiers standing in front of it. Above the photo was a group of four medals, including a *Croix de Guerre,* which Bill knew to be an award for bravery.

"Time to finish this," Roland interrupted and slapped Andre on the back, who grinned at him. He nodded to Bill, then marched out the door and back to the truck. Bill and Andre turned and watched through the glass as he struggled to get the engine started back up.

"We're going to find the rest of the guys, get this city cleared, and then try to find where they moved Leo," Andre said.

"Moved him?" Bill inquired.

"That's right. He was arrested shortly after you two were, as we were leaving the cabaret lounge that afternoon. As planned, we went separate ways, but he got intercepted and taken in. Some time went by with no news. Then, we got word that they were moving two prisoners from the Gestapo building. A woman rumoured to be one of your lot, probably your friend, Violette, and Leo. We headed down to the bottom of the avenue to follow them, but we arrived too late. I need to find out where they sent him. He'd do the same for me. We have been brothers in arms right back to Verdun. Nineteen sixteen was a long, tough year. Leo saved my life. More than once. The Boche thought they had us then, and they thought they had us this time, but we proved them wrong, right Willy?" His little inset eyes looked like black onyx buttons pushed into a ball of putty.

"Sure did, Andre."

Bill now realised who it was he'd witnessed get murdered by Misselwitz that day. Should he tell him? It was never good to break a man's spirit before combat. Bill had seen this happen, and it never ended well.

Bill stared at Andre, building the courage. It seemed too

cruel to let him go on a wild goose chase. Maybe he might get hurt or worse trying to pursue his friend when he was already lying cold somewhere, thanks to the young, depraved Nazi, Ernst Misselwitz.

"Here, sit down. I need to tell you something." So, they sat, and Bill waited, searching for the words. "Listen, Andre, I need to tell you something."

"What is it, Willy?"

"That day they came to collect Violette? Misselwitz executed Leo outside number eighty-four. Right there, out on the street. I was so sure it was Jack. He had a black hood over his head. He would not have known what was about to happen."

"Hood? So, he had no idea?"

Andre sat in stunned silence. His breathing grew shallow. He reached into his tunic, pulled out a matching pair of medals, and placed them on the table in front of him. Small brass-coloured discs suspended on silk rainbow ribbons. Everyone who had served in the Great War on the front lines for long enough got one. The other was Leo's. Andre had been holding it for him, perhaps rescued from the old safe house before they vacated. He sat and just looked at them for several minutes.

Bill looked at Lena. Lena was squatting near the table, and Jack was propped up on his elbow on the mattress by her. They were both just silently watching Andre. Rene was now also staring in their direction from behind the counter. All around, the various other conversations continued. Andre was a veteran of Verdun, one of his best friends, Jean, had gone missing whilst in Gestapo custody, and now he had the news his only other friend, Leo, had been murdered by the same butchers. He looked to be devastated.

Andre carefully turned over one of the medals and felt the raised letters' surface as if it were Braille. *LA GRANDE GUERRE POUR CIVILISATION 1914-1919.* He smiled as he gazed down with his small rodent eyes at the award. Then, after a few moments, he shoved it off the table and onto the floor. He said nothing as he stood, walked around, and carefully pushed his chair back in. He picked up his rifle, slung it onto his shoulder, and headed towards the door. He stopped suddenly, placed his hands on his stomach, then spun around, walked back towards the toilet, disappeared inside, and closed the door behind him.

"He'll be alright," Bill tried to reassure the others.

Rene looked out at the still smoking vehicles in the street and shook his head. Lena gave a small smile and nodded to Bill. She then stood and made her way to his table. Bill automatically rose back to his feet.

"Look after Jack. Make sure he gets plenty of water," Lena said, thrusting the half-filled water bottle into his hand.

"I guess I'd better make sure the big bugger lives. Thank you, Lena."

She grabbed his head on either side, pulled him close, and planted a kiss on his lips.

"I feel better already."

"That was a kiss goodbye, Bill. Buckmaster is sending for me to assist him in wrapping up the French networks." Tears had welled in her eyes. She blinked and sent one cascading down her cheek. "I'll not be returning to Paris. You are to contact the French command upon their approach and assist however you can in the city. Baker Street said they would be sending forward a British medical unit to collect you both from here once the city's liberation is complete. The hospital is not ready to accept civilian casualties yet, so get him recovered here. Hopefully, the French medic will be along soon."

"Understood. Look after yourself, Lena. Maybe our paths will cross again one day."

She turned away and hurried out of the cafe. Bill waited for her to look back. She never did. She turned right, walked the length of the glass windows and disappeared from view.

Bill wandered over to the picture on the wall. He squinted at it and then recognised a very young-looking pair of men he had come to know in Paris. An older-looking Rene was maybe thirty-five, but it was hard to tell with all the dirt and grime on his face. He had his arm around Andre, and just beside them stood the taller, far more handsome, Leo. Rene seemed like one of those blokes who looked old, even when they were young. The other two looked like teenagers. The enthusiasm of young men amid the great adventure of war. They held their rifles casually, like toys. All three of them beaming from ear to ear.

"I had no idea."

"Happier times. I wasn't always an ungainly cripple, you know," Rene replied. "Took a piece of shrapnel to the head and another to the pelvis. Messed my eyes up and my walk, plus it's pretty hard to stay in shape when you run a cafe."

"I'm sorry about Leo."

"Just another one lost. You start to lose count in the trenches, you know. Coming back to the real world after the war, I needed something to do. No one wanted to employ a half-blind cook, so I opened up this place with my wife. You lose them all. In the end, I mean. She died a few years before the Germans arrived. Cancer. I'm glad she never had to see them on our streets, not after what we all had to go through to keep them out last time," he said, pointing at the photograph.

Just then, Roland came in from outside. The chugging truck engine intensified and throbbed through the cafe as he opened the large door. The glasses behind the bar danced and rattled together like a miniature orchestra made up of only crystal maracas.

"Where the bloody hell has he got to, then? I've been waiting to go! This war won't win itself!"

"Oh shit!" a voice yelled out from the back of the cafe as Bill spun around to see where it had come from.

He made his way over to the gathered huddle and, pushing his way through, at the now-open doorway, found a pair of old farm labourer's boots. They were attached to the swinging legs of Andre, who was dangling from a plumbing pipe running across the high ceiling, his small eyes bulging out of his lifeless, reddened face. Around his neck was the sling he'd removed from his rifle, which was neatly propped up in the corner of the small water closet.

"And another lost," Rene said from somewhere behind.

13

The Defeat of Victoria

Berlin, 15th February 1947

He could hardly believe it. He knew having friends in the right places would pay off. The Ink Spots wailed at him from the small gramophone in the corner.

"Whispering grass, don't tell the trees."

His spine tingled, and he put the letter back into its manilla envelope and placed it neatly on the polished coffee table. He may be on the brink of disturbing a hornet's nest, and this knowledge did not sit comfortably in his whirring mind. These hornets wore cheap brown suits and had greasy hair and even greasier palms.

The kettle whistled for attention in the kitchen, so Bill stood up and wandered out to rescue it. He filled the small teapot and, cradling it in both hands, gave it a swirl. His Aunt Nelly used to tut loudly when he did that at home: *If you're going to make tea, make it like an Englishman!* Bill smiled at his late aunt's memory and carefully placed the teapot on the worktop. It was a strange-looking art deco piece of lime-green ceramic he had swapped for a packet of American cigarettes on Unter den Linden.

Barter was the new currency in Berlin. When society collapses, the man holding the most valuable goods is king. In this city, that was usually cigarettes. Enough cigarettes could get you fed, drunk or laid.

Barter-central was in the Russian sector of the city. The streets were mostly filthy, and most of the inhabitants and their new masters were even filthier. It was a strange sort of huddled mass of bombed-out Berliners, refugees passing through, and other poor souls. They were selling their worldly possessions for enough to buy a bite to eat at one of the makeshift beer halls or to swap for a threadbare greatcoat to keep out the worst of the biting winter. The winter of 1946 had not arrived on time. Its tardiness had been a great blessing for Bill, who had turned up in November expecting the worst. It had given him enough time to make some contacts and settle into life in this alien land before the worst weather hit.

Bill peered out of the window at the dirty moonscape below. The omnipresent rubble and dust that plagued everyday life gave this new Berlin a strange other-worldly air at dusk. His apartment block looked out onto a giant stone-filled crater where there were once grand facades and other buildings more in keeping with the street than this newly obliterated quarry, care of the Royal Air Force. Since Bill arrived, the walking dead locals seemed to be making slow progress clearing the site. They often sneered in contempt as he passed by to get home. He watched as the last two dust-covered workers gathered their coats and scrambled down the rubble mountain. It was bitterly cold out, but the two ghosts walked off down the street in shirt sleeves with their coats under their arms, their hot breath visible in the dying of the light.

Bill poured a cup of Earl Grey into a chipped china cup and returned to his chair. He leaned forward, carefully placing another log from the wire basket into the fireplace, and picked up his pipe. He watched the dancing flame of the match for a moment, then lit up. A sip of his tea and he returned once again to the letter to see if the text had changed while he was away. To his disappointment, it hadn't. He had work to do. He gathered up the telephone and, lifting the receiver to his ear, dialled the number. He then gave the operator the two-digit extension of the office.

The Berlin telephone system was nothing short of a miracle. Straight after the occupation, the allies had quickly got an efficient telephone system running. Most telephones in the city could be dialled directly, with most significant buildings and military departments requiring assistance from an operator for the extension only. Moreover, they had set up Bill's apartment with the ability to dial internationally, too, a novelty usually reserved for those that had pre-booked at the rather hefty sum of 120 Marks. That was about twelve US Dollars.

"Mr Fuchs to speak to Mr Weber, please."

"Hold, please," replied the female voice.

There was a long silent pause.

"Yes?"

"Mr Weber, it's Mr Fuchs from the BBC. I was wondering if we might meet to discuss the story I am working on?"

"Ah! It's good to hear from you so soon. I would love to

meet to discuss the story. I will go and get my schedule book from the drawer, just one moment."

In a somewhat muffled voice, Bill could hear him ask his secretary to retrieve his diary from her office.

"Okay, she's gone. Did you get my letter, Bill?"

"I did. Where can we meet?"

There was an uncomfortable pause. In the background, the Ink Spots continued to offer their melodic advice. "Whispering grass, don't tell the trees."

Bill was all too aware of how insecure the telephone lines were. He even had an operator in the exchange in his pocket who listened to calls for him.

"Do you remember where you introduced me to the Hamiltons?"

"Of course," Bill quickly replied.

"Tomorrow at thirteen hundred hours." Bill could hear the secretary had re-entered the room. "Yes, here we are. How does midday on Thursday sound?"

Bill hung up. He knew Albie would give the secretary a good show but ultimately cancel the appointment. He looked down at the note one last time before throwing it into the fire.

NEED TO MEET. VITAL INFO ON YOUR MAN. AMIS BACKED US OFF. BLUE EYES IN BERLIN - HAVE ADDRESS.

So, final confirmation that Misselwitz was indeed in the city. Bill clenched his teeth as he watched the letters on the page dissolve into ash and up the chimney, just as Ernst Misselwitz had helped so many disappear up chimneys. Bill thought back to the old SOE file on him. SD, Gestapo and police special actions in France—Nazi euphemism for mass murder.

* * *

Bill took the time to loop through the giant park they laughably still had the audacity to call the *Tiergarten*. The centuries-old woodland was once a cultural celebration of all things German, back when there was anything worth being proud of. Wagner, Mozart and many of the kings and emperors of old Prussia used to keep a watchful gaze on the transient visitors and Berliners out enjoying a walk or a picnic surrounded by their stone heroes of old.

Rumour had it that apart from the forlorn statues now resting on their side in the mud, some had been buried somewhere nearby to protect them from the Russian artillery. The trees had long gone. Just another two hundred thousand Berliners wiped out for a pointless war. Due to the dire shortages of coal, they had been methodically cut down to provide the city with firewood. Bill remembered the warm apartment he had left earlier in the day and tipped the invisible forest a nod, silently thanking it for its sacrifice.

He watched as barefooted children dragged a toddler around in an old toy cart. The exuberance of youth was all around the city. Most of what was left were the old and the very young. They knew no different. The ruins of Berlin were their playground. Hardly the quasi-Roman new world planned by Hitler's personal architect, Albert Speer, as a tribute to his thousand-year Reich. The grandiose Nazi plans had been cancelled, although evidently, no one thought to tell the Russians, who had continued with the demolitions on their behalf.

Bill passed through the various allotment plots where, among patrolling soldiers and police, feeble old men and their bedraggled wives tended to potatoes and other vegetables. It made him wonder how the gardener back at his home in Kent was doing with the vegetable garden. Bill was one of those people who was happy to eat vegetables but had no idea how they worked.

He pulled up the collar on his navy-blue long overcoat over his scarf, tipped forward the peak of his heavy felt fedora and continued briskly into the biting Prussian wind. His leg started to throb. The old wound always gave him pain in the winter.

Arriving twenty minutes early had given Bill time to survey the area, double back twice to ensure he wasn't tailed and find a dark corner to wait for his man. Albie Weber arrived a little before one o'clock and waited under the Brandenburg Gate like a rabbit in the headlights.

"Take it easy, Albie. You'll have a heart attack. Let's take a walk. Look casual."

"I really don't like any of this, Bill. What is this all about?"

"What do you mean? I'm just looking for this guy to follow up a rather sensitive story."

"L ... look, Bill, I want to help, really I do. I don't understand what the BBC wants with this guy or why the Amis are interested in him."

Bill stopped and turned. "Yes, the Americans. What did they say?"

Albie looked suddenly spooked. "Well, your man with the blue eyes showed up. There was a crash in the American sector, a couple of guys in a Jeep got injured, the paper covered the story, and one of the witnesses gave his name as Ernst Witzer. That's him, right? Your man? Anyway, we went down and took some statements and had a photographer with us. This Witzer really didn't want his photo taken. Anyway, we used a few quotes from him, among others from a couple of beggars on the corner there, wrote the article and sent it off for print.

"I was just about to telephone you and let you know your man was on the radar when my secretary took a bizarre call from the US Headquarters, Berlin District. The gist was to remove any mention of Ernst Witzer's name and censor a crash scene photograph. They didn't leave a name or number. Later that day, we had a visit from the Berlin Police to check the changes had been made before the full print run. Anyway, I figured a simple message to let you know might be better than a call they may listen in on."

"Good thinking. It sounds to me like the Americans contained the incident. Maybe one of the casualties was a VIP or something? Did you get their names?"

"No, by the time we arrived, the ambulance had gone. We know only that one was a sergeant in the Air Force and the other a lieutenant." Albie looked over Bill's shoulder, noticed a police patrol, and turned to continue walking.

Bill followed his lead. "Do you have anything else to help me find him?"

"Here's the address he gave us, the photo and the article pre-edits."

"Thanks, Albie. I can tell you the BBC in Berlin appreciates the help. Let me put your mind at ease, you did what they asked, and nothing will blow back on you. Dollars again?"

"Ideally, thanks. If there is a decent story at the end of all this, will you give *The Post* a chance to get it to print before the rest get their claws in?"

"Sure. Take care, Albie, head back and let me know if you hear anything else." Bill pulled out eight ten-dollar bills and handed them to Albie, who looked down in his hand at the green-hued Alexander Hamiltons, smiled and headed back towards the Gate.

The address was in the American sector. He would need to be paying Ernst Misselwitz a visit. Bill watched Albie leave, looked up at the statue of Victoria, the Roman goddess of victory, on top of the half-destroyed gate guarding the city and shook his head at the irony.

* * *

Bill smiled as he gave the young woman the notes. The Allied Occupation Marks, as they were clumsily called, were merely supposed to be temporary. But, over a year on, they were still the only official currency in Berlin. Used throughout the city in all sectors was proving a gold mine for the US troops who were swapping their soap and cigarette rations for thousands of marks and then using them to buy US postal orders to send back home. Highly illegal and exploitative, the practice was outlawed, and the powers-that-be were keen to stop the practice among their troops, to little avail.

As Bill passed the blue-and-green Monopoly money over to her, he noticed the remnants of old stitching marks on the breast pocket of her tunic. She looked down and, pulling her shawl across herself, attempted to hide the unmistakable star-shaped outline ghosted by the sun and dust. Bill reached into his pocket and added a few more notes. She nodded obligingly and continued to stare at the earth.

The apartment building was large, impressive and largely undamaged. There was a small rope around the entrance, not unlike the Ritz in London. Through the spotlessly clean windows, Bill could see there was a concierge at the front desk in a cartoonishly large maroon-peaked cap and matching uniform. Glancing around, he spotted a small cafe almost opposite with a clear view of the front entrance. It had a grand flagpole above the large windows. No flag hung there. Its absence made it all the more apparent. The ever-present zeitgeist of Nazism still loomed large. Crossing the quiet street and opening the heavy glass door with its giant brass handle, Bill took off his hat and sat inside facing the window.

"Could I take your coat, sir? What can I get for you?" the wide-eyed young waiter asked in a kind of mock high-German, copying the ludicrous forced accent of the late Führer. Bill guessed this manner of speaking had become synonymous with class in Berlin high society.

Bill would be keeping his coat and his gun close to hand. "What time is it?"

"It's just turned eleven, sir."

"Excellent, then I will have a Scotch."

"We only have American whiskey, sir."

"I guess that will have to do then … Hans," Bill replied, reading from the man's name badge.

Bill had spent a lot of time with Americans. Living in the American sector, now it was almost a necessity. He found them loud and brash, with little to say and taking far too long to say it.

He had become a big fan of jazz, blues and swing music from his frequent trips to Café de Paris in London before the war and was now finding it increasingly difficult to get hold of new records. Ironically, even the black market here didn't care for music of that particular hue. Bill could never understand how the Americans could hold the moral high ground over anyone while their own people lived entirely segregated lives.

The jazz bars had some records, of course, but were hardly likely to want to sell them on when replacements were nigh-on impossible to obtain.

The waiter returned and placed a cut-glass tumbler, a third full on a small card coaster and a little steel cup of ice with a set of toy-like mini tongs, like something straight out of *The Nutcracker*. He pulled out the *Berlin Post* he had brought with him and pretended to read. The building opposite was as quiet as the bar. He might be wasting his time here. Bill noticed Wagner was playing subtly in the background as two elderly women forced their way into the airlock to get safely out of the bitter cold. They walked with conviction towards some destination beyond him. He felt their disapproving look at his chosen beverage as they sat behind somewhere and ordered a pot of English tea.

Bill flipped once again to the article. Misselwitz had not changed much. His hair was a little longer and unkempt, but he still had that chiselled bottom jaw. His youthful appearance had perhaps become more mature than pin-up-boy. The intel was good, though. He was going under the name Witzer. The rest of the article was of no interest, the crash appeared unconnected, and the quotes used were of no value to intelligence. It looked like Misselwitz was just in the wrong place at the wrong time, and now his cover was blown wide open, much like his head would be if Bill got his way.

* * *

Entering the building, Bill could smell the distinct fragrance of lavender. The floor was like an ice rink of curiously patterned marble, and the front desk looked like it could have withstood the Hiroshima bomb. The concierge stood up to greet him, and Bill placed his hat down on the monolith between them. The small man beyond it looked dwarfed by both it and his oversized uniform.

"Hello, sir, my name is Schmidt. I am the concierge here. How may I be of assistance?" the polite shrunken man announced.

"I'm looking for an Ernst Witzer. I believe he lives here?"

"He does indeed, sir, but I'm afraid Mr Witzer is not currently here."

"Do you know when he is due back?" inquired Bill.

"I'm afraid to say; I am merely covering for the usual concierge who is temporarily away due to ill-health. So, whilst I know the faces and names of our residents, their routine is still unknown to me."

"I would like to leave a message for him if I may?"

"Of course, sir. I will ensure he receives it immediately upon his return."

"Thank you, Schmidt." Bill slid the envelope across the desk with a crisp ten-dollar bill on top. The Allied Occupation Mark may have been the legal currency in Berlin, but Uncle Sam's coupons were king.

Schmidt's face lit up, pocketing the note as he took a cautionary look about the marbled lobby. Then, turning, Schmidt placed the empty envelope into one of the small pigeon-holes behind him, and as Bill collected his hat, he looked to see a small brass plaque below the slot with the number six engraved in copperplate font.

14

Confessional

Berlin, 16th February 1947

The dishevelled church in the Berlin-Wedding District, part of the French sector, stood defiantly among the chaos of crumbling buildings and rubble surrounding it. Bill squinted into the wind and emerging twilight of the crisp winter morning as he made his way towards its formidable entrance. The stone pillars that guarded the door were peppered with bullet wounds and seemed to be straining under the weight of the grey tiled roof they had unwillingly held up for more than two hundred years. Bill pushed the giant oak door and was surprised to find it unlocked.

He looked down the wide aisle toward the altar. Some of the pews had been uprooted, probably for firewood. Their absence made the left side of the church into a sinister toothless grin. The right side was almost entirely bereft of seating altogether. A sizeable ornate crucifix stood on top of the Roman-inspired white altar. Christ was staring down at Bill with a disapproving scowl. Bill didn't hold it against him. He had been forced to witness his church being stripped of its benches and valuables and had been unable to intervene. Neither the Nazis nor divine intervention had been able to stop the Russians from ransacking the historic city.

There was a small makeshift replacement confessional booth to the right of the altar and a small doorway beyond that. Bill didn't know what he was looking for here, but he hoped he'd know if he found it. The floor was surprisingly clean. Most of the windows were missing at least some of their glass, and the light wind whistled from various gaps in the boarding that replaced them.

Bill checked again the card he had found in Misselwitz's apartment. One of many, all neatly kept in the writing desk drawer:

> *You have a friend at St.Bernhardt Church. All sins cleansed. Escape in the arms of our Lord.*

A large balding man appeared from the small doorway and announced his presence.

"Good morning, my son. I'm afraid it's a little early for me, but please make yourself comfortable, and I will be out presently."

"I don't wish to intrude, but my name is Bill Fuchs, and I was told you may be able to help me with the whereabouts of someone I wish to speak to." Bill couldn't help but wonder about the kind of donations the church received to enable the priest to maintain his ample bulk in the present climate and with such food and fuel shortages.

"I see. Of course, please just allow me a few minutes to make myself presentable."

Bill wandered over to the altar and saw various remnants of fixings visible in the stonework where ornate trim used to be held in place. In the days following Berlin's capitulation, the Russians had taken everything that wasn't screwed down, and as it now appeared, most that was. The Nazis, too, had persecuted the Catholic church and stolen many of its treasures and much of its land. But, unlike the Jewish synagogues, most of the churches still stood and had been reoccupied shortly after liberation. Many priests had returned to their flock after living in hiding or from places like Dachau concentration camp.

Bill made himself as comfortable as he could in the cold church. He had uncharacteristically kept his hat and leather gloves on, through fear of succumbing to hyperthermia in the freezing building. A short while later, the fat priest came back out. He wore a black shirt, his dog collar visible, and an oversized brown woolly pullover with large patches on the elbows. His trousers looked well-worn, but he had a pair of almost brand-new brown Oxford-style shoes. They were well made, probably in London.

"How may I assist you, Mr …?"

"Fuchs."

"Of course, Mr Fuchs. Sorry, it's been a long week."

Bill could smell his odour and the Schnapps on his breath.

"I am looking for a man by the name of Ernst Witzer, as I believe he witnessed a car crash recently, and I am seeking further clarification of the events," Bill lied.

"Hmm, I would like to help you, Mr Fuchs, but alas, I have

not seen him for a long while. He indeed used to come here from time to time for confession and the like, but I have not encountered him for many weeks. Do you work for the police?"

Bill wondered why he hadn't asked why he would think to look for him here? Instead, he seemed more concerned if Bill was law enforcement.

"No, nothing like that. I am a correspondent for the BBC, and I am just researching the story and have some follow-up questions."

"I'm afraid I cannot help you, and if you'll excuse me, I must prepare the church for the day."

Bill could tell he was getting a little nervous and evasive. Finally, he added, "If you do happen to see him, could you please ask him to contact me? Here is my card. He may reach me at the BBC in Berlin, extension thirty-eight. It's all on the card. Many thanks, Father."

As he turned away, Bill could make out the unmistakable slight bulge in the small of his back that could only be made by the shape of an automatic pistol.

15

New Smell, Old Bat

Berlin, 16th February 1947

As he entered the building, the usual smell of disinfectant lingered in the immaculate wood-panelled, large reception area. Bill instinctively readied his pipe. The carpeted floor did much to dampen the noise of the conversations happening all around in small seating areas. There seemed to be well-dressed mannequins in every corner drinking coffee and chatting.

The large counter that made up the bulk of the rear of the reception area was flanked on either side by little post boxes, each with its own miniature door. People occasionally walked up to one of the walls of pigeon-holes and opened one to retrieve some mail, or internal memos or some such. Bill suddenly envied the office staff. Sitting on his arse all day smoking, drinking coffee and occasionally retrieving mail seemed suddenly very appealing.

Bill walked up to the grandiose front desk. Behind it was mounted *BBC* in three-foot-high metal letters. He resisted a joke to the cute brunette receptionist about the fact that Berlin was bloody cold and instead announced his arrival.

"Mr Fuchs to see Mr Errington."

He already knew where he was headed and didn't wait for the answer. He greeted the diminutive, Asian-looking cleaning lady as he walked through the double doors and along the corridor. Bill didn't know her name, but she always said hello to him whenever he visited. He reached the office marked World Service - Head of Operations - BBC Berlin and entered the small waiting room. As he entered, he said nothing to the wrinkled effigy sitting behind the typewriter. She made some of Picasso's monstrous portraits look handsome.

The old receptionist peered at him over her half-moon reading spectacles and then returned to her violent hammering. She never had liked him, from the first time he'd walked in dripping wet from a rain storm. If looks could kill, she'd be a wanted serial killer. Bill did his best to ignore her as she bashed the old typewriter to within an inch of its life. He looked up the wall beside him at the painting of a spitfire through his pipe smoke. A light faintly glowed above the far door.

"Mr Errington will see you now," the old bat croaked from behind her machine.

"Thanks," Bill replied as he rose from the red leather chesterfield. He walked through the door and into the office.

"Ah, Bill! So pleased you are alive and well. Surviving all the German winter can throw at you, I trust?"

"Barely. There is a distinct lack of Scotch in Berlin."

Stuart Errington was B1, the officer in command of operations in Berlin for British Intelligence. He was an old friend of Buckmaster, the head of the now-defunct F Section, who had busied himself with shutting down networks and debriefing the various resistance groups, while Vera Atkins had extensively researched the whereabouts of all the missing agents, including Violette. Bill closed his eyes briefly and exorcised the demons.

"Of course, of course." Errington stood and walked over to a large walnut cabinet, opening up a hidden kingdom of cut crystal decanters and all manner of glassware and polished stainless-steel cups of every size. He chose a decanter and poured a large slug of brown liquid into two beautiful glass tumblers. Bill looked on like a dog waiting for a juicy bone. He drew hard on his pipe and attempted to calm his anticipation.

"I take it you two still haven't made up?" he remarked, chuckling and gesturing at the door back towards his secretary.

"She still hates my guts. I'd only just arrived in Berlin. How was I to know she was her daughter? She barely acknowledges me now and that suits me fine."

Errington smirked and shook his head. He was a tall, wiry and likeable man with a perfectly formed full-black moustache and black, slicked-back hair. Bill often thought he had styled himself on the Italian American gangsters in the movies. He wore a black chalk-striped suit, white silk tie and a light pink shirt, all tailored and made to measure, of course. A man of such breeding would hardly wear the off-the-peg suits of the type Bill would purchase from his meagre wage. His gleaming silver cufflinks caught the light as he gathered up the glasses. He was the son of some viscount or baron, and

Bill got the impression that his posting to Berlin was irksome to the easy life he expected.

"There you are, Bill," Errington said as he placed a hallowed glass in front of Bill, "twenty-year-old single malt."

"Thank you, sir. I appreciate it."

"Cigarette?" he asked, offering up a pack of American Luckies.

Bill just continued to puff his pipe and frown at him.

Errington shrugged and grinned. "If I thought you'd take one, I wouldn't offer."

Bill sipped the smoothest whisky he had tasted in many months. Before swallowing, he allowed the peaty nectar to flood across his tongue a moment. Maybe the winter wouldn't drag on so long if he could find reasons to keep checking in.

"I'm glad you're here, Bill. It saves us the trouble of contacting you. There is news straight from the top. There have been rumblings from Westminster about double agents in our midst. With this new uneasy peace with the Russkies, the red wall is pushing back against our agreements in Berlin. They are even hinting at removing the free movement through their sector. At the moment, the politicians are keeping everyone happy on the face of it, but the bottom line is that we can expect they have agents out probing for intelligence."

"I see," Bill said bluntly. Errington had been good to Bill when he first arrived in Berlin. He had set him up with a fine apartment with a concierge in the American sector and ensured it was well furnished, hot running water, gramophone, the whole nine yards, as they'd say in his neighbourhood.

"Of course, we are sure which side your bread is buttered, Bill. A man with a reputation such as yours is exactly what we need out here. Berlin is to be our new front line."

Bill thought back to the war when everything seemed a lot clearer. Then, you knew, for the most part, who your enemy was. Now it could be almost anyone. Bill sipped his whisky and casually glanced into the large onyx ashtray on the desk. There were a few scrunched cigarette ends. On one was a faint lipstick mark.

Errington caught him looking, then took the ashtray. "Apologies, I meant to empty it earlier," he said as he tipped the contents into the little brass bin next to the desk. He then continued: "With that in mind, Bill, we have brought in some of our best agents. I needn't remind you that this is not SOE anymore. Those amateurish days are behind us. No discussing your case with other agents, including our own. I know you've heard all this before, but I'm reminding everyone, so don't take it personally. How are you two getting on with locating Misselwitz?"

"Well, it seems he is indeed in Berlin. A journalist at *The Post* passed some information on. I am following up on several enquiries, including at a church in the French sector. I believe he is working with the Americans, but nothing tangible yet."

"Good work, Bill. Go easy around the Americans. Allies we may be, but they don't trust us these days. Things are hot in the city. Be careful out there and let us know when you have him. Alive if possible, please. We need this bastard after what he did to our people."

Errington shook Bill warmly by the hand. Bill finished his drink.

"Let me get your hat and coat," Errington said as he rushed around the desk.

This was unusual. Bill knew to be cautious of unusual. As

he watched, Errington picked up Bill's coat from the wrought iron hat stand. He opened it up to help him put it on. No one had done this for Bill since he was a boy. As Errington helped his coat on, Bill felt him make the tiniest contact on his left side pocket. Bill said nothing as he picked his hat up and made for the door.

He ignored the secretary as he crossed the waiting room, down the corridor and out into the freezing Berlin morning. Then, perching his fedora back onto his head, he checked that the coast was clear and carefully pulled the slip of paper out of his pocket. It was written beautifully on ivory-coloured Basildon Bond paper:

> *Meet with Irene. Call 02 0236. Caution. Suspect B Section infiltrated. Good luck. Burn this.*

Bill memorised the number and then placed it back in his pocket. A match wouldn't light in this wind anyway.

* * *

Bill reached the cafe opposite the opera house fifteen minutes early and noticed Irene was already there. She had sat near the back with a view of the street. Her auburn hair was longer than the last time he had seen her, and as her gaze locked with Bill's, she began to smile. There were no other customers in the cafe. He removed his hat as he entered, and Irene stood to greet him.

She threw her arms around him and exclaimed, "Bill, it's so good to see you."

She smelled good. Something French, Bill thought, no

doubt.

"You too, Irene. It's been a long time."

"More than two years." The Cheshire cat smile was still playing on her face. Her voice was rich and husky. The Berlin telephone system's thousands of yards of copper wire had sterilised her tone when they had arranged to meet here at the most upmarket of all the cafe bars in the theatre district. Her long red dress clung to her shapely body. Bill had been familiar with several female voices, not to mention their owners' bodies, in the last few years, but it was this particular pairing he had longed to reacquaint himself with the most.

They chatted in English, as Irene could only speak English, French and Flemish-Dutch.

"Can I get you something, sir?" the skeletal waiter asked from somewhere behind.

"Scotch, please, and another for the lady."

"I'm sorry, sir, but …"

"Whiskey then, whatever you have." Bill interrupted, "Goddamn shortages."

"Most people are worried about the coal situation," Irene said with a giggle.

"Well, you know me. I have different priorities than most people."

Irene's dainty white cotton-gloved hand perched a short, black Bakelite cigarette holder between her teeth. Bill pulled his little silver vesta case out and struck one of the red-tipped matches to life. He held the flame aloft as Irene leaned in. As her cigarette lit, she pursed her lips around the holder and looked straight at Bill, who now returned a schoolboy grin.

"Your whiskey, sir. Your *martini,* madam."

Bill noticed the strange emphasis the waiter put on the word martini. Irene saw his reaction.

"No vermouth. It's just gin," she explained. "It does get tiresome trying to explain to waiters, but a truly perfect martini involves just ice-cold gin with nothing but the slightest of glances in the general direction of Italy."

"Nice." Bill chuckled and threw the whiskey back. "Another," he demanded to the waiter. Bill decided this night might need a head start. "What is this hell you're putting me through? I feel like a penguin."

"It's called Faust, and there I was, assuming you were an avid opera fan," Irene joked.

The grand-sounding Renaissance Theater on Hardenbergstrasse, in the British sector, was one of the few in the city that often had performances in English.

"Can't we just blow all this out and head to a jazz bar?"

Bill's second drink was placed carefully before him by a bony hand.

"No. I have the tickets, and you will pretend to be a perfect gentleman for the next few hours. There is a bar, don't worry," she teased.

"It's pretty close to the zoo. Will I need to hold my nose? How far is it from the elephant house?"

She looked good, better than he remembered. But, of course, any woman would look better in an expensive dress and wearing a set of pearls than the pair of them had looked back in '44.

"You'll like this one, Bill. It's about a man who sells his soul to the Devil. What would yours be worth, I wonder?"

"Not much these days," Bill replied, only half-joking.

Bill sipped on his drink as they talked about all the missing time. He told her about his home in Kent, the large garden maintained by the groundskeeper there, and all the apple trees they had planted just before he'd flown out to Berlin. She told him a little about her failed, short-lived marriage and the Triumph Roadster motorcar she had recently bought.

The hour went by in a haze, helped along by the alcohol and pleasant company. Bill had not felt so relaxed and happy in a long time. He almost forgot they were the first line of defence in this bizarre new invisible front line Churchill had called the *iron curtain*.

Until this afternoon, he had no clue Irene was even in Germany, let alone re-employed as an agent in Berlin. As they got up to leave, Bill helped with Irene's fur coat and white chiffon scarf, and she pressed against him. He held her there for a moment and whispered into her ear.

"I'm so happy it's you, Lena."

"I'm happy to see you again too, Bill. But please remember, it's Irene now."

16

Old Friends

Berlin, 17th February 1947

It was only a short journey north from Irene's apartment in the British sector back to the church, but he'd managed to arrange a car. The concierge at Irene's building was, as she had pointed out to him, *one of us* and had the black two-door car brought to the front of the lobby. It was far more modern and cleaner than his own car, and Bill wondered how much higher Irene was in their organisation. Bill paid the baby-faced youth that had delivered it with Occupation Marks, and he ducked into the front seat out of the cold. He'd much rather have stayed in Irene's warm bed, but the car was, at least, warm enough to remove his hat. Placing the flask of coffee and the paper wrap of sandwiches on the seat beside him, he carefully packed his pipe and lit it.

The car purred into life, and he pulled away into the morning mist. The purr became a growl as Bill's foot grew heavier. The devastated world of Berlin blurred past the glass on either side of him. Children waved as he passed, and mothers instinctively pulled at their arms to keep them moving. They had learnt it didn't do well to attract the attention of anyone driving a black Mercedes-Benz in Nazi Germany, and the instinct remained strong now that their city was full of foreign cops, politicians, and soldiers. The roads were quiet. Bill stopped at an intersection to see a large military truck pull up and decant its olive-green contents of French soldiers onto the pavement. He continued up the street, avoiding the numerous potholes, and saw the soldiers entering some anonymous ruined building behind in his rear-view mirror.

Arriving now, opposite the empty block of devastation that surrounded the grey church, Bill pulled up alongside a matching but slightly inferior and far dirtier version of his motorcar. The windows were misted on the inside, and a thin layer of ice had formed outside.

Switching off the engine, Bill ventured from the warm and supreme comfort of his steel and leather sanctuary and walked around to the second Mercedes.

"Wake up, you bastard!" he shouted as he rocked and bounced the car with his hands on the frosty roof.

The outline of the occupant shifted inside, and the ice cracked and fell from the glass as the window creaked open, and Bill was presented with the business end of a Walther P38 semi-automatic pistol.

"Well, that's a fine way to treat a man who brings you breakfast."

"Fucksakes, Bill, I thought I was a goner!" Jack exclaimed. "Waking up an armed man like that is a good way to catch a bullet," he added, redoubling his vociferation. Then, putting his gun down on the seat between his legs, he paused and asked, "Bacon?"

"Sorry, partner, only corned beef. I didn't get home last night."

"I wondered why the flash new motor. Jump in."

Bill forced the half-frozen door from its hole and jumped inside. "Start the engine and get some heat going, would you, Jack? It's frostier than a disciplinary meeting at the Kremlin in here."

The engine strained into life. Holding his pipe between his teeth, Bill poured the coffee into the two white mugs on the car's dash and passed over a tired-looking sandwich.

"Thanks ... I guess," Jack grunted.

"Any sign of our man?"

"Nope. Just Father Lard-Arse and a few of the regular God-botherers the past couple of days. Strangely, no one seems to gather here at any one time. They all come and go individually throughout the day and evening. The last visit is usually around twenty-three hundred hours. Lardy pops out for essentials to the small shop over there on the corner fairly regularly. I had a word with the little old shopkeeper there called ..." Jack pulled out his little notebook to check and carried on, "... Mrs Krause. Lardy's essentials mainly consist of copious amounts of bread, sausage, cigarettes, and schnapps. Not necessarily in that order."

"Maybe it's time to talk to Lardy?"

"No, wait. There's more. One character, a well-dressed man with a black suit and tie and long leather overcoat, visited twice within a couple of hours, went to the shop, returned to the church, and never came out. That was the day before yesterday. I stayed up all night, but he never re-emerged. I know I didn't miss him, as he had a ridiculous Hindenburg moustache and a distinctive maroon scarf. There is no other entrance than the one on this side. The church seems to go dark every night at midnight, and no one comes or goes after that."

"Cracking work, Jack, thanks, pal. It looks like I need to get in there and have a proper nose around. Here, finish the coffee and sandwiches."

"Where are you off to? He'll still be in there."

"I'm going to see Mrs Krause."

* * *

"A pound of sausage, please," asked Bill politely.

"Certainly, young man. Is it cold outside?" enquired Mrs Krause.

"Erm, yes. I'm afraid the winter has finally hit."

She was at least eighty. The thin curly hair perched only on the top of her head was devoid of colour. Not grey, but white. She wore a moth-eaten brown woollen cardigan, the same colour as her teeth. There was a prominent scar down her left cheek, and she wore threadbare, knitted, fingerless gloves on her small, bluish, withered hands. The shop was as hot as Hell's waiting room, with a roaring fire in the large open fireplace. The obscenely large sausages hanging from a hook behind her were half-baked from the ambient temperature.

"So strange for the time of year. It was only cold in the winter when I was a girl."

"Well, it is February."

"Is it? Is it really? Well, I never! It's not easy keeping track of the time. I've not seen you in here before. My name is Mrs Krause. My Husband is Mr Krause, but he is not here now. He's fighting the Russians, you see. You are very smartly dressed. Are you from the Gestapo?"

Bill looked quizzically at her, "No, I'm British. I'm a journalist here in Berlin. The Gestapo are long gone. They disappeared over a year ago. You don't remember the big battle here and all the bombing?"

"Oh my! Are you British? But you speak such perfect German!" She picked up a small photograph in an ornate gilded frame of an elderly man wearing a black felt, floppy peaked cap. He was holding a Panzerfaust single-shot anti-tank weapon whilst grinning proudly in a heavy grey greatcoat with a full, bushy, even greyer moustache. On his arm was an armband with embroidered eagles and the bold lettering, Deutscher Volkssturm Wehrmacht. "My husband is a hero in the war against the Bolsheviks. He is a tank destroyer. He was so brave in the last war that they wanted him to help in this one!"

On the man's chest was an Iron Cross, Second Class, evidently from the first war. "Yes, he is clearly a brave man. They don't give those Iron Crosses out to just anybody."

Bill thought back to the turmoil thrust upon his own family before he was born in that futile war that did little for European relations except to start them all on the path for this last one.

The Volkssturm were Hitler's grand plan for a last-ditch final stand against the invading Russians. Hitler was so sure of a last-minute victory by sending the children and elderly of Berlin to their deaths that he went and hid in a bunker and shot himself.

Mr Krause was, without a doubt, very much a hero, but he was also clearly very dead. The bravest of heroes usually are, Bill reminded himself.

"I ask those nice men from the Gestapo who pop into the shop occasionally, but none of them seem to know where he might be."

The Gestapo? The old lady had clearly gone senile and was imagining things.

"Not everyone in a black coat and hat is from the Gestapo, Mrs Krause. Do you know the priest from the church?"

"I do! He is such a lovely man. He comes in for his sausage and schnapps every day! He also sends his friends from the church here to buy cigarettes and other things," she proudly announced.

Bill looked around the pathetic store. Apart from the bare essentials, like cheap schnapps, beer, sausage and bread, there were a few dozen tired-looking potatoes in a small basket, some soil-covered carrots, apples and a small hardware section with brooms, clothes pegs, dustpans and shovels. Bill wished he'd bought shares in whoever made the shovels and brooms sold in Berlin. Sales were booming.

He stifled a chuckle to himself and placed a small half-bottle of fine cognac he'd obtained from the concierge at Irene's apartment down on the counter along with enough marks to buy the pound of sausage he'd asked for, plus another.

"I'm going to need a favour if you can keep a secret, Mrs Krause?"

"What do you need?" she whispered. "I was a nurse near the trenches in 1916. The men used to bribe me to do all kinds of sexual things!" she said excitedly.

"No, no, no! Nothing like that. I need you to delay the

priest next time he comes into the shop. Don't serve him too quickly. Buy me some time."

"A surprise birthday party, is it?"

"Er, yes. A surprise, so don't tell him anything, just keep him talking a bit longer than usual. Here is a bottle of brandy for your trouble and a few extra marks."

"Thank you, young man, that is very thoughtful of you. I will save it for my husband, for when he returns."

"Take care, Mrs Krause," Bill said as he collected the sausage.

He placed his hat on his head as he left the roasting hot shop with the cold hitting like a sledgehammer to his face and made back across the deserted street towards the cars. He turned as he heard Mrs Krause call out after him.

"Young man! Young man! You forgot your bottle of brandy!"

What a great plan this was, Bill thought. It was going swimmingly.

17

Divine Indifference

Berlin, 17th February 1947

Thankfully, Father Lardy had left the door unlocked. Bill made his way to the back room of the church. Was it a vestry? Bill wondered. Churches and their geography were never his strong point. He made it a rule to spend as little time as humanly possible asking anyone, invisible or otherwise, for forgiveness. Whatever it was called, it was where he was headed. Bill had no idea what he might find, but whatever it was, he was confident that's where it would be.

Making his way through the open stone archway, he found himself in an untidy, makeshift bedroom-cum-kitchen. A filthy sunken mattress sprawled across the floor to the right, below a solid oak table covered in crumbs, had deep knife cut marks all over it. On one end was a pile of empty paper bags, the same as the one Bill had taken his sausage away from Mrs

Krause's store, neatly pressed flat and stacked.

Bill noted that there was only enough space for one to sleep as he rechecked the mattress.

He stopped in his tracks as his mind flashed back to Bergen-Belsen. On the day of liberation, the overcrowding had seen dozens of emaciated spectres crammed onto tiny shelves to try to get some rest after the forced death marches from other camps to the east. Filth and disease were rife, and there was no food and very little water. From the very outset, the Nazis had designed suffering into the very fabric of these ghastly places. The meticulous records they had kept there showed the deaths in March 1945 alone had been over eighteen thousand.

He shook the memory and noticed the knuckles of his right hand were white due to his tightly clenched fist. He carried on his search. He had no idea how long he had left in here. Lardy and the man with the Hindenburg moustache and maroon scarf had left together. Lardy had gone, as usual, to the shop, the other man down the hill and away, out of sight.

Looking to the far side of the cold room, Bill spotted a small wood-veneered writing desk, the kind he could imagine Jane Austen or Charles Dickens sitting to write. It might have once been quite in-keeping with the interior of a church, but now it found itself entirely out of place among the squalor of this dishevelled room and under the command of an imposter. Bill was quite sure the man masquerading as the priest was anything but.

The lid of the writing desk yawned open in despair at its current situation, and Bill made his way towards it. He didn't have much time.

There was a small glass ink well with a well-worn pen poking up like a flag pole, a small, blank notepad with about half the pages torn out, a folded paper bag like the ones on the large table, and a little card shoebox.

Opening the shoebox first, Bill found four brand new Berlin ID cards with all the fields left blank. Worth a small fortune on the black market, but only if you could somehow fake the required rubber stamps, photo style and signatures of the genuinely completed document. There was no sign of a printing press or stamps, so they were either better hidden, or Lardy was outsourcing.

There was also yet another paper bag folded up, which upon inspection contained a wad of paper money. There were French francs, US dollars, marks, and even a few British notes. Closing it back up, Bill spotted the letters EW scrawled on the outside. Ernst Witzer, Bill thought. It had to be. Why would a wanted war criminal like Misselwitz risk getting caught over a few dollars for spinning fake IDs in Berlin?

There was some other loose money, but not much, a few odd crumpled travel tickets to various locations, and an Adox branded folding camera. Bill quickly checked for a film. It was empty. Bill flicked through the tickets. U-Bahn, S-Bahn and trams to places all around the city, but quite a few into the American sector. Particularly Wannsee, in the far southwest.

He replaced the box's contents and quickly peeked into the other, loose package. There were no markings on this one. Inside he found a brand-new ID card. There was no photograph, no stamp and no other details.

Placing everything back in its place, Bill tore off the top page of the notepad and pocketed it.

* * *

"What do you reckon then? The fat man is clearly running a fake ID business, but there isn't much peculiar about that. This is the city of split personalities." Jack spoke with his mouth half full of chewed-up bratwurst.

"We could have him arrested on that, alone, but it doesn't get us any closer to flushing out Misselwitz or finding why he's even in Berlin at all." Bill sighed.

Jack poured a small cup of, now cold, coffee from the flask, swirled it a little and threw it down his throat. "That reminds me, did you hear they awarded Violette a posthumous George Cross?"

"Yes, I read it in *The Times*. A surprisingly honest account, considering what we do is meant to be secret. You don't hear about many members of the Nursing Yeomanry getting parachuted into hostile territory and holding off a German onslaught with a submachine gun."

"Her little girl, Tania, collected it from the king. She must be, what? About five now? Poor kid. Never met her father, killed at El-Alamein, and now no mum."

"I'm sure the king's trinket will bring her comfort. Maybe she'll prop it up and ask it to read her a bedtime story?"

"Come on, you and I both know that a GC is a hell of a thing, Bill."

"Agreed. I'm just pretty sure she'd rather have a mother."

* * *

Another hour had passed as they sat, chatted, and waited. Lardy was back in his holy pied-à-terre, and there had been no further developments. The warm car made the outside appear to be all the colder. A northerly wind whipped between the few standing buildings and made the air vents wheeze like a sleeping old asthmatic bloodhound.

"Lena is in Berlin. Calling herself Irene now." Secrecy or not, Jack was his partner and had a right to know.

"Really? Well, that's a turn-up. *One of us*?"

"Yes. Probably technically our superior, based on my new wheels."

"I take it you have, er, reconnected then?"

"Who do you think prepared us the flask this morning?"

Bill saw Jack shift in his seat and instinctively scratch the scars on his chest through his jacket. Just then, a tall, thin gentleman in a long pale overcoat strode confidently up the hill and entered the church.

"Probably just another church-goer," Jack said.

"You don't honestly still think any of these people believe this is actually still a church, do you?"

"Why not? Perfect cover. Anyway, it's no more ludicrous than them still thinking God has any sway over the goings-on in Germany," Jack bluntly pointed out as he gestured around at the devastation caused by the Russians.

"Well, if he is up there; the more I see of Germany and hear about what they got up to in the east, I think he must be long past giving a shit."

"If Misselwitz is collecting payments, presumably he is running this tin-pot setup?" Jack asked, with as much incredulity as Bill.

"I guess. He's too clever to turn up here to pick up the money. He'll be using a drop somewhere, or Lardy is delivering." Bill brushed breadcrumbs from his makeshift snack off his front and onto the floor of the car, then continued, "He hasn't been in his apartment for weeks. The concierge didn't even fit in his uniform. He's obviously a plant. If he does have contact with him, he'll already know that someone, who left him nothing but an empty envelope, was sniffing around."

"And the real concierge?"

"Sacked? Dead? Who knows?"

The tall man appeared from behind the solid door of the church and shiftily looked around. He spotted their two almost matching vehicles and then walked quickly, head down, back towards where he had first emerged.

Bill tutted, "So I guess Lardy knows we are here too."

"Not very good at this spying lark, are we, mate?" Jack put on his leather gloves, picked up the P38, which had still been between his knees, and placed it carefully back into his inside coat pocket. "So, which one of us is following the tall man?"

"What? Why?"

"He has a small, folded paper bag in his hand."

* * *

Jack cracked his knuckles, rotated his neck around and removed his hat.

"What the hell are you doing?" asked Bill as he put his empty pipe back in his pocket.

They were in the more up-market part of the French sector now. They had carefully followed the tall, thin man down the hill, away from the church. He hadn't looked back or looked particularly suspicious or cautious, but Bill had a feeling he may well have known he'd been followed.

"I'm just preparing. That bloke might have a billy club in his hand by now."

"Hardly likely. Did you see him? He looked like he could play hide and seek behind a flagpole."

"Well, you never know."

The area was full of tailors, shoe shops and leather goods, all trading from smart-looking storefronts. It was apparent where most of the French money had gone for the rebuilding. Vast swathes of the sector were still rubble and desolation, and yet, here, the shops looked to be lifted straight from Saville Row in London.

Bill checked the street. All clear. He then pushed open the glass door, one hand gripping the revolver inside his right coat pocket.

A little brass bell rang as they entered, and Bill removed his hat and placed it down on the back of a chair near the door. The bookshop opened up into a double-floored atrium. A dead fire sat in the open fireplace to their right, but its warmth remained in the room. The wooden shelves were neatly packed with row upon row of leather-bound books, all carefully colour-coded. The upper floor was accessible by a small iron spiral staircase, and the open side was lined with a brass railing, meticulously polished to a high shine.

This place reminded Bill of the library from his time at Cambridge. There wasn't much he enjoyed about university, but the library was one of them. He'd spend hour after hour in there, reading as much as possible. Some days it would be Voltaire and Satre, in French, of course. Other days it might be Shakespeare, Twain or Poe. Bill had loved to read once upon a time. He had even set up a proper library in the house, although, he admitted to himself, it had been mainly to sit among the great works and enjoy a whisky and his pipe.

When the war began, there had been no time for such

distractions. Since it ended, he didn't ever find enough downtime to enjoy a book properly. Perhaps he'd never find the time again. He'd even forgotten most of what he'd read. Seeing piles of decaying bodies and innocent people executed will do that to you.

He had brought one of his Arthur Conan Doyle books with him to Berlin but had ended up using it to prop up a broken chair. At that moment, he resolved to find the time to read more often.

The room had the glorious smell of the rich must of old literature and very faintly of wood and tobacco. Passing a little seating area with worn chairs and a smoking stand, they made their way towards the counter at the back, where a large cash register sat among a messy sprawl of books and loose papers.

The thin, tall man appeared from behind the bookshelves like a stick insect.

"Please. Don't hurt me!"

"Why would we hurt you?" Jack asked.

"You are cops, aren't you? I've not seen you two before, but I have paid Müller this month already. I already apologised for last time. So, there was no need to follow me."

Bill and Jack waited for more. They had practised the silent-pressure technique.

The thin man continued, "I'm only doing what I have told you about, no extra jobs off the record, I swear. I only sell my books and do the special custom printing work."

Bill glanced over at Jack. His partner looked as perplexed as Bill was.

"Well, the price just went up. It gets expensive keeping the prying eyes out." Bill tried his luck.

The Berlin Police were under the control of the Russians. They operated as a supposedly independent force throughout all the sectors, but in reality, all that meant was the crooks, whores and forgers across Berlin all paid the communists to be allowed to operate. It also meant they were not only in their pocket, but any intelligence of interest filtered back, through the police, to Moscow. It was the perfect protection racket and a genius move by the Ivans.

"I can't afford any more!"

"Well, we'll have to take some of these books then. There must be some value in them, as fuel at least," Bill replied.

"No! Please. This is my livelihood. You're new up here, right? Look, maybe if you come around the back, I can show you the setup, and we can find something that you may be interested in."

"Sure. We are not unreasonable men. We have been relocated from the American sector, so I am curious to see your setup in person."

The thin man led the way around the bookshelf, and Bill and Jack followed close behind. Bill kept his gun aimed from within his jacket pocket.

The back of the store was a whole other world. It was a workshop. There were a few different printing presses and two large wooden workbenches. On top of one was what appeared to be a giant's wooden thumbscrew, surrounded by all kinds of peculiar hand tools scattered carelessly around. A giant ball of string sat on the other bench, which had a large vice attached. At the rear of the workshop was a door with a light above it and yet another bookshelf, curiously out of place and only half-filled with books. Carefully packed down and leaning against it was a camera tripod.

"I have some photographs I have developed, which you may be interested in."

The man picked up a wooden box and pulled out some photographs, all of the same woman in various states of undress. Each image was more graphic than the last. Her dead-eyed stare at the camera made Bill feel deeply troubled. She had dirty blonde hair and large breasts, and Bill knew he had seen her somewhere before.

"What is this? Is this what all those books are filled with?" Jack demanded.

"No, no." The man cowered away from Jack. "It's only a hobby. Please, I just bind books."

"You don't pay us protection to bind books. You pay us to look away while you print the fake IDs," Jack said menacingly.

"Well, not quite. Look, I don't expect a simple policeman to understand what I do here. I simply fill out the papers they provide me and sort out the photos. Like I say, it's a hobby of mine. I bet you got your job using false papers, like most of the rest. You're a big fellow. What were you, SS, Gestapo? If you know anyone that needs papers, send them to me, won't you?"

"Is that what you are doing for the priest?" Bill asked.

"Of course. What else?"

"Why don't you print the ID cards here?"

"I do. I mean, I did. But, I mean, I still do, just not for him."

"What are you babbling about, you lanky streak of piss?" interrupted Jack.

"The priest, he gives me the cards. Only one at a time, but they are the best forgeries I've ever seen, totally indistinguishable from the real thing."

You bet they are indistinguishable, Bill thought.

"I take their photographs, complete the details here, sort out the rubber stamps, then deliver the cards back to him."

"The latest order is for a man with a moustache like Hindenburg's?"

"Yes, that's him. A lovely man."

"Where is he now?"

"I don't know. I took his photograph about an hour ago before I headed to the church to collect the card. He really wasn't here long. I don't know their names, you know. Always quite hush-hush, as you can imagine. I only get the details required for the card. Some of the customers are downright scary, like your mate here," he said, gesturing towards Jack.

"I suppose if you had to, you could get me a copy of the photographs of the customers?" said Jack, his arm hanging down by his side. His hand had his gun in it.

"Please, there is no need for this. If you are working on a case and need my help, I will help. I owe the priest nothing. Part of our deal is that I return the card and the negatives. Photographic film, chemicals and paper are not easy to come by or cheap, so I don't make additional copies. Why would I need them?" Then, suddenly remembering, he added, "I have one of the last chap. You could take that one?"

"Yes, and we're taking this garbage too. Say anything to Müller or the others, and we'll be back, and it won't be pretty," Jack said as he gathered up the smut from the table and rolled it up into his pocket.

18

Red Light

Berlin, 17th February 1947

"Who is Müller?" Jack asked as they wandered down the extravagant street.

The lavish amount of glass and polished brass hurt Bill's eyes, which were more used to boarded-up windows, rubble and dust.

"Chief of police for the French sector, so presumably a communist or at least pretending to be."

"I like him already," Jack said with a smirk. "Those blank IDs are genuine ones, aren't they?"

"I think so, yes. Misselwitz must be lifting them from somewhere for the priest."

"From the cops?"

"No. Not even the Russians are stupid enough to let the police department handle identification and record keeping. That's handled by government offices of each district, separate from the bulls."

They made their way back up the hill towards the church and the cars. Along the way, they encountered an old man, hunched over, shuffling towards them. He looked like he would over-balance and roll down the hill at any moment. He carried a little net bag with a couple of anorexic carrots and a half-mouldy potato. He shuffled past them as they parted and carried on down the hill.

"I almost feel sorry for them," Jack commented. "More than twelve years under the fascists, and now this." He gesticulated his arms around for added emphasis.

"They made their bed," Bill said unsympathetically.

"There wasn't much they could do once the big ugly Hitler-ball started rolling. The Weimar government wasn't great, but anything was better than what came next."

"I suppose they should have let the Bolsheviks take charge?"

"Maybe. I think they would have been almost as bad. I might joke about it, but I'm no communist, Bill."

"I know, brother, you just like to sound like one. Head home and get a good sleep tonight, then swap your car and find a better spot for a lookout for tomorrow. Keep an eye on that church, and if you see our friend with the scarf and moustache, follow him. It would appear he is the latest customer of many."

"Where are you going?"

"I need to catch up with the girl with dirty blonde hair and big tits. I've just remembered where I have seen her before. She's one of Anna's girls."

"Well, don't have too much fun."

* * *

Bill pulled up to his building at around seventeen hundred hours. The darkness was drawing in. The ghostly apparitions from the building site opposite were packing away their equipment and smoking and gossiping in huddles here and there. Bill tipped his hat at one of the women, who nodded politely back.

Entering his building, he tossed the car key to the concierge and headed upstairs. Bill never trusted lifts. He walked down the red-carpeted hallway and opened the door to his apartment. He filled the kettle, placed it on the stove, and then washed his china cup and teapot. He sat down with an audible groan in his wingback chair. It wasn't worth lighting the fire, as he would soon be leaving again. In any case, with all the carpet and the other apartments around, it never got overly cold.

He placed the pipe from his pocket onto the table near the kitchen window and opened the top drawer. Selecting a brand-new tin of tobacco, he prised it open and packed his spare pipe. He didn't have the time or inclination for cleaning right now. Instead, he went to the bathroom and started to draw a bath, then went back to the lounge, took off his trench coat and hung it on the back of the chair.

Gathering up the telephone, he dialled Irene's building and then gave the extension to the operator.

"Hello?"

"Irene, it's me."

"Ah, hello me. Are you still coming over?"

"I'm afraid something has come up. I'll have to cancel, sorry. Duty calls, and it's going to be a long night."

"Nothing dangerous, I hope?"

"It's always dangerous, sweetcheeks," Bill joked.

"You really are a creep, Bill. See you soon, I hope."

"Definitely." Bill put down the receiver.

As the kettle boiled, Bill pulled out the notepad page he had taken from the fat priest's pad. Holding it up to the light to check the words hadn't miraculously changed in his pocket, he studied the indented path caused by the pen on the page above, with the slight ink bleed, one final time:

Anna's place, Alexanderstrasse. Ask for Dorothy.

* * *

Bill parked his car a block away from the notorious house in the Russian sector. As he locked the door, two local policemen eyed him warily. He waved at them and gave his best *go fuck yourselves* grin, then swaggered off in the direction of Anna's Place.

The once-grand facades along the river Spree were now barely standing. Many buildings had succumbed to the Russian onslaught in '45 and simply slumped haphazardly to the ground. Many hiding civilians had been killed. Bill paused to think about it as he looked across the river back towards the destroyed Reichstag. They were the lucky ones, he concluded.

Bill checked over his shoulder to see that the two cops had decided he wasn't worth the effort and hadn't bothered to follow him. He paused in the doorway of a half-destroyed house and waited several minutes, just in case. Besides, they weren't likely to follow him all the way. He was heading to the one place in Berlin the cops never ventured.

Emerging from the darkness, he carried on his way past one of the many bars that had sprung up in the past year. This one played some awful Russian noise and seemed to be half-packed with Russian soldiers. Despite what had happened in the weeks following the fall of the city, this long after Yalta, the Russians generally behaved as if they were at least pretending to be human. Another Berlin cop kept a watchful eye on the place and ignored Bill as he passed by, the smell of cheap cigarettes clouding the way ahead.

He passed by several destroyed buildings and two more beer halls, finally arriving at the pristine building, complete with a new sign which proudly displayed, in Germanic gothic font, Anna's Place.

He greeted the two giant brutes on either side of the entrance. The uglier one of the two suddenly lit up as he recognised him.

"Bill! We haven't not seen you for, in ages! How you are, my friend?" he asked, gleefully, in broken German, with his thick Polish accent, taking Bill's hand to shake it in a rough, vice-like grip.

Igor's slightly less ugly friend just glared at him cautiously. He wore a tight suit jacket over an open-necked shirt, which looked like a pyjama top. The whole ensemble was too small for him, showing off his well-defined biceps, which were approximately the size of Belgium. Igor said something to him in Polish, but Bill had little idea what, only that his name was Fabian and that he now seemed slightly more accepting of Bill's presence.

"I'm fine, Igor, just been very busy with work. Plenty is happening in Berlin right now."

"Yes, is always," he replied.

"I'm going to be busy this evening, so if I don't notice you on your breaks, please get yourselves a drink on me," Bill said as he handed each of the doormen a fistful of marks.

Fabian's face finally cracked into a grin as he gratefully accepted the money. In Bill's experience, it was always good to get people on your side early on, particularly if they happen to be the biggest couple of bouncers in the neighbourhood, well known to the local law, and look as though they could burst your head like it was a grapefruit without so much as breaking a sweat.

He removed his hat and entered the large open doorway, descending the semi-lit stairs to the welcoming glow of the jazz club. The sweet smell of rich cigar smoke hit him in the face as he entered. This was one of Bill's favourite haunts. He had discovered it while doing his rounds of the city in the first couple of weeks of his arrival. If you were looking for someone in a city like Berlin, it was good to have as many telephone operators, journalists, doormen and concierges as possible in your pocket. If you were looking for someone like Misselwitz, you'd better add many of the criminals and whores of the Berlin underworld to that list too.

Anna was neither. She ran one of the most up-market dives in the whole Russian sector. She had acquired this building during the final days of the Battle of Berlin. Her years of service with some Polish partisan group had earned her a lot of respect among the Polish officers. They had secured her this place to ensure they had a place to relax away from the hoi polloi of the ranks, particularly the Russians and local peasantry.

Whilst some Russian officers were often down here, the lower ranks were forbidden. Civilians, civil servants and Polish soldiers were welcome, though. These days, the Poles were thin on the ground on account of most heading home or being secretly sent away to one of Uncle Joe's gulags. The Soviets hated dissidents even more than the Nazis did. The disproportionally high prices kept most people out anyway, regardless of who they were. Aside from a good supply of quality vodka and good cigars, Anna often bragged that she offered up the best tail this side of the Spree.

The numerous luxury apartments upstairs were payable by the hour, with appropriate company supplied. Bill wasn't into that, but they had the best jazz in the city here every night. It was strictly recorded music only, as not many touring bands fancied playing in the brothels of occupied Berlin, least of all black ones.

Bill sat at a vacant table near the bar. The lights were low, and the music was good. Bill caught the attention of the waitress. She must be new. She had dark, bobbed hair, green eyes, and a smile that could stop hearts at thirty yards. She shimmied seductively towards him and leaned over just a little as she stopped at Bill's table, her ample cleavage visible above the mock-Bavarian maid's blouse. Her short red gingham skirt made the most of her shapely, black stockinged legs.

"What can I get you, handsome?" she asked in perfect German, with just a hint of an accent that Bill couldn't quite place.

"I'll take anything you have to offer, gorgeous, but a Scotch will have to do for now."

"Sorry, kid, I'm not for sale, only vodka or beer tonight."

Bill laughed. She was about twenty-five, seven or so years younger than Bill.

"I wasn't offering to pay. I just thought you might fall lovingly into my arms."

"Not until you at least buy me dinner." She winked and

grinned at him.

"I might hold you to that. Vodka it is then, for now, and one of your fine cigars."

"Coming right up, kid."

Bill surveyed the room. Louis Armstrong's "Jeepers Creepers" played in the background. The loud, melodic trumpet washed through the bar like some tuneful cleansing tsunami. Then Armstrong's mellifluous baritone warble pierced the muted chatter of the room. Bill tapped his foot and, among the unknown faces, noticed an elderly Russian officer sitting with Anna. He had large, red, felt patches on his lapels. Bill didn't understand Russian uniforms but assumed he must be a high-ranking officer.

The tall, shapely waitress brought over Bill's vodka and set it carefully down, along with a clean cut-glass ashtray, upon which she carefully balanced a sublime-looking Corona-sized, hand-rolled cigar. The band had already been removed, the end pre-cut with a clean V-shape. She then placed a little paper book of matches on the table, along with a handwritten check for an eye-watering amount of money. She smiled seductively, then turned and walked back to the bar, with a little bounce in her step that made her skirt rise at the back, intentionally almost *too* high.

Finally noticing Bill's presence, Anna raised her small glass at Bill from the Ivan's table and nodded his way. The Russian officer, seeing this, copied her. Bill returned the double gesture in kind.

Anna was a little older than Bill, perhaps forty. She was short and plain but attractive enough. She had blonde, short hair and, unlike the other women in the bar working their way around the tables, wore very little makeup, choosing only a peculiar shade of pink lipstick. Bill knew enough of her recent history to understand her slightly world-weary appearance. However, she made up for what she lacked in glamour in intelligence and the deeply protective love she had for her girls.

Igor and Fabian may have been the ugly faces on the door, but Anna and her Russian-made Nagant revolver were the real danger to anyone who misbehaved in her place. She carried it around on her hip, in a holster, like a feminine version of Buffalo Bill.

Bill picked up the cigar and smelled the wonderful, fermented aroma. He then struck one of the little matches on the plain, white book and charred the tip of his cigar to the point he almost burned his fingertips. He inspected it, then lit a second, and drew through the stogie to get the fine long filler tobacco glowing.

The jazz music played on from the gramophone in the corner, the records occasionally swapped by one of the waitresses. There were, quite noticeably, never any men working in the bar, apart from Bill's large acquaintances up on the street.

One of the girls across the way got up and led a young, uniformed Polish officer by the hand out through the door to the far side of the bar. His night just got very expensive, Bill thought.

Bill sipped his cold vodka and then closed his eyes and drew on his cigar. His mind drifted back to the war and those no longer with him to enjoy such simple pleasures. He wished he could just stay here for all eternity. His perverse enjoyment of occupied Berlin was due, in no small part, to his reacquaintance with Irene, and the various other pleasures of the grain and leaf, courtesy of the British government who, thankfully, never seemed to require receipts.

Anna rose from her seat with the Russian, then, as she made her way towards Bill's table, said something inaudible to the waitress. She greeted Bill with a warm smile, and as Bill rose from his chair, she hugged him and kissed his cheek.

"Good to see you again, Bill. How are you enjoying the winter now it's finally here?"

"Too cold for me, Anna. How's business?"

"Very good. These Reds miss home more and more each month, so business is brisk. How's life at the *BBC*?" she asked, putting a sarcastic emphasis on BBC.

"Fine, fine." Bill shrugged off the implication.

"And how's that fine drink of water of yours. Jack, was it?"

"He's very well too."

"Tell him Apolonia misses him and would very much like to see him again." She chuckled.

"I'll do that."

The waitress brought over two glasses of vodka and placed them down, taking away Bill's empty glass. Bill, again, silently admired her shapely rear as she waltzed away.

"So, you like the new help?" Anna teased.

"Very much so. Where did you find such a fine specimen?"

"She came to me looking for work from the American sector after her release from custody. The Yanks had arrested her in Saltzberg, who had sent her to their so-called de-Nazification training. But, really, they just wanted intelligence. She worked as a secretary for some Nazi officials in Austria in the last year of the war. She told them she had been helping the resistance there, feeding them information about the planned attack of Castle Itter near the end of the war."

"You certainly have a good eye for staff, Anna. But, look, I need a little help." Bill pulled out the two photographs he had brought with him. The least obscene image of the girl and one of his man with the Hindenburg moustache.

"And this would be, what? Research for a story?" she asked knowingly.

"Of course. This girl, I've seen her in here before. Does she still work with you?"

"Yes, that's Katya. She is in tonight but not working. To be honest, she is not very popular among our clientele. Too dour. Hardly surprising with what she's been through. What most of them have been through. I don't know how long I can keep her on. Where did you get that photo? It was taken here, wasn't it?"

"I was hoping you'd be able to tell me that."

"Yes, that looks like her room. I recognise the bed and velvet walls. Each of the girls has an apartment. Nothing fancy, just a bedroom, a little kitchen and seating area, and another room for their dates. It helps them to keep things separate and clean. We have cleaners that change the linen and deal with fluids or breakages. Anything they can't fix, the boys usually help out with." She gestured towards the main entrance. "Photography is allowed, as long as the girls agree. I can check her entries in the book to see what was agreed if you can estimate when it might have been?"

"I've no idea. Perhaps she'll remember?"

"I'll ask."

"I believe the photos were taken by a tall, thin beanpole of a man, German, around fifty."

"We don't get many Germans coming here, and I'm not here every night, but the description rings a bell. Shifty looking man, greying hair."

"Sounds like our *John*," Bill confirmed.

"Feel free to come and see her when she's working, but you can't see her tonight."

"I can't just speak to her?"

"Not unless you are a cop, but they know better than to come down here anyway. You wait to see her when she is working and pay like everyone else." Anna started to get up to leave.

"Please, Anna, I'm sorry. I didn't mean to push it. Just one last thing."

She nodded graciously and settled back into her seat, pulling out a pack of cigarettes and tapping one out. Bill took a match from his book and lit it. She eyed him as she pursed her lips and coaxed the cigarette to life.

She had these piercing eyes. She was pretty in her own way, but her eyes could look into the darkest corners of your mind. It reminded Bill of the thousand-yard stare the Americans talked about among their infantry troops. Bill had once met a man from the US Airborne, who had been rescued at the Battle of the Bulge, with this permanent vacant look. Anna's was different, though. She seemed to see all your secrets like a hawk circling its prey. Bill suddenly felt like a mouse waiting for the inevitable strike from on high.

Bill swallowed, then continued, "Who's Dorothy?"

"What?"

"Someone told me to ask for Dorothy."

Anna broke character and threw her head back into a raucous belly laugh. She could hardly contain herself. Bill just sat, confused, watching as she gathered her emotions and wiped a tear away. Everyone in the bar had turned to look at her, then Bill, wondering what he could have said that was so funny. Bill wondered the same.

"Something I said?"

"Oh, ha ha, sorry, Bill, it's just I never took you for a fairy!"

"A f…? No, I'm not! Is that what this means?"

"Of course! Have you never heard of a *friend of Dorothy*? Like in the Wizard of Oz?"

"Clearly not. Look, it's not really for me. I'm following a lead. Someone was sent here to ask for Dorothy."

"Alright, sure, I believe you," she teased. "We do cater for that sort of thing too. Well, not here, you understand, but there's a building a few doors down where we send them, down a little alleyway to a red door. Of course, the Russians don't really approve but leave them well enough alone." She reduced her voice to a whisper, leaned in and then continued, "Between you and me, some of the fairies are Russian officers."

"That's really useful information, thanks, Anna."

"Any time, Bill."

Bill came to his feet as she stood to go, and she hugged him tightly. Then, with her arms around him, she reached down and felt the snub-nosed Colt revolver he had tucked in the waistband at the small of his back.

"Ah, standard BBC issue," she joked. "Your secret's safe with me, Bill."

"I don't know what you are talking about. I have a permit for that. You can never be too careful as a British journalist in Berlin."

"Of course, of course. Stay safe, and don't even think about touching that while you're in here, or you'll be dead before you hit the ground."

"I would expect nothing less. One last thing, I forgot. Do

you recognise this man?"

He pushed the other photo of the man with the moustache across the table towards her. She didn't even look at it. She had obviously spotted it earlier and made the connections Bill hadn't.

Without even breaking eye contact, she waited, smiled, and then said, "He was here earlier today. That's your fairy."

19

Matador

Berlin, 18th February 1947

Bill made his way back towards the river and the inviting sanctuary of his Mercedes-Benz. The streets had mostly cleared. It was far too cold to be lingering around. An ill wind blew in off the Spree, and Bill pulled down his hat to keep it from freezing his eyes. He felt a little drunk. The vodka had given him a warm protective thermal layer and a slight feeling of giddiness. He felt like a newborn foal trying to work out how his legs worked.

He forced his feet to keep moving. Bill had no intention of staying among the Russians any longer than he had to. Everyone knew what the Ivans could be like. If you fell asleep here, one of the bastards would have your gold tooth when you yawned. There was no way you'd survive falling asleep on the streets alone on the East side of the city with these crooks at the best of times, let alone in this icy hell.

Bill was craving the warmth of his bed. He would take a slow and careful drive home. Shuffling along, he wondered about the investigation. He seemed no nearer to locating Misselwitz. So far, the only link Bill could make was the stack of business cards in the drawer at Misselwitz's mostly empty apartment. No dirty dishes, no worn clothes. Nothing that might give away recent occupation.

He pulled out the card and mulled over the message again:

> *You have a friend at St. Bernhardt Church. All sins cleansed. Escape in the arms of our Lord.*

Maybe it was some secret society for homosexuals? Why would Misselwitz be in Berlin at all, let alone run a lonely-hearts agency for the locals who were light in the loafers? What about the IDs? Why would anyone need fake papers in Berlin when you could just make up your own identity and claim your documents were destroyed?

It seemed to Bill that he had more questions than answers. First, he needed a good night's sleep, then to touch base with Jack and see if he had any ideas. He also had an overwhelming urge to visit Irene but decided that arriving at her apartment in the early hours of the morning stinking of vodka and cigars might not be the best thing for their budding relationship. No, he told himself, just head home.

Reaching his shiny, frost-covered, black refuge, he fumbled around in his pocket for his key.

"You won't need that," a disembodied voice said from somewhere.

Turning and reaching for his revolver, Bill saw the voice emanating from a weasel-faced Berlin cop. The cop placed his large truncheon onto Bill's right arm, which was now gripping his gun, about to draw.

"You won't need that, either," Weasel's grey-haired colleague announced. His black Walther PP pointed at Bill's chest.

"Well, if you are the weasel, I guess that must make you Badger," Bill said to them, releasing the grip on his gun and slowly revealing his empty hand.

"Oh, look. A fucking comedian," the Weasel shouted to no one in particular as he reached around and grabbed Bill's gun. Bill stood perfectly still. There isn't much you can do when someone is holding the hot end of a pistol at you, just out of arm's reach.

"We are going for a little drive. Turn around. We need to cuff you," Badger ordered.

"Great, I could use a tour of the city's underbelly from the local vermin."

* * *

The cell was large, poorly lit, and very cold. Bill pulled the meagre blanket up around him and lay on the bare wooden boards that were masquerading as either a bed or a bookshelf. He wasn't sure which. He was shoeless, still wearing his best suit, and conscious that he could now feel the fabric catching on the splintered timber under him. He shuffled around a little, but comfort eluded him. He drifted into a sort of semi-sleep a few times, waking to change position as the numbness of cold and his aching limbs kicked in.

Eventually, he gave up trying to sleep altogether. The beginning of a hangover was hacking through the nerve endings in his brain, somewhere behind his eyes. He cursed himself for drinking too much when he was not only on an active investigation but also in the Russian sector, having just that afternoon tap-danced on the Berlin cops' toes.

Just as the sun rose outside, he was finally roughly shoved through the cell door by two young cops and down a stark white corridor towards another room, presumably for questioning. One of the young cops left and stood outside, visible through the glass panel in the door's tiny window. The other, just inside the door. The room was empty but for two small chairs on either side of a square table.

"What's this, the dining room? When is breakfast?" Bill asked the cop.

He stared straight ahead, ignoring him. Bill tried again.

"I'll take my eggs over easy."

Tough crowd. Bill resigned to just sitting and humming, trying his best to appear unperturbed.

A short time later, a dark-haired man in his fifties wearing horn-rimmed glasses barged into the room, almost knocking over the young cop.

"Alright, piss off," he said to the guard as he pulled out the chair opposite and took his place opposite Bill. Then, with a stern look, he emptied the small box he'd come in with onto the table between them. The young cop closed the door behind him but remained visible with his colleague outside.

"Right then, what do you and your pal think you were doing pretending to be police earlier today?"

"What? I don't know what you are talking about. I want to call my Lawyer."

"Tough. No lawyer. Who are you, and what are you doing questioning people and claiming to be cops?"

Bill's mind raced through the day's events, trying to recall exactly what he had done to upset the Berlin bulls. His brain struggled through the hangover and pain caused by nodding off on the hard wooden bench.

The forger. Of course! The bookshop. The tall man had loose lips, it seemed. Maybe he needed another visit to loosen his jaw, too, Bill thought.

"If you are charging me with a crime, I suggest you do so, and I will consult my legal representation. Otherwise, I do not wish to converse with you further. I am a British citizen and an employee of the British Broadcasting Corporation. Therefore, you have no right to detain me or obstruct me from my legal activities as a journalist."

"I'm afraid I don't like your attitude."

"Please don't be afraid. I get that a lot."

"Lousy punk. What did you do in the war, sit at a typewriter writing about real heroes, or just typing up the shipping forecast for your betters?"

"I mainly played cards and drank a lot. You? Communist in hiding returned from the Steppe?"

"Red? Ha! Fuck off!"

"Ah, we are getting somewhere. So how many old Jews' skulls did you smash on the pavement? How many helpless disabled children did you euthanise for the glorious thousand-year Reich? SS, SD? Which was it then? If I lift your arm, I bet you have your blood group tattooed under there, as per SS regulations. You sicken me."

His face reddened. Bill had hit a nerve, and he moved his jaw around like a cow chewing cud, wondering what to say to that. Bill wondered if he'd just given him the excuse he was looking for to beat the hell out of him. He tensed up and waited to get hit. The way Bill saw it, everyone takes a beating sometimes, and besides, that would confirm Bill's suspicions about what this big lump had done in the war.

To end up a detective in this born-again Berlin Police, he must be well connected, Bill supposed. Communist? Possibly, but more likely ex-Gestapo. The old Red Castle at Alexanderplatz was the main police precinct for the whole city. At least it was until Uncle Joe, and his red storm destroyed it. The real cops had mostly perished in the last days of the liberation. The rats with the blood group tattoos had scurried and hid in the rubble of the city. If the Americans had chosen Berlin to drop their new bomb, all that would be left would be cockroaches, the SS and the Gestapo.

The allies needed a tough police force to keep order in the decaying city, and who better to instil fear than the very same mob who had been terrorising the country for the past twelve years? The terror from the Russians had been brutal but brief. The long shadow of the men in black coats would last a generation.

This particular phoenix had risen from the ashes of the war, and he was probably hungry but certainly angry and resentful.

"What would you know about anything? Limp-wristed, glorified typist. Fucking pen-pusher. What sort of a journalist carries round a revolver, and an American one, at that? You'd probably do more damage to yourself than anyone you tried to fire it at."

"A paranoid one who likes his gun to work when needed," Bill quipped.

"Look, you smart-arsed punk, the French sector is my town. You and I both know what you were up to, intimidating people just to get them to talk and get your story, whatever the hell it is. So don't piss up my leg and tell me it's raining. I have enough trouble as it is with the bloody Yanks breathing down my neck."

He suddenly stopped his speech short. Whatever he wanted to say, he prevented himself from saying it.

"Oh?" Bill asked.

So, the Amis were shaking him down. What about? First, the brown suits had threatened Albie at *The Post* not to publish the photograph, and now they had their greasy hands on the throats of the cops in the French sector.

"Nice try, punk. I've checked your credentials, and it seems you are well connected. Your carry permit is valid. They even vouched for you at the BBC office. Unfortunately, I can't hold you with no real evidence, but, Hell-be-damned, next time, I'll just make sure I'll find some, understand?"

"Are you suggesting you will fabricate evidence to charge me with a fictitious crime?"

"Maybe next time, I'll just kick your teeth in and dump you in the Tiergarten with the other vegetables. Now, take your crap and get the hell out of my sight," then he added, "and stay out of my town."

"I'll be sure of it, Mr …?"

"Müller. Chief Müller."

* * *

"So, what was he like?" Jack enquired, sipping carefully at his steaming milky coffee.

The cafe was bustling. Never had the chasm between the classes been more evident to Bill than right there. There were no shortages for the middle class and foreign diplomats. While they sat in the heated cafe drinking hot drinks, they watched as, outside, three bedraggled children, no older than ten, begged the passers-by for money and cigarettes. They wore torn coats and had grubby, threadbare trousers. Two of them had hob-nailed boots on—the kind you see worn by farm labourers. One had fashioned some laces using twine. The other shuffled along with the tops wide open. The third, smaller boy had wrapped his feet in canvas sandbags to give at least some protection from the cold.

"He was a belligerent old prick," Bill answered as he stirred a third sugar lump into his tea. He would drink coffee but had always preferred tea. "He obviously rules the French sector with an iron fist, and we stepped on his toes."

"You think he's in on the ID business?"

"I expect he's cut into everything that happens on his patch. The cops are more bent than the villains in Berlin. Especially the ones that used to wear the long black coats."

"So, he's ex-Gestapo?"

"Undoubtedly."

An even younger boy appeared in front of the other three urchins. He was small and looked malnourished. The city was full of these feral children. The various governments had little desire to be burdened with their care. Some were orphans, whilst many had been sent out by their mothers to obtain whatever they could to help keep the family fed, whether it be through begging, barter or just plain old theft. The smaller child appeared to be looking for something and was pointing down the street.

"Well, all has gone quiet at the church. So, what's the next move?"

"We need to get on the trail of Misselwitz. It feels like we are chasing our tails. He's in the city, so he'll have to surface sometime."

"What about Schmidt? I could pay another visit to Misselwitz's building and see if he'll talk."

"I don't think he's using it. It's a front in case he needs to give it out. It's probably the address on his ID card. Let's not shake down Schmitt just yet, in case it spooks Misselwitz to go even further down his rabbit hole. Then there's the fat priest. I don't see any other leads at the moment if we can't catch up with the moustache man. I'll head back to Anna's tomorrow to try to speak to her girls. Perhaps others have *made acquaintance* with our amateur photographer. I'm still none the wiser about how this all fits together."

Bill lit his pipe and slouched back in his chair. Jack stared thoughtfully out the window at the four kids.

Jack was something of an enigma in the service. Since the war he rarely smoked while on operations. In England, he occasionally smoked, and he was never bothered by Bill's pipe, even in the confines of a vehicle or small room, but Bill had, with maybe one exception, never seen him smoke while overseas in the past year.

Bill looked up at the diminutive beggars just as he got his pipe to stay lit. The two largest boys started to shove the new child to the ground as the smaller of the three kicked him in the leg.

Jack rose slowly and deliberately from his seat, then, whilst muttering something in Polish under his breath, made his way to the cafe door. As he pulled the giant door open, the air pressure changed in the room, and the cold air rushed to fill the vacuum. Bill knew something had gotten to him, as Jack seldom spoke Polish these days.

The three boys stopped tussling with the younger boy,

who was now in floods of tears and stared in terror at Jack's looming figure approaching them. The boy with the laced boots turned to run, so Jack grabbed him by the ear and spun him back around. Bill couldn't hear what was being said, but the three belligerents quietly listened and nodded as Jack harangued them in a raised voice, his arms gesturing all around him. Finally, the three boys looked down at the ground and spoke to the youngest boy, who was wiping away tears.

Bill looked on as Jack reached into his pocket and handed the three older boys something. Placing a few objects into each of their outstretched palms. Bill looked back at the table to see the little bowl, which had held the sugar cubes, was now empty. Then, smiling to himself, he swivelled back around just as Jack added a banknote to each grubby little hand. Now beaming with smiles, they each shook the hand of the littlest kid, thanked Jack, and then made off in the direction of the city centre, Mitte, where the Reichstag once stood proud near the famous Brandenburg Gate and the grand facade of the Adlon Hotel. These days, the hotel was gone, and the gate was simply a sorry, tired, inconvenient obstruction to the progressives' brand-new political divergence of the Russian, British and American sectors.

The politics were hanging by a thread. The allied nations seemed to eye each other distrustfully, like two Rugby teams ready for a scrum, but with guns. The Russians appeared to be distancing themselves from the clique more, day by day. Indeed, if Errington was right, their spies were even probing their organisation for intel.

Jack led the young boy into the cafe, much to the disgust of a uniformed British officer sitting at a table near the door with a couple of suits. Jack ignored their screwed faces, nodded to the waiter, and sat the boy down at their table.

"I hate bullies," Jack grunted as he sat down. "This whole country is full of them."

"They are just boys with no fathers, Jack."

"Hello, sir," the young boy said to Bill, almost avoiding eye contact.

"Hello, young man. Are you hungry?"

"Yes, sir."

"Good, then this is indeed a good day to get a kicking," Jack interjected.

The waiter appeared and bowed his head. Jack shook his head and pointed to the scruffy boy.

"Sir?" the waiter asked, confused.

"Ask him what he wants," Jack added.

The waiter, perturbed, turned to the boy, "What would you like … sir?"

The scrawny little kid looked to Jack, who nodded encouragingly. "Whatever you want, kid."

"*Schnitzel*?" he said, unsure if he was allowed.

"Very well."

"Plus a basket of bread and a tall glass of milk," added Bill.

20

Brown Suit

Berlin, 22nd February 1947

Bill rolled over to find a space where Irene's warm, naked body used to be. He glanced around the room and saw there was no sign of her. Instead, a small, handwritten note was on the pillow in a beautiful looping cursive script:

Gone out to see B1 man about a dog. Talk later xx

Bill thought about Errington's office and, more specifically, the aged single malts hiding in his drinks cabinet. He lay on the bed and stared blankly at the note for a few minutes remembering the golden nectar, then shook himself from his stupor.

Bill wondered about this imagined dog. Maybe it was the *red* one Errington had warned him about. If such a thing were possible, the Russians were becoming even more of a threat to stability in Berlin lately.

Of course, Bill hadn't mentioned what he was doing in the city but had told her Jack was around too. She was keen for them to meet up, but it would have to wait for now, as it appeared all three of them were currently operational.

Bill dragged himself from the bed into the chill of the kitchen and prepared some tea. He then hunted around for his clothes, discarded in some hurry the evening before, and got himself dressed. The gold-framed, full-length dress mirror stood inanimate by the door and showed him a moving image of some overly-creased homeless man. He would fit in nicely among the numerous refugees hiding in the ruins throughout the city. He needed to change suits and desperately needed a shave.

Out the window, Bill could see it was trying to snow. The beginnings of the inevitable harsh cold were now blowing in more misery from the east. But, late or not, the winter was now, indeed, here.

After finishing his tea, he pocketed his revolver, collected his coat and hat from the stand, and headed out into the cold Berlin hell.

* * *

"Bill, we need to talk about the Hamiltons again."

"Sure. Just let me know when."

"Today. I've uncovered one heck of a story. But, to be honest with you, I am a little concerned about my safety."

Bill looked at the dancing flames in the fireplace, and his heart sank a little that he would have to face the weather again today. He had left his shiny new car at Irene's apartment and taken an S-Bahn train back. They were running pretty efficiently, despite the difficulties with the weather. Berliners sure knew how to overcome adversity. The services were no longer running first class, though. Since the war, it was strictly second and third class only, and neither had any heating.

"Budget is tight, but I'll get you some protection if necessary, depending on what you have for me. Let's say, three-ish?"

"Great. See you then." Albie hung up.

Bill looked down at the sheet of paper at the childish drawing. Violette used to try to work out the best plan of action by drawing out what she called a spidergram. Put all the known facts down and try to draw links between them. It hadn't worked out for Bill, whose mind worked better when he smoked, eyes shut, whisky in hand. Whilst Violette had drawn elaborate charts and diagrams with perfect handwritten annotations, Bill's art career had barely stretched further than crudely drawing penises on his friend's exercise books at school. He screwed up his pitiful attempt and threw it into the fire.

Trailing around Berlin, picking up half-clues, spending a small fortune of the king's money on fuel and liquor was as elaborate a waste of time you'd find anywhere outside of the Houses in Westminster, but how else would he bring Misselwitz out into the open? All was quiet. The rat had gone to ground, and Bill had to think of a way to dig him out.

Bill numbed his brain with another jazz record, and it crackled its melody through the cloud masquerading as his mind, an extension of the pipe smoke about him. He closed his eyes and tried to draw the links.

All paths he took led to the same destination. An answer that lurked in the darkness. Somewhere among the faceless agents in brown suits, the men in long black leather coats and the topless dancing girls from a cabaret that only existed in the past. Somewhere in the dark. Forged IDs, homosexuals, dangling boots, photographs, scalpels and guns. Somewhere, in that misty dark corner of his mind, there was the answer.

The record ended, and the rhythmic ticking of the run-out continued. Finally, Bill dragged himself back to reality and stood to switch off the gramophone. The attempted mind map had got him nowhere. He carefully placed the record back into its paper sleeve and, in turn, into the wooden box on the floor.

Bill sighed and collected his hat and coat. This was driving him mad. It was like banging a brick against a wall made out of heads.

As he pulled on his leather gloves, he muttered to himself, "Back to the grindstone, Bill."

* * *

The chill wind slithered through a gap in Bill's cashmere scarf, and he quickly adjusted it to keep the cold, wintery fingers off his neck. He clapped his hands and stamped his feet waiting under the once-grand, now crumbling, stone gate.

Two Russian soldiers in uniform walked past and curtly nodded at him. They each had a woman on his arm. All four wore fur *ushankas* pulled down to just above the bridge of their noses. The girls had released the ear flaps and tied them under their chins. Locals, Bill assumed. Their Russian cohorts probably gifted them the hats. No proper Russian would have the ear flaps down in anything less than a full blizzard. Strange they may be, but they were a tough sort. It was a different breed that survived the winters out there to the East. No one could accuse a Russian of being frightened of a bit of snow.

Bill checked his wristwatch. Five minutes to three. He had been standing for a full quarter of an hour. His nose was running, and his toes felt like they were freezing inside his shoes. He decided right there to get better socks and decent boots at the first available opportunity. He briefly missed the army boots he used to have to wear. What he wouldn't give to be wearing them right now. Bill tipped his hat forward to keep the wind from his eyes and tried to forget the icicles where his toes used to be.

Albie swept into view out of the haze, dragging his heels with every step, leaving strange skid marks in the gathering thin white veil on the ground.

"I'm not late, am I? Have you been here long?"

"Bang on time, Albie. Don't worry about me. I thrive in the cold." Bill flashed him a smile, then added, "Now let's get back into the British sector, out of this bloody awful cold and into a bar."

"Couldn't agree more."

The bar of the Grand Hotel was nice and quiet. It was only just past three p.m., after all. They picked a table in the back corner and, removing their various outer garments, handed them to the waiter, who placed them as carefully as if they were the crown jewels onto the faux-gold hat stand by the wide entrance to the bar. Bill needed Albie to be comfortable, happy and willing to talk. The five-star service here might just give him the edge he needed.

Bill pulled out a packet of Lucky Strikes and placed them on the table next to a large glass ashtray. Albie nodded and smiled, then helped himself to a cigarette. Noticing this, the waiter darted to the long art deco, emerald-coloured bar, retrieved a cartoonishly large amber table lighter, and looked back towards their table. Bill just frowned and shook his head as he struck a Swan Vesta to life with his thumbnail and held it aloft for Albie. The waiter clicked his heels together and bowed his head, returning the ridiculous object from whence it came.

"What do you have for me, Albie?"

"Well, out of curiosity, I did a little digging into the victims of the Jeep crash. I might have disturbed something big here, Bill."

The waiter appeared. He was about fifty, with slicked-back grey hair and a small moustache that still held some black pigment. He was a handsome man and, in another life, could easily have been in the movies. He stood silently, with a small pencil poised to take their order.

"I'll take a large beer. Anything dark," said Bill.

"We have lovely local Dunkel, sir, on tap."

"Perfect, thanks."

"And a Weissbier for me, thanks."

"Would you care to sample our snack platter, gentlemen?"

"Sure."

The waiter drifted effortlessly back to the bar and placed the little ticket on a giant metal spike.

"Look, Albie, whatever it is, I'll do my best to keep you protected."

"Alright, fair enough. I told myself I wouldn't, but I looked into the crash, and it turns out that the two US airmen were killed, not injured. The lieutenant was straightforward enough. Failed the cadet program to be aircrew, delayed entry, missed the war by a few months, and ended up a glorified Jeep jockey, moving around prisoners."

"Prisoners? So, the sergeant was a prisoner?"

"I don't know. The sergeant has no records at all. He appeared in the files barely three days before the crash. I have a contact in the US Army Air Force that guards the perimeter at Tempelhof Airport. He said he wants to talk to you directly. The Jeep had come up from Wannsee headed for a flight out, bound for Wiesbaden in the American-controlled region in Bavaria."

The waiter returned with their drinks and a large silver platter with little dividers for the four sections. It had all kinds of sliced sausage and dainty small pieces of rye bread. Bill ate a piece of sausage and took a long swig of his beer.

Albie continued, "This is where it starts to get strange. I also managed to get an off-the-record chat with the local coroner who looked over the body. When the Americans turned up and requisitioned the corpse, they made him sign some non-disclosure contract. When he refused, they held a gun to his head and told him they'd help him to sign it with his brains."

Bill packed his pipe as he listened intently. Albie had stopped and noticed he was busying himself.

"Please, Albie, continue. I was hanging on your every word. Smoking helps me think."

"Well, after that performance, my guy held back the negatives of the initial photographs he took of the cadaver and stashed them away. He didn't know what to do with them until I came calling. I had to put a few dollars his way, which I'd appreciate if you would cover."

"Of course. We'll come to an arrangement."

The Americans, again. Bill let it filter through the colander of his mind. The brown suits were meddling everywhere in this case, it seemed.

The prominent figure of Jack appeared in the lobby of the hotel, and as he removed his lightly frosted hat, he smiled and raised his eyebrows at Bill, then made his way into the bar. He removed his coat as he walked, throwing both it and his hat carelessly at the stand as he passed. The astonished waiter rushed to the stand to rearrange it. Jack ignored him.

"Albie, this is my friend and colleague, Jack."

"Pleased to make your acquaintance." Albie stood and shook Jack's hand.

"May I get you anything, sir?" The film-star waiter had interrupted yet again.

"What's that?" Jack asked as he jabbed a finger towards the table.

"That's our famous snack platter, sir."

"Alright, I'll have two more of those and a couple of beers. Surprise me."

"Very good, sir." The fawning waiter scurried off.

Jack sat, brushed down his black suit, and adjusted his tie. He grabbed a fistful of the sausage slices from the platter and dumped them unceremoniously onto the small plate in front of him. Ever the gentleman.

"I'm starving," he said to no one in particular and shoved two pieces into his mouth.

Bill smirked, shook his head and then said to Albie, "So, these photos?"

"Right. I got the negatives processed at the lab at the *Post*'s office. They didn't mean anything to me, but I showed them around, not mentioning where I got them, and another journalist recognised his face. He was sure it was an ex-SS officer he had the misfortune of coming across when he was on the Eastern Front. I told him you might want to speak to him. That's all I know so far. I thought you'd like to hear about it as soon as possible."

"Fantastic work, Albie."

Bill turned to Jack, who had hungrily cleared the platter and was now nodding in appreciation, still chewing. Bill wondered if it was the food or the story that had him so pleased. Much to Jack's delight, the waiter set down the other two platters and Jack's beers, one of which he swiftly emptied, then asked for another. Bill nodded at the waiter's silent tip of his head, a confirmation to order another round.

"How does this tie in with your guy? Ernst Wizer? Just a coincidence?"

"There are no coincidences. The universe is never that lazy," Jack spluttered, his mouth full.

"I do wish you wouldn't do that, you uncouth oaf," Bill scolded as Jack had a large slurp of his second beer.

"That's better. I hadn't eaten at all today."

Turning back to Albie, Bill said, "I'm sure there must be a link, but I'm yet to make it."

"So, who is he? Another ex-Nazi?"

"I'm afraid, as I told you when we first met, I can't tell you that."

"You're right. Sorry, Bill. Here are the details for my guy at the *Post*. He knows to expect your call."

"What about this USAAF guard? Do you think he saw

anything regarding the crash?" Jack interrupted.

"He was present on the day. I can give you his name, but you won't be able to talk to him by telephone or at the airport. The military strictly forbids the men from talking to the press. However, he hangs out at the Victory Club, nearby, most nights."

"I know it well. It's near the airstrip, not far from my apartment."

"You have been a great help, Albie. The BBC want to show their appreciation for your efforts." Bill slid a little stack of green bills across the table to him. "Jack here will stay with you this evening. Head back to the office and see if you can persuade your colleague to meet you there and see if he can remember a name. Best stay the night together until I can arrange some proper protection for you. You have been asking a lot of questions, so it won't take long for the Amis to realise something is afoot."

* * *

The short walk to the tram stop was interrupted only to rewrap his scarf and occasionally wipe his nose, which was now running like a tap. The investigation had been stalling, but now he might just have a lead.

The streets were quiet. The light was fading out, but the blanket of snow reflected what little there was, giving the surroundings a lacklustre glow. It would not get truly dark with this thin white carpet all around. He passed by the Brandenburg Gate, out of the British sector and back into the city's red zone.

The streetcars in Berlin were run down and dirty. They

buzzed and clattered their way through the city like the rattling of a half-empty matchbox. But they were only twenty pfennigs, and Bill could suffer the discomfort this once. He hadn't fancied driving in the snow, and the trains would go too far out of his way. As he crunched through the snow, his shoes getting heavier under the weight of the acquired mass, he could distinctly hear an echo of his steps somewhere behind him.

Bill stopped and pulled out another pack of Luckies from his coat pocket. He didn't know how many he needed to keep Albie talking back at the hotel, so he had brought backups. He had swapped a full wax carton of the awful things with an American soldier he'd met while hanging out in the Castle Club near his apartment.

It paid to familiarise yourself with the local drinking establishments in the city and their selection of American whiskeys, especially ones in your neighbourhood, particularly when the US military and undercover agents frequent those bars. You never know when you might need to squeeze someone for information or swap some pipe tobacco for US cigarettes.

He needed an excuse to stop and take a surreptitious glance back. He hated cigarettes. The Berliners called them coffin nails. Bill would sooner drive a nail through his tongue than smoke a whole one. He dragged one of the white sticks from the pack and held up his coat collar. Tucking his head down behind it, Bill struck a match and paused to light it. The slightest of peeks back in the direction he had come from confirmed he had a shadow. A stocky man hesitated, then suddenly diverted into the dull light spilling from one of the bars.

Bill put the pack and matches back into his pocket and continued on his way. He walked unhurriedly along and then crossed the broad avenue. As he reached the opposite curb, he threw away the disgusting cigarette, looked down the street, and caught the shadow in the corner of his eye, further back now, following him once again.

Bill turned left down a narrow alleyway. Even down here, the snow had laid down a thin veil of white. He passed a narrow doorway entrance to some apartments. He continued another fifteen yards, then veered left down an off-shoot alleyway. He quickly walked backwards, retracing his footsteps back to the entranceway, and jumped sideways into it, hiding in the shadows. He hadn't had time to be too precise and had missed his old footprints ever-so-slightly, leaving a double print in places, but he hoped the shadow would be in too much of a hurry trying to catch up to notice.

He waited in the dark cover of the doorway, collar up, hat tipped down. His leather glove gripped his gun in his coat pocket. The stocky man passed by, following Bill's footprints in the snow. He was wearing a brown fedora, lightweight brown trench coat with an ivory-coloured scarf wrapped around his neck, snow-splattered brown brogues and brown trousers.

Could this guy look any more like an American agent if he tried?

As he continued out of sight, Bill stepped quietly from the doorway and pointed his revolver at the back of the sepia shadow.

"Hold it right there," said Bill in English.

The shadow stopped and sighed. It had confirmed his suspicion. Bill had chosen his words carefully. Most locals,

Russians and even the French would know the word *stop*. He had contemplated *freeze*, just for the ironic comedy, but had decided it wasn't the time or place.

"Now turn around slowly and keep your hands where I can see them."

The stocky man turned to face him. His face was almost obscured, but Bill could see his bushy eyebrows perched above his eyes like a couple of hairy caterpillars. Yes, of course, his eyes were brown, too.

"Why are you following me?"

"Can't a man just take a walk?" he said arrogantly.

"Into the Russian sector in the middle of a snow flurry? I'm afraid I do not believe even an American would be quite so stupid."

Bill approached the man, then circled him and kept his gun barrel pointed at the man's back. Then, swapping hands, he snaked his right arm around him, unbuttoned his coat and reached around to retrieve the gun he had spotted under the man's left arm. He pulled it gently out of the shoulder holster with his thumb and index finger.

"A Colt," Bill said, inspecting the gun. "Detective special, a man of good taste. Or a man who had no choice in the matter and was issued it by Uncle Sam."

"I have a permit for that."

"Yes, I'm sure you do."

Bill checked the man's pockets and found the permit and a United States Army ID card.

"Lieutenant Frank Malone. US Strategic Services Unit. I wonder what Americans want with a journalist from the free British press? Especially one dressed in such a strange uniform."

"Look, I don't know anything. I was supposed to tail you and report back to the office," said Malone.

"Keep talking."

"Seriously, that's it. I don't know shit."

"I sincerely doubt the US government would send an agent who *doesn't know shit* to tail a mark into the Soviet sector of Berlin."

At the far end of the alleyway, a pair of armed Russian soldiers patrolled by, chatting and smoking. Malone looked back over his shoulder at Bill. Bill held his breath.

Malone got as far as forming the start of the first syllable of "Help" before Bill smacked him on the back of the head with his revolver. His brown hat fell onto the cold ground, followed by a tumbling Malone shortly afterwards. Bill checked him over for a pulse and found he was still alive and breathing. He dragged him into the dark alleyway, out of the wind and weather, and propped him up against the wall.

Checking the unconscious man's pockets, Bill found a couple of hundred dollars, some Occupation Marks, and a fancy Zippo branded petrol lighter. Leaving him the money, ID card and gun permit, he carefully placed his hat back on his head. Bill noticed some blood dripping down onto Malone's collar. The red made a nice change from all the brown, Bill noted.

Bill reached into his jacket pocket, pulled out a half-bottle of whisky he had forgotten to give to Albie earlier, and placed it carefully into Malone's inside pocket. The bloke would need it when he woke up with the headache Bill had left him with. In any case, he was now heading to the Victory Club, anyway.

Bill emptied the chambers of Malone's gun, pocketed the

extra rounds, and dropped it back into his holster. He then crept back to the alleyway and checked for the Russian soldiers, who were nowhere to be seen. He needed to get as far away as possible, fast. Bill had well and truly shaken up the brown hornets' nest.

21

Victory

Berlin, 22nd February 1947

The tram hummed and groaned off into the distance. Bill cursed his choice as he rubbed his back, sore from the bare wooden bench seat. He made his way down the street, past the Castle Club and its lavish exterior.

"Evening, Bill!" shouted Ronnie, the smartly dressed gatekeeper of the ornate shrine to the gods of pre-war art deco. The Roaring Twenties had never ended at the Castle Club. It was full of smartly dressed US Army officers, pretty barmaids, and even prettier female patrons. They all seemed to have the same sculpted hair, styled in voluptuous victory curls, with even more curvaceous figures. They all looked like Betty Grable, which was no bad thing at all, as far as Bill was concerned.

"Good evening, Ronnie. How's business?" Bill moved out of the wind into the grand doorway.

Ronnie was a tall, muscular man with a boxer's squat face and a prominent wonky nose. His neck had a sizeable scar ear-to-ear, apparently from a drunken argument with an Egyptian arm wrestler one night near Cairo. Of course, when you spend most evenings drinking near closing time with the staff, they tell you all sorts of stories.

"Good, my friend. You know the Yanks. They love to throw away their beer coupons like they are going out of fashion. Are you coming in tonight? I'll make sure one of the girls looks after you, you know, priority service, that kind of thing."

Ronnie was an ex-con-turned war hero, originally from South London. He had fought with the French Foreign Legion in North Africa and later, Italy. By the end of the war, the bright lights of a new adventure were calling him, and yet, somehow, Ronnie ended up in Berlin. He had intended to assist in setting up the new sectors but landed a job here instead. This diamond in the rough, the Castle Club, was among the trendiest in the south of the city and right on the doorstep of Tempelhof Airport.

"Thanks, Ronnie, but I have business down the road this evening. I hear Charlton's having a decent run in the cup?"

Bill had little interest in sport, but it always paid to do your homework. Ronnie could be a handy ally sometimes, especially when a drunk American fly-boy gets belligerent over a spilt drink.

"That's right. The only thing I miss about home is the football. So where are you off to, the Victory?"

"Indeed. I need to find someone and speak with him. While I'm here, though, do you know anything about the Jeep crash near here just over a week back?"

"I did hear about it. The girls told me there was a real fracas out here, but I sleep most afternoons and don't get here until six p.m. Some Yank officer bought it, didn't he?"

"That's right, and another man, a sergeant."

"Can't help you with that one, pal. Perhaps I can ask around?"

"Let me know if you find out anything; gossip, rumours, anything. You know where to find me. I must dash."

"Will do. The music's better down there anyway."

"It is that. Look, maybe I'll stop by before I head home later. Get yourself a drink in case I don't see you, though," Bill said as he handed Ronnie a ten-dollar bill.

Ronnie smiled and looked at the crisp bill before stuffing it haphazardly into his front top pocket. It was below zero degrees outside, and this lunatic was only wearing a dinner suit.

Bill continued down the busy street. The wind had dropped to an icy breeze, and the snow had ceased to fall, leaving only its thin carpet here and there to remind of its visit. All around were couples walking arm-in-arm, wrapped up like Scott of the Antarctic. American voices, gentlemen in military greatcoats, and ladies in mink furs were all around. But for the street names, one might mistake the street for Broadway. The numerous bars spat their neon glow onto the reflective damp of the pavement.

A young woman wearing a small, fancy hat smiled at Bill, who politely smiled back. However, he got a distinct impression there was slightly more behind her sparkling eyes than just innocent politeness. Her male officer companion noticed this, too, and jolted her by the arm as he hurried her along.

Bill chuckled to himself as he turned off the main drag onto

Dorfstrasse and walked the short way down to number 22, the address of the Victory Club. Bill had spent a lot of time around the Americans and had picked up much of their odd language, but even though he had been down here a few times before, it never ceased to surprise him. If the Castle Club was the classiest joint in Tempelhof, the Victory Club was surely the hippest. For good reason. It played all kinds of jive, fast blues and swing music.

The road was run down and dirty. This certainly wasn't Broadway. It was more like Lewisham Broadway. He was barely a hundred yards from the main strip, yet this place was a world away from the bright lights and affluence of Berliner Strasse. Gone were the officers and their ladies, replaced with local men, dressed in worn grubby moleskin trousers and oversized boots, smoking spitty, little, roll-up cigarettes, thinner than a hermit's address book.

Bill looked back behind him to see if anyone had followed him, then ducked through the doorway of a very generic looking building. Above the door was a wooden sign, with hand-painted black lettering, reading: *Colored Troops.* He didn't know what to hate more, the disgusting segregation, even within their forces, or the awful spelling.

The former beer hall had been converted into what the regulars called a juke joint. The owners were apparently Berliners but had been more than accommodating of their new clientele, and the place had slowly become what it was now, a drinking and dancing bar that looked to be plucked straight out of the Mississippi Delta.

Bill couldn't place the music, but it sounded good. The place was already busy, despite the early hour. They served no food at the Victory, but people were drinking, chatting, and smiling all around. The black troops were no different to the other American soldiers when it came to spending. There were stacks of green bills being exchanged on the various tables where card games were taking place. Some of the men had evidently picked up local girlfriends, as Bill had to squeeze by a couple who were busy eating each other's faces, totally oblivious to their surroundings.

Bill spotted a familiar face across the room. Chester was a short, skinny man with white, curly hair and a face as creased as Tutankhamen's comfort blanket. Everyone knew Chester, and he knew almost everybody. If you were a spy with a new face in Tempelhof, you came to the Victory Club and befriended Chester. It didn't take much. The old man wanted for nothing. He had a decent townhouse just down the street, and the boys from the nearby base would deliver groceries or whatever he needed. What he usually needed was wine. Bill had never seen anyone put away wine as Chester could.

"Hey! Billy-boy! How you doin', my buddy?" he said as he paused the game he was playing against a young soldier at the bar.

"I'm doing fine, thanks, Chester. How are you getting on in the cold weather?"

"Boy, my old bones sure don't like it one bit. Ain't seen you in here for a couple of weeks. So pull up a stool and prepare to lose some money!"

Chester gestured to the stack of bills in front of him, his winnings from the evening spent stitching up the young servicemen who were keen to try to pull off the impossible and outwit Chester at a few rounds of dominoes.

"I may be stupid, but I'm not silly! So, I think I'll stick to watching you milk the youngsters dry."

The young kid at the bar stared in despair at Bill, only now realising his foolishness. Bill laughed and shrugged at him.

"Well, they gotta learn sooner or later not to stick their heads in a gator's mouth," he said as he turned back to the game and placed down tile-after-tile with no reply from the teenager, except to pick up another. "Marie, get Billy here what he wants and put it on my slate."

"I'll take a bourbon, thanks." Bill knew it was an exercise in futility to ask for Scotch anywhere in Tempelhof. He pulled out his tobacco pouch and pulled out a couple of the small flakes, placing them on top of Chester's money stack. He looked around and smiled at Bill, nodding in appreciation, then laid another tile, much to the young man's despair as he collected up yet another as a forfeit.

Bill collected up his drink and leaned back on the bar, placing down his hat upon it. Chester was a marvel. Bill would never understand how anyone could cheat quite this well at dominoes. The regulars all knew he kept a couple of tiles tucked under his elbow. The older and more experienced guys all knew that playing him was a trap and found it all the more entertaining when he had managed to snare another recruit into one of his games.

The bar had the smell of smoke and exuberant youth. Half the men in here were under twenty-five. They had arrived in Germany too late to see action and had ended up part of the so-called Army of Occupation. There were a few long-timers around tonight, all wearing ribbons and stripes on their arms. Most were drivers, cooks and camp guards. The US didn't want too many of their Afro-American boys earning a good reputation for themselves, so few were given a chance.

"Damn it," the young soldier at the bar said as the old man

won yet another round.

Chester collected the green Lincoln from the bar and placed it on his stack, but not before removing the tobacco flakes and balling them into his leathery fist.

A sergeant rose from his chair at a nearby table, laughing heartedly, and clapped the young man on the back, offering him up a full glass of beer and a seat. The veteran soldier winked at Bill and then sat back down, still chuckling at the young man's orchestrated misfortune. It was all part of the hazing of recruits in the Victory. The patrons would often treat a white face like Bill's in here with a general distrust, even animosity at times. Bill had seen it more than once, including when he'd first ventured in. Now he was a semi-regular here and was left well enough alone.

The women, of course, were a different matter entirely. Many locals were curious about these new soldiers from faraway lands. Most chose the up-market bars on the strip, but some of the more adventurous would come in here to find solace in the arms of one of these even more exotic strangers. An absolute taboo under the Nazis was now a blissful throwaway escape from reality. The language barrier was no real obstacle to either party, as they both only had one thing they wanted anyway and always seemed to have no problem achieving it.

"Another bites the dust, eh, Chester?"

"Sure was fun. That's my bills paid for the week."

Chester pulled out his old, charred pipe. A genuine curiosity to Bill, who had only ever seen a corncob pipe in the Popeye cartoons. He watched as he shoved the rubbed tobacco carelessly into the bowl and packed it down with a rough finger.

"Here. I've brought you a present," Bill said as he placed down Malone's steel Zippo lighter on the bar.

"Nice. I've never had my own one of these."

"I remember, you told me before. So, I thought you'd appreciate one. It's no good to me. I like matches too much."

Bill pulled one out from his vesta case and lit his own, then Chester's pipe. He looked briefly at the knocked-about little silver box his father had given him, smiled, then placed it back in his pocket. Chester nodded to the pale white barmaid, who poured him out another full half-litre glass of red wine. Bill looked again and wondered if it was just that she was here that she appeared quite *so* white.

"I need to speak to someone, a Sergeant James Pheonix. He works on the base."

"Yeah, I know Pheonix. He's right over there," Chester replied as he pointed to the far side of the club. "Tall fella, big nose, smoking a cigar."

"That's a real help, Chester. Thanks." Bill rose to leave him.

"Wait up, Billy. You got any of that fine tobacco going spare?"

Bill sighed and fished out his pouch. He pulled out a bunch of flakes and placed them into Chester's dry, cracked, awaiting palm.

"Always the hustler, old man."

"Play to your strengths, Billy boy. Play to your strengths."

Bill ordered four Budweisers, gathered them up and made his way to Sergeant Pheonix's table. He was mid-flow telling a story about an old Chevy truck he and his father worked on back home. Bill quietly placed a beer bottle down before him and his two friends, both corporals. He ignored Bill and finished his story. The two corporals eyed him warily.

As he ended and silence fell around the group, Bill finally interrupted. "Sergeant Pheonix, isn't it? I'm Bill, a friend of Albie and Chester. I'd like to have a quiet word with you, if I may?"

The sergeant peered at Chester, who replied with a slight nod. "Oh, you must be the Brit reporter from the BBC. I've seen you in here from time to time. Let's take a quiet seat over there and talk, and you can call me James."

The sergeant bade farewell to his companions and followed Bill over to a table in what they referred to as the saloon, a quieter area to do serious drinking or have clandestine chats like these. Black market transactions often occurred back here too. Pheonix relit the cigar that was clenched in his teeth, drew on it rhythmically, puffing out little streams of smoke like a steam train chugging up a hill.

"I guess you want to know what I told Albie, right? All I know is that this guy is German, and it ain't the first time. There have been at least three others. They show up at the airport from elsewhere by military transport, then catch a flight out to Wiesbaden. The weird thing is, they are always in an American uniform, like some kind of cover. So they think we don't notice, but they end up talking to some of the Germans we got working at the airfield."

"What did he look like?"

"Shit. You white mother fuckers all look the same! I guess about five foot ten, blond."

"And why are you so keen to tell the press about this?"

"Look, I ain't had the best time since the war. It sure beats going back to the States, but they still treat us like dirt here. I fought right up through Italy. I took a hit in the right shoulder and another through my ass. I got awarded a Bronze Star,

Combat Infantryman Badge, campaign medals, the works. Then one day, there's no one left to fight, and we're right back to where we started. Getting fucked-on by the man. Guarding a damned airfield in a half-destroyed city, a thousand miles from home, that no one gives a shit about. Berlin is just the same as back home. We are soldiers. I lost a lot of friends, and now it's all over. I'm just another Negro in the white man's army. I don't owe them shit. I ain't keeping their secrets for them. They are recruiting Nazis from somewhere and flying them out of this dump, off to some fancy hotel somewhere, while me and the guys get a lousy bunk in a barrack block."

"I can see why you aren't so keen to keep a lid on it. Can't you call it a day and head home?"

"And go back to what? No job and no respect. I send half my money home to my ma, the rest I spend here to help forget. Well, almost everything. At least in Berlin, I can go nearly anywhere, and not be made to go through the back door like some animal, or stand on a bus for some white dude who's never been closer to combat than when his mama whooped his ass for stealing candy when he was ten."

"I'm sorry they have treated you this way, James. For what it's worth, I don't much like Americans, either. The hypocrisy makes me sick to the stomach. Thanks for your service. I appreciate the information. I'll try to make sure it does some good. Let me buy you another drink. I have a few more questions."

22

The Ghost of Paris

Berlin, 22nd February 1947

Bill usually looked forward to visiting Anna's Place, but it had already been an immensely long night. Thankfully, the U-Bahn had brought him up to Unter den Linden in at least some comfort and warmth. Bill headed down the famous street. As his footsteps fell into theirs, he could have sworn he felt the presence of Hitler, Napoleon, and other narcissistic parasites around him, like flies around a carcass. However, it could just as likely have been the beer and whisky doing the thinking.

He passed a Russian patrol who had stopped in the awkwardly named but once-grand Kaiser-Franz-Josef-Platz and tipped his hat. The smaller of the two greeted him in German, and then the pair continued conversing in their alien dialect. The colossal structure of St. Hedwig's Cathedral stood forlorn in the devastated square. The eighteenth-century Catholic church was little more than a shell. The roof and interior had been destroyed by allied bombing. The front mock-Roman pillars were covered with patches of bare stone where the Russians had blasted away the ornate, carved sculptured facade during the final fighting.

The ubiquitous rubble surrounded the square. Bill thought perhaps if someone were to design a flag for this strange new fractured city, it ought to be red, with a mountain of rubble as a centrepiece. He walked swiftly through the square, smoking his pipe as he went, feeling numerous Russian eyes burning into his back.

He headed once more over the river. The water smiled unwillingly, full of indignation at the state of her banks, piled up with destruction and squalor. The old river had snaked through the city, bringing life for millennia, only for people to offer up death and destruction as a reward. No wonder she was pissed off.

Anna's Place was quieter than usual. Perhaps the cold had kept the customers away. There was an amorous couple in the far left-hand corner past the end of the bar and a few other people scattered here and there. The place looked much larger without the throng of patrons and heavy cloud of smoke hanging in the air. Not everyone came to Anna's to look for unrequited love. Many went for the jazz, excellent vodka and risqué company. Bill could think of no other reasons to want to be in the Russian sector at all.

Anna spotted him as he approached his favoured table, not too far from either the exit or the bar. "Bill. Good to see you again. A bit late for you, isn't it? You usually like to start your drinking by eight o'clock at the latest. Not always the one that's in the evening."

"I had a head start," Bill replied as he slumped into a trendy, modern, bucket chair.

"Well, don't let that slow you down."

Bill grinned. "I never normally do. I believe Katya is working tonight. Is she busy?"

"Never is these days. Most of her regulars stopped coming to see her. I don't know what's up with her. She won't tell me anything. I'm going to have to ask her to leave soon."

Anna seemed too keen to get Katya out of her hair. For one as protective as she was, it curiously only seemed to extend as far as the girls who were still financially viable. But then, she had never claimed to be running a charity.

"Let her know I would like some time with her in half an hour."

Anna nodded and then raised her eyebrows at the tall, gorgeous waitress from before, who was standing behind the bar. She winked at Bill, then jotted down something in the prominent red leather-bound journal which stood on a plinth, like a guestbook at Windsor Castle. The spine was finished in gold leaf, and there was a large velvet bookmark with a yellow rope lanyard embellishment. It was hilariously ostentatious and far more than is required to keep a record of bookings in a knocking shop—even one this classy.

"For what it's worth, I don't think Katya is your type. Buxom, but too plain in the face." Anna smirked.

"You know I only need to speak to her. It's business."

"All our clients are here on business, Bill. It's the oldest business there is."

"Fighting is the oldest business there is, and this city has seen more than enough of it."

"Fighting, fucking, drinking. It's all the same to me. War

has been an excellent business opportunity. Maybe I should expand and add a pay-to-play boxing ring too?"

* * *

"Katya, my name is Bill. I need to ask you a few questions."

"Your face is very familiar."

"I come in here a lot."

"Yes, I've seen you around in the bar, but I could have sworn I have seen you somewhere else. You looked younger. Perhaps from somewhere before."

"I doubt it. I think I just have a familiar face. I need to talk to you."

"You only want to talk?" she asked, surprised.

Katya's *date* room was just as ludicrously over-embellished as the journal downstairs. The old wood panelling was covered with faded purple velvet, and the window was blocked up as if the blackout in the city had never ended. The whole room was depressingly dingy and smelt strongly of disinfectant. The floor was bare, with a sheepskin rug at the foot of a large double bed before a large standing dress mirror. The sheets were all pristine, pressed white cotton, and a grey woollen blanket was placed neatly on top. The whole thing reminded Bill of his days at Sandhurst, where it was all ironing, pressing, polishing and hospital corners.

"Yes, only talk. I will, of course, pay for your time. I'm sorry if that message wasn't passed on to you. I will wait here, and you can get dressed if you like."

Katya perched on the edge of the bed. Her sheer floor-length purple robe was half-open and had fancy feather trim. It looked like something you would find draped around the mistress of some member of the aristocracy. It held its colour better than the wall coverings. However, it did little to hide her body, but it was designed to titillate, not throw on when collecting the morning milk. Although Bill supposed, it would depend entirely on how you felt about the milkman.

She wore white lace knickers beneath the transparent robe, but her ample breasts were entirely on show. In the light, Bill could see her hair was indeed a dirty blonde colour but well-kept and clean. She certainly took good care of her appearance, no doubt a requirement for the job. Bill could certainly see nothing at all that might put off her clients.

"I'm fine, thank you. I am used to men seeing me naked. Most aren't as handsome as you, though."

"May I sit?"

"Please, be my guest."

Bill dragged the wooden chair out of the corner towards the bed and noticed the sign above stating that *all financial agreements and physical inspections are made before any contact.* The euphemistic language seemed pretty redundant if you had already made it this far. The physical examination was undoubtedly due to the current epidemic of sexually transmitted diseases in Berlin. Much like the bitter cold, it was another unwelcome gift brought by the Russians.

"Would you care for a drink? Smoke?" Bill asked. He noticed a slight trace of the dead-eyed stare evident in the pornographic photographs they had obtained from the tall, skinny bookbinder.

"I would take a smoke. Unless they are Russian?"

"No, you're safe. Here," Bill replied as he handed her a pack of Luckies.

She placed one between her pale red lips and accepted

the flame Bill held out to her. Some of the raspberry-coloured lipstick came away with the cigarette as she perched it between two manicured fingers.

"Do you like working here, Katya?"

"The money is easy enough. The Russians will hump you anyway, so it's better to charge them than get a punch in the jaw first."

"I'm not a fan of them either. Are they as bad as everyone says?"

"You really don't know? You obviously haven't been in Berlin long," she scoffed. "I came here looking for work after the war but had my fair share of trouble from the Ivans. I came here thinking I could get work but just found misery. They raped anything in a skirt. On my way into town, I met two little girls, six and nine years old. They had lost their mother. I promised to help them find her. Sure enough, we did a couple of hours later, on the way into the city on the road through Spandau. On the ground, dead, totally naked with her throat cut. She had died thrashing around on the street while a group of Soviet soldiers looked on. When they saw the girls screaming and crying over the still-warm body of their dead mother, they started laughing and shouting insults at them. Then they came over. I tried to get them away. By God, I tried. But ..." She stared into some invisible middle distance, and her voice trailed off.

"I don't know what to say. You have been through a lot."

"That's not even the half of it, Bill. Anyway, all I know is I have a roof, a bed and food in my belly. If I have to let a few drunks hump me now and again, so be it."

"Anna said your business is down lately."

"Most of my clients change their mind once they are up

here and ask to see one of the other girls."

"How come?"

"I don't know." She shrugged off the question.

Bill changed the subject. "Do you remember seeing a man with a fancy curled-up moustache like Hindenburg? He would have been well-dressed, perhaps wearing a maroon-coloured scarf? He was a queer, but he came in to look for the house down the street."

Katya shook her head. "They only come in downstairs the first time. After that, they cater for those Johns across the back square, the house with the red door. I go over there sometimes, on my nights off. Sometimes when I ought to be working. The men are kind, and there is precious little of that left in Berlin. The back of this building opens into a small garden courtyard, shared with the other buildings on this block, including that one. You can also find it by walking straight past Anna's Place's main entrance. A few doors along, there is an open alleyway. Once Anna sends them the first time, they book appointments directly in future. It's not really hers as such. I must not have been around that night, as I normally remember faces."

"What about the tall, skinny man? I know he was here and took photos of you." Bill pulled out the one he had brought with him.

Katya stared at the ground.

"Sorry, Katya, did I embarrass you?"

"No. Nothing like that. It's just *that man*."

"Has he been here previous to the photography visit?"

"No. But I know him. From before."

Just then, there was a single gunshot outside somewhere, then, a few moments later, a shout, followed by a loud piercing scream. Bill rushed to the window and pulled off the blackout board. But there was very little to see. The window looked out onto the courtyard, which was in almost total darkness, except for a tiny slither of light coming from a doorway just out of view. The yard was neatly bordered by flower beds, although the vegetation was dead or dying, like the dark mound at the courtyard's edge.

With the last twitch of an arm, the body lay still. Bill dropped the blackout board, perched his hat on his head and moved toward the door.

"How do I get out there to that courtyard?"

"Back the way you came, down the stairs, then turn left. The door at the end of the corridor. You won't be able to get back in that way without a key, though."

Bill was already through the door and halfway down the hall.

Turning back as he ran, he replied, "Keep everyone in here. Don't open that door again once I'm outside."

He sprinted down the stairs, skipping every other step, and rounded the bottom like an acrobat. He made the twenty yards through the long corridor in mere seconds, pulling out his revolver as he barged the back door open. Keeping low, he crouched and moved around the outside wall towards the body. He dared not show he was armed in case a nervous vigilante or a Russian patrol were watching. Holding a gun over a dead body, in the dark, among the Russians in Berlin was a guaranteed one-way ticket to, well, probably somewhere better than Berlin among the Russians.

Bill looked up to see panic-stricken faces all around at the upper floor windows. Curtains twitched, and doors creaked open. Everyone was trying to get a glimpse of the city's latest victim. Another name to the ever-growing list of those who met a grisly end in these godforsaken streets.

With a quick look about him, Bill saw no threats, ominous shadows or bystanders at all. He carefully placed his gun back in his pocket and cautiously made his way over to the victim. The body lay just in front of a narrow opening in the buildings. Bill looked to his left as he reached the body and saw three men standing in a doorway. One was sobbing, and one had his arm around him. The third man was standing behind, slightly in shadow, just looking out. The door of the building was painted red. Some other people gathered at the far end of the alleyway on the main street.

Bill knelt and took the dead man's hand, checking for a pulse. The lack of one confirmed what Bill already knew by the copious amount of dark, sticky blood around the body. He had taken a direct shot to the heart. He would have been dead in a matter of seconds, although the shock probably rendered him incapacitated instantly. Bill grabbed the head by the back with a fistful of hair and gently lifted it. He peered at the face of a man with a curled-up moustache like the late Field Marshal Paul von Hindenburg used to have. In his lifeless hand was clamped a maroon scarf.

Bill knew he had maybe five minutes before the police or the Russians would be here. It didn't matter which it was. Bill would undoubtedly be arrested for questioning. He quickly checked the dead man's pockets, finding a small amount of US dollars, a relatively large amount of marks, an old, half-torn ID document, a Nazi party membership badge, and a brand-new, freshly printed ID card with a very recent photograph.

Bill replaced a small amount of the marks and pocketed the rest. As he looked up at the men in the doorway, the calmer of the two at the front used a shaking arm and outstretched finger to point Bill in the direction of the main street. Following the man's lead, Bill scanned the group of unknown faces and then spotted one very out of place. As the face realised Bill had clocked him, he turned away, pulled up his coat collar and quickly disappeared from view.

The killer. That was the killer, Bill told himself. Get up and run, you stupid bastard!

He bounced to his feet and sprang into a full-tilt sprint down the alleyway. The shocked gathering crowd gasped and parted as Bill carved through them, clipping one in a glancing blow to the shoulder, sending the youngish man sprawling to the ground. There was no time to slow. He spotted the killer running into an opening across the wide street. Bill grabbed for his Colt once more as he followed him. He checked up the road as he entered the battered stone archway of the old brewery building and saw two uniformed policemen heading to the alleyway from which he had just escaped.

He ran across the stone courtyard and through an open door. Bill came to a halt in an old, damp, paved warehouse. Ahead of him stood the killer, silhouetted by a small amount of moonlight shining in through a barred window in the far wall. He was calmly pointing a pistol at Bill's chest. The killer coaxed his face into a twisted, demonic grin and pulled the trigger. Bill inhaled sharply, but there was only a metallic click. The gun had jammed.

The killer barely had time to look shocked, as Bill had already closed the ten-foot gap between them. In the next half a second, Bill thrust his open palm up into an angular jaw while he snaked his left arm over his opponent's right shoulder and squeezed with the power of his own. With an audible crunch, the killer's arm went limp, the Luger he was holding falling to the ground and clattering away. The unconscious man dropped, too, as Bill released the pressure. He knelt briefly to check he was still breathing.

Bill collected the gun, cleared it, putting it and the magazine into his pocket, and then moved to the barred window to check out on the street. Over at the alleyway, the crowd had grown larger, as everyone wanted to get in on the latest drama. The man Bill had knocked over was shouting and waving his arms around, trying to be heard. He was so far failing. It would not be long before he directed the police over to the brewery building. Bill needed to get out of prying eyes. More importantly, he needed to get the killer safely detained.

Bill turned back towards the helpless man on the ground, then decided, as an afterthought, to apply Sykes' training. So, with the bound of a rugby player approaching for a conversion attempt, he sent a swift kick into the man's groin. He barely moved, but Bill was satisfied he would get to suffer it later.

* * *

The apartment was cramped and untidy. The plaster ceiling was cracked and nicotine-stained. Newspapers were scattered around the floor, and a single, old wingback chair stood in front of a small, black metal stove. On top of the stove was a heavy iron pan, half-filled with water.

"What you will do with him now?" Igor asked in his usual, broken German.

"I really don't know. Let's keep this between us, though. I'll pay you back for the trouble."

"Yes, you will. Although, I owe you for helping me before

and getting me work."

Igor checked the rope ties on the killer's legs and wrists were good and tight, then opened a small, olive-green canvas kit bag that he had stood near the front door next to a large rusty but sharp-looking hatchet and thrust a large fist down into it. Then, pulling out a slightly damp half-log, he gave Bill a broad smile and placed it in the fire.

"Get a little warm in here. They don't cost me anything. I'd better get back to the club. I hope no one saw you drag your friend up here. You know how the Russians be."

"Of course, you had better get back before Anna notices you are gone."

"I hope you know what you do, Bill. I come home around five, for to sleep."

"We'll be gone by then. This is the best way. There will be no justice if he winds up in the hands of the Russians. I need to get him back to the British, but first, I need things to quiet down outside. What are your neighbours like? If they saw something, might they report us?"

"No, they not talk to police, and they more scared of me than the Russians. Make some calls and get him gone from here, Bill."

"Thank you, Igor."

Igor left the apartment, and Bill locked the door and pushed across the large bolt. He then settled back into the chair and gathered up the telephone. He dialled the number for Albie's office. Silence. He replaced the telephone, tried calling his own building, and finding it able to ring out, decided to speak directly to the operator.

The killer groaned and stirred in the corner. Bill looked up, then continued to ignore him. He thought briefly about simply cutting his throat and letting him bleed out but didn't want to dirty his knife and also realised he would be worth far more alive and in custody.

As Bill waited for the operator, the killer lifted his head. Blood trickled from his mouth and down his chin like the drool of a baby. Bill and Igor hadn't tried particularly hard not to bash his head along every tread of the stairs coming up. Bill grinned and narrowed his eyes, pulling his F-S knife from his inside pocket and admiring its thin blackened blade as it glinted slightly in the dull glow from the bare filament lamp hanging by a flex from the discoloured ceiling.

"May I help you, caller?"

"Yes, hello, I'm trying to contact a number in Wilmersdorf."

Bill gave the operator the number, and she asked him to wait. The killer tried to look out through his bruised, half-closed eyes. His neck gave up trying to hold up the weight of his head and dropped it back onto his chest.

"Hello, sir. Thank you for holding. I'm afraid the phone lines are down in that vicinity. An engineer is due out early tomorrow to investigate."

"Right, thanks." Bill hung up. "For nothing."

He watched the twitching killer trying to either escape or, more likely, work out if he was even still alive. He couldn't just hold him here forever. Bill stood, moved over to the small window, and looked out onto the street. He could see Igor back at his post outside Anna's. Fabian was just coming back upstairs from the bar to join him. Bill had been lucky Fabian was taking a break. There was something about him he didn't entirely trust.

Who could he ask for help? Jack was with Albie and his colleague at their office, and the phones were down. He didn't fancy his chances out on the street trying to drag the killer around bleeding and in his catatonic stupor.

Bill lit up his pipe and sat back down to think. He also readied his tobacco pouch and matches. This would be more than a one-pipe problem. Gazing up at the dim lightbulb, he had an idea but realised it might be dangerous. He lifted the telephone receiver, paused, and then dialled anyway. All his ideas were dangerous ones.

"Hello?"

"Irene, it's me. I need your help, fast."

"What do you need?"

"It's dangerous. Bring a gun. I can't tell you any more. There is no one else I trust right now. I know I shouldn't involve you in my work, but I'm in a real fix here. I have a prisoner who is in no state to be easily moved alone, and I need a car."

"Who is it?"

"It's Klaus Barbie."

23

Hard Heart

Berlin, 23rd February 1947

Bill stoked the dying fire and fished out another damp log from the bag. It had taken two whole newspapers and numerous slivers of wood to finally get the thing lit, and he wasn't going to let it die now. He left the dry wood he had asked Irene to bring in a stack next to the canvas bag. Cigarettes and dry firewood are the two most valuable things in Berlin. Apart from a foreign agent in your custody. Particularly one you didn't expect to find alive, let alone still in Germany.

"Been looking up old friends, have we, Klaus?"

Barbie just sat staring up at him through bloodshot, angry eyes. A trickle of blood had dried a brownish streak down his face.

"I know you killed our fiend with the moustache. Why? I have no idea, but you will tell us. If you don't tell me now, you will tell the police later."

"The police!" he croaked with incredulity. "You think the police are going to care about some degenerate? I've done the world a favour."

Bill, of course, had no intention of taking him to the police. He would get him directly to Spandau and in a cell. There were things in his head that an interrogator would do almost anything to extract. Bill would almost feel sorry for him if he didn't know this man better.

"Why him? There is a house full of homosexuals over the road, but I'm sure you know that. It wouldn't have anything to do with this, would it?" Bill replied as he showed him the Nazi party membership badge recovered from the body. Barbie glared at him, breathing heavily. "Your friend, though, won't be identified for quite some time. If at all, I'm afraid. You see, I recovered his ID."

Bill pulled out the two differing ID documents and held them up for Barbie, who tried to lean forward to read them but stopped with a wince and sharp intake of breath.

"Are you in pain, Klaus?"

"You broke my arm."

"It's only dislocated. I'll get someone to fix it for you. Eventually. Maybe."

Bill moved over to the window and peered out to see the Russians' stepped-up patrols were starting to dissipate into the misty darkness, like a fart in a picture house. He didn't want to stay here much longer. Irene had got in without issue, but getting Barbie out quietly would be almost impossible with so many eyes watching.

"What is the plan here, Bill?" Irene asked. Her eyes widened as she looked out at the patrolling soldiers. She was still wearing her fur coat, with her white chiffon scarf tied tightly around and over her chin.

"It's started to calm down out there now. So, we'll wait for an opportunity, gag him and get him down to the car."

"I wonder who you are?" Barbie remarked in French, coldly. "Do you realise the danger your friend here has put you in?"

Bill looked to an alarmed Irene and reassuringly shook his head. "I won't let anything happen to you."

"Thank you, Bill, but I don't need protection. Not anymore. I have been through too much to be scared of bullies like him. He is a has-been. A never even was." She turned to face Barbie and continued, "You are only a man. A small, twisted evil man, whose sick ideas are long dead and buried, like your awful politics."

"Dead and buried?" he sneered. "You think our ideas are gone? On the contrary, National Socialism will live on. No longer allowed in the open, it has moved behind closed doors, in the minds of the righteous. Every time white European politicians meet, our ideas are docked in the safe harbour of their minds. Outwardly they will be every part the obedient servant of American Jewry. Still, they will drip-feed our ideas back into a hungry society, reawakening the centuries-old knowledge that we are the superior race. We have always been there, and we will always be there."

Bill moved towards Barbie and grabbed him by the throat, pinning his head against the solid wall with a dull thud. He swept up his blade and held it barely millimetres from Barbie's eye.

"One more mistimed remark or false move, and I will have your eye. The intelligence boys will still get what they need from the shrivelled corrupt mess you call a brain, and I will have my revenge. The revenge for all the people you killed."

Barbie stared back into Bill's eyes. Bill saw there was nothing. Just empty, endless pools of evil. The man was so filled with hate. It had consumed him entirely. Cutting his throat might even be a kindness.

"What of your friends, I wonder. Violette? Yes, that was her name. She was a fighter. She took down six men before they captured her. One died of his wounds. Yes, a real warrior. Not like you. We picked the three of you with no real trouble. What became of her, I wonder?"

"You know exactly what happened to her." Bill's blood was drumming in his ears in some ancient tribal rhythm. Like druids marching to some death beat towards a waiting human sacrifice.

"*Au contraire,* I have no clue what became of her, but I hope she survived. A spy she may be, but she told us what we needed. I'm not some kind of monster, you know, no matter what you think of me. I persuaded Ernst to let you all live. Our methods may have been," he paused, searching for the right word, "unorthodox. But we had no desire to add to your misery any more than we had to."

"Not a monster? Do you think we don't know about what you did in Holland or the thousands you sent to their death from Lyon? Your repulsive ideas and your charlatan Führer are extinct."

"Those were not people, Mr Hoffmann. They were merely Jews."

Bill gritted his teeth and clasped the handle of his blade tightly. It was all he could do not to stick the thing in Barbie's neck.

"Don't listen to him, Bill. It will only cause more pain. The man's a beast, and they will hang him."

Bill grabbed the spare rope and used it as a gag around Barbie's head. He pulled tightly, hoping it might cut off the thoughts in his brain from reaching his mouth.

* * *

"Do you think he knew we were in Berlin?" Jack asked as they walked out of the main doors of the prison.

"I have no idea. I tried to reason with him or get some decent intelligence one final time, but I wasn't focused. Anger was getting the better of me. With Irene there, having to look into that monster's eyes. I shouldn't have involved her."

"You had little choice. If you hadn't got him out of there, or the Russians had arrested you, it would be you getting interrogated and tortured now, instead of him, and we both know who deserves it more."

They strolled along the cobblestone-paved wide road that led out onto Wilhelmstrasse. Either side were sentry posts. A British military policeman waved to them as they left.

"Cheerio, chaps. Mind how you go."

"Thanks, goodbye," Jack replied.

Spandau Prison was barely seventy years old but similar to the old Police HQ in Alexanderplatz. It was curiously built in mock-medieval style out of red brick. Its looming towers and portcullis archway had a formidable appearance. Bill looked up at one of the watchtowers that made up part of the perimeter wall and nodded to the marksman that manned it. The soldier smiled back. About a hundred yards farther, they were through the chainlink and razor-wire fence that marked the outer boundary of the complex. Taking a left turn, they headed back towards Jack's car.

"It's starting to add up. The cards that Misselwitz was handing out," Bill said, handing it to Jack for added effect, despite him having seen it before.

> *You have a friend at St.Bernhardt Church. All sins cleansed. Escape in the arms of our Lord.*

Bill added, "You have a friend at the church."

"Father Lardy, right?"

"I guess so. Plus, we know the sins. Being ex-SS, having worked in any capacity, administrative or otherwise, is tantamount to being a war criminal in the eyes of all the allies."

"Then, who is the Lord?"

"Misselwitz? We know he is arrogant enough to compare himself to the almighty."

"Fine, so, if the victim was on board for a long ride on this ratline, why did Barbie kill him? We already know coincidences don't happen." Jack unlocked the car, got in, and then leaned over and unlocked Bill's side.

"Because he was a queer, I guess? Maybe they had already set him up to leave the city, and with Barbie tailing him to ensure he wasn't a snitch, he made one final visit to Anna's pretty boys. Barbie realised what he was and so took him out."

"So, a crime of passion? He had no idea previously?" Jack asked, not entirely buying it.

"Who knows? I guess the Intelligence chaps will get the truth. They can be very persuasive."

"Yes, so I've heard."

"The only thing bugging me is that the new ID card would only get them so far. It might be good enough to get them on a train out of Berlin into one of the allied-controlled areas to the West, but how long would the cover last? Someone would be bound to recognise them eventually."

"There must be another ratline out of the country somewhere. Didn't *they* find one getting ex-SS officers out to Argentina from somewhere?"

Jack started up the engine and eagerly awaited some warm air. Bill started to fill the bowl of his pipe. He struck a match and, stopping briefly to light his pipe, looked up at the vast prison.

"At least one. This would be a first for Berlin, though. If you were a Nazi, would you hang around in this city? You'd likely want to get as far from the Russians as possible."

"You don't have to be a Nazi to want that."

"But Misselwitz hangs around the city with his old comrade Barbie, reminiscing about old times, plotting world domination and maiming small animals, or whatever Nazis do, then decides to set up a fake ID operation and runs a ratline to get the old SS alumni out of the city? Why wouldn't he just get out of Dodge and set himself and Barbie up with a new life somewhere?"

"All good questions. All of which I have no clue about. However, I have some more details about our man in the Jeep crash. Albie's colleague said he remembered him. He had served in an army unit in the war, driving supplies to the Eastern Front. Ukraine, or somewhere. Anyway, our crash victim was an SS captain, in charge of some kind of anti-partisan operation out there. He gave me his name." Jack found his notebook and, pulling out the top page, read aloud,

"Grüning. He said he couldn't remember ever knowing his first name, but he had to report to him several times over about a month to sign over ammunition resupplies. He was certain it was him. The autopsy confirms it, as Albie's guy at the mortuary also photographed his blood group tattoo under his arm."

"So, we have two dead ex-Nazis. Sergeant Pheonix, the Tempelhof guard, said he and another guy saw the Jeep veer off the road and crash. He didn't notice Misselwitz but said there were some civilians around."

"But we know he was there from the photo and interview."

"Correct."

"And, there are no coincidences."

"Right."

"Still doesn't get us much closer to finding where he is, does it?"

"No, but at least we know what he's up to. I have the moustache man's ID documents. I'll get Albie to hunt through old news reports, anything that might give us some more info on him or this Grüning. There must be a link other than what we already know. Maybe they knew each other?"

"Maybe. I believe the Nazis burned most of the military records. But I agree it's worth a try."

"Once we get back, drop in and see Apolonia. Anna said she has been pining for you," Bill said, laughing.

"I'm afraid she only really misses the marks, not the man. But, I'll go and see her all the same."

24

BBC2

Berlin, 26th February 1947

It had been a pleasant few days. With Albie pouring over all the records he could access and calling in favours from all over the country, Bill had managed a couple of days of, well, almost rest. But, of course, getting a loaded gun pointed at you and someone pulling the trigger doesn't do much good for your mental well-being, so he had run a few errands, and done a little asking around, but mostly stayed away from trouble.

They dared not confront the fat priest just yet, lest they should scare off Misselwitz. It all hung in the balance. They simply could not let Misselwitz slip the net. It was their sole purpose now to bring him in.

Bill sat in the large open foyer, absorbing the atmosphere of people busying themselves or crossing the carpet to leave and enter, mainly carrying briefcases. One particular man hurried through the grand glass revolving door, crossed the carpeted lobby area and approached the front desk. He spoke briefly to the cute girl on the front desk, then disappeared through the large double doors and down the corridor that Bill knew well.

Bill had arrived too early, and rather than sit in Errington's office with the old battleaxe of a secretary of his, as she tried to destroy her typewriter with her infernal typing, he had decided to sit in the lobby and have a smoke and a coffee. Despite letting the pressure off in the last two days or so, the investigation was stalling, somewhat. He would need to help Albie hunt the archives, or find him an assistant to get things moving along a bit quicker.

Bill entertained himself with people-watching. Mainly, though, he had just watched the girl on the front desk as she smiled to greet the visitors and afterwards always licked her lips. Occasionally she shifted in her seat. Bill soon realised that he had been watching a bit too much. So instead, he turned his attention to the various visitors and tried to guess why they were there.

The hurrying man had drawn Bill's attention far more than the others. Not only had he headed down *that* corridor with the double doors, but even from twenty paces away, his permanent scowl and broad flat face reminded him of a young Orson Welles in *Citizen Kane*. He even had the slightly too-long side-parted dark hair of the famous actor.

Bill returned his gaze to the receptionist as she stood, turned around and, with one knee on the seat, leaned over the back of her chair to retrieve some documents from the open drawer of a filing cabinet behind. As Bill tilted his head, she turned and sat back down. Not even getting a glimpse of stocking-top, Bill sighed, sipped his coffee and glanced back at the unread newspaper he had on his lap.

After sitting for some time, watching the clock, Bill rose from his seat and made his way through the double doors and down the corridor. Entering the office, he sat down and did his best to ignore the secretary, who, thankfully, seemed oblivious to his presence. The stranger appeared in the doorway a few moments later, laughing and shaking hands with Errington. As they noticed Bill waiting, they composed themselves, and the man who had stolen Orson Welles' face avoided eye contact with Bill and headed quickly for the exit.

Bill thought little of it, as it was an unwritten rule that you don't communicate with other agents without good reason, orders or invitation.

Bill's mind wandered. *Don't communicate.* And yet, it had been Errington that had set up Bill with Irene.

"Bill! Thanks for coming in at such short notice. Come through. A drop of whisky?"

"Yes, thanks."

"I'll come straight to the point. It's not good news, I'm afraid."

Bill kept quiet as Errington poured out two whiskies in case interrupting him might make him change his mind about sharing. He placed the glass stopper back into the decanter and handed a glass to Bill, who knocked it back in one hit. Usually, Bill minded his manners around Errington, but today he had a feeling that it wouldn't matter what he did. The bad news would still be bad news, just the same. Errington smiled as politely as he could in the situation, then refilled Bill's glass and left the open decanter in front of him.

Returning behind his enormous leather-topped mahogany

desk, he sat down and lit a fancy-looking cigarette with a slim gold Dupont lighter. He offered one of the ostentatious black-coloured sticks to Bill from an engraved silver case. Bill summarily dismissed them with a wave of his hand and shake of his head. Errington knew Bill didn't smoke cigarettes but always offered anyway. Just the way he was raised, Bill supposed.

"Are you going to tell me you couldn't get any information from Barbie? If so, I'd say you've gone too easy on him."

"Not quite."

"Well, he can't be dead because that would be good news, not bad."

Errington nodded his head and looked down at his untouched whisky. "Bill, we had to release Barbie."

"You what! What did he have, a *get out of jail free* card?"

"We had no choice. It was a decision that came from the very top."

"Who? God?"

"No, more important than him. I got the orders from Attlee himself. The US secretary of state requested Barbie's release into their custody, and the prime minister is trying to appease them after some deal to sell the Russkies some military hardware left them a sour taste. We all hate the communists, but some hate them more than others."

"But we only had him a couple of days. So how did they even know? What do they want with him anyway?"

"It was less than twenty-four hours. The top brass seem to know something, but they haven't told me what. Maybe they want him for war crimes, just like we want Misselwitz?"

"Hmm. Maybe. Perhaps I should have just shot him while I had the chance."

"Perhaps you should," Errington said through his glass, taking a small sip and returning it to the table.

"Someone obviously leaked it that he was in custody. But, let's be frank, he is a murder suspect, on top of everything else."

"We wouldn't want the Berlin Police to know that regardless, we'd only lose him to their investigation, then you know where he'd end up next."

"The Russians."

"The Russians, indeed. Justice is nice but, at the moment, depriving the Reds of intelligence is far better."

Bill refilled his glass once more and slumped back in his seat. "So, there is nothing we can do about this then? I risked my backside for nothing?"

"I'm afraid so, Bill. Politics."

Bill stared into his glass. Then, his cheeks inflated slightly as he exhaled a huff of air. Finally, he shook his head, sank his drink and placed down the empty glass.

"Politics," he repeated, just to exorcise the word. It was like poison in his mouth.

25

One Night in Berlin

Berlin, 26th February 1947

"Thanks for your help the other day. Sorry I had to drag you into all that."

"I'll always be there for you. Although, of course, I'd rather it wasn't to help you capture a murderous Nazi, but I'll be here." Irene shuffled over in the bed and laid her head on Bill's chest. "It just got me thinking about Violette. I still miss her."

"We all do. She was the best of us."

"Why did they have to move her when they did? She might still be alive if they had left her a little longer at that house on the avenue. Her poor daughter."

"I ask myself the same thing all the time. Barbie said they left us alone out of the goodness of their hearts. But they don't have hearts. I'm not sure what was planned for Jack and me, but it wasn't freedom. They left in a big hurry, I think.

We were the least of their problems."

Irene looked up and had tears in her eyes. A tear ran out of one corner down her cheek.

"I've lost everyone, Bill. My parents died at the hands of the Nazis, my best friend, and even my husband. I don't miss him, but I did love him once. I don't want to lose you, too."

"I'm right here."

"What happened to your family, Bill? You've never mentioned them."

"Not much to tell. My dad died when I was young, and my mother and her sister brought me up, although much of the time, I was at boarding school and then university. My mother died while I was at Sandhurst, finishing up officer training. So, she never got to see me pass out in my uniform."

"It's sad you never knew your father."

"I knew no different. He was a hard-hearted man by all accounts. All I remember of him was the one time we visited him on the Isle of Man. He was held there in a place called Douglas Camp as a prisoner of war." Bill shook his head. "Ridiculous. Prisoner of war? The man had only ever held up a pen. He was a journalist. The assistant editor of a newspaper for German immigrants living in England. He died while in captivity when I was four. No one knows what happened, or at least they never told me. All he was ever able to give me is this," Bill said as he held up the silver vesta case that had been on the bedside table, "and an empty house full of sad memories."

"Wow. What a terrible way to treat people."

"Yes. It's what governments do, Irene. What made you ask, anyway?"

"Trying to take my mind off things in the here and now. I'm

just scared. You and Jack are playing a perilous game. Barbie knows what he is doing and wasn't worried about capture. He knows we're working for the government."

Bill had no intention of worrying her further, so he kept Barbie's release into the hands of the Americans to himself.

"He's safe under lock and key now. So, who's he going to tell?"

"What if he already has?"

Bill stopped and thought about it. If he had been following them, maybe he had already passed information. To whom? The Soviets? Not likely, but not impossible. He hated their ideology, but he was also undoubtedly the mercenary type. The currency people like Barbie appreciated, though, was not money. It was power. Or at least a corrupt simulation of it. One where they got to decide if you live or die. If you were a Jew, gypsy or homosexual, there was only one answer you could expect, and as it transpired, a tiny blood group tattoo under your arm would not stop him.

"I think rats like him tend to work alone," he lied. The truth was far too worrying.

"You know we broke the rules today, don't you? We shouldn't even know what we are each doing in the city, let alone wrestling with a prisoner or sharing a bed."

"Errington must have set us up for a reason." Bill paused to think about it. *Set us up*. It made him feel uneasy.

"I asked him to. I told him what close friends we had been. I knew you were in Berlin, as I had spoken to Vera."

"How is she?"

"Troubled. Deeply troubled. The places she had to go. The things she had to hear about Violette and all the others. She traced almost all of them. One hell of an undertaking."

"She is a good woman. None of the families will forget what she has done for their memory."

"Aren't you curious about what I am doing in Berlin, Bill?"

"Of course, but I know better than to ask, and you should know better than to tell me."

"You have trusted me. I think I ought to trust you."

"Don't, Irene. I'm not even sure I trust myself."

"But it might help your investigation."

"Then, sleep on it. If you are sure, you can tell me in the morning."

"Alright. I love you, Bill."

"No, you don't, and you shouldn't. It complicates everything too much, and in this city it could get us both killed."

* * *

Bill woke with a start. He thought he had heard something. He instinctively looked around the room. Nothing. Just the faint glow of the moonlight through the slatted blind. He closed his eyes and tried to drift back to sleep.

Somewhere in his half-dream state, he could hear footsteps and shouts in German voices. He could see dangling boots, old artillery guns and cigarette haze at some old Parisian cabaret. Then there was a face he recognised in the smokey mist. It was Violette. Young, bright-eyed. Alive. He looked about him and found he was now in a muddy field. He saw long wooden barns that were walled on all sides, but these elongated huts housed people. Hungry, emaciated, dying people in striped pyjamas.

He caught the recognisable smell of cordite in the air and turned to see a group of schoolboys drinking and shooting off fireworks. One of the boys dropped to his knees, and his head sank. Chin on his chest. He was holding a short-barrelled revolver. As he lifted his head once more, Bill squinted through the smoke to see it was Andre. He was younger than Bill remembered him. He had the same face from an old photograph he had seen once in a cafe. Where though? Bill couldn't recall.

A shot rang out, and as he spun around, he realised he was surrounded by barbed wire. Violette was on her knees, blood gathering in a pool around her. An SS officer stood over her. He was holding a pistol and laughing. His face was daubed in Violette's blood. Bill could not place it. He tried to move, but the barbed wire tightened around him, sending sharp pain throughout his body. As he felt the last of the air squeezing out of his lungs, he tried to scream but was now paralysed. The face. It was the blood-speckled face of Ernst Misselwitz.

Bill jolted himself awake violently. He realised he had been dreaming and tried to lick his dry lips with his tongue. He was covered in sweat but cold. Dragging himself from the bed, he paused briefly to check Irene was still asleep.

Bill made himself a glass of water. As he sipped his dry mouth back to life, he peered out through the window onto the street below and then checked his wristwatch. It was just before midnight. He looked up at the sky to see the moon was shining brightly. The last of the thin snow clinging to the grassy areas that surrounded the tree stumps that lined the paved road glistened under the white limelight. The familiar sound of a motorcar broke the silence outside.

A pristine pre-war BMW roadster appeared in view, slowed down outside the building, and then carried on up the avenue. It was a strange maroon-almost-red colour, but curiously the driver's door was painted black, like the canvas roof. Bill leaned and tried to see the occupants but could not make out anyone inside as it disappeared from view. He heard it pull up somewhere nearby, farther down the street. The door opened, then closed. He could still hear the engine running.

Down below, a man in a black hat had appeared on the wide pavement outside the building's lobby. He was ambling and looking around him. He was wearing a long wool coat, gloves and a dark scarf. From the angle, Bill could not determine what he was doing, but he moved warily and watched behind him as if he had been followed there. Bill felt very uneasy and left the window briefly to put on his clothes. As he picked up his coat, he dropped the tobacco tin that had been resting on top, sending it clattering onto the coffee table and spilling its contents on the carpet.

"Bill?" Irene murmured. She sat up and rubbed her eyes.

"It's alright, go back to sleep."

"Where are you going?"

Her hair was sticking out in every direction, and in her half-awake state, peering through the darkness, she frowned, trying to make out Bill's outline.

"You look cute when you are still half asleep, you know."

"I look awful. Come to mention it, so do you. What's happening?"

"I had a bad dream. So, I thought I'd get some air and settle my nerves."

"You are lying, Bill. Why are you taking your gun?"

He looked down at the little Colt he had picked up without thinking. He put down the pistol and donned his jacket. Bill thought it was better not to alarm her. He quickly but calmly tied his shoelaces, then moved back over to the window and peered carefully at the street. The man was still there. He put his hand to the top of his hat and looked up. For a split second, Bill could have sworn their eyes met. Bill reminded himself that he couldn't see him through the blind.

He could just make out who it was as he continued to peer down. When he recognised the man, he wondered if he was still dreaming? No, of course, his mind was not playing tricks on him. He was very much wide awake. The man outside appeared to be the actor Orson Welles.

Bill went back and collected up his gun.

"Do you have one to hand?"

"Of course, here in the bedside drawer, but what's going on?"

"I'll explain when I get back. If anyone except me comes through that door, slot them," he said as he rushed out. Then, just as he closed it behind him, he added, "I won't be long."

Bill strode down the long, lit hallway and the stairs. Crossing the empty lobby, he could see the concierge desk deserted. All the lights were switched off, which was very out of the ordinary. The backroom door that was almost always open was closed, without even the tell-tale glow of light from under the door giving away its occupancy. He looked out through the glass frontage, but Orson had disappeared.

Carefully moving towards the door, he slipped the lock and slowly pulled it open. The calm, cold night air slapped Bill across the face with an icy open palm. Squinting into the darkness, he let his eyes acclimatise to the twilight of the open street. He could see the upstairs hallway lights every time he blinked. He glanced around, looking for the agent, but the road was empty.

The car door, Bill thought. He was suddenly acutely aware of the possibility of a second person in the vicinity. He instinctively gripped his pistol inside his coat pocket. He kept his back close to the wall as he skirted around the edge of the building and along the street. There was an empty plot next door, another casualty of the Russian bombardment of the city, or maybe it was the Royal Air Force. Either way, Bill was thankful for the small amount of cover it would give him.

Bill recalled his old schooldays. They always seemed to hijack his thoughts at the most inopportune moments. He had been made to study the ancient Saxon epic, *Beowulf*. At first glance, it was all gibberish, but his English master had a particular way of explaining things. To bring the old text to life and present it concisely. The most memorable part for Bill had been the shadow-goers. They were mythical beings, neither alive nor dead. They stalked the forests and coexisted with the people of the villages. They were the rustling in the leaves. They were the darkness of the night.

Bill gripped the handle of his revolver and slipped into the shadows. He *felt* the night. He had to *become* the night.

He moved silently across the empty square of moss and mud and slid up against the opposite wall. He peered around by carefully shifting to the edge of the building's corner. He spotted the agent in the black hat slip away from the street and down a small alleyway that led to another adjoining empty lot.

This could work out perfectly, Bill thought, as he turned back, crossed his muddy square and popped out in the rear of the buildings. He hopped easily over a short wall and into the neighbouring gardens. Following a path topped with flagstones, he reached a gate, which he found mercifully unlocked. He quietly lifted the latch and squirmed through the tight gap, carefully closing the latch behind him. He was almost to the other empty lot. He scurried, bent low across the next courtyard, and then bashed his head on a wooden planter mounted on the wall at about waist height.

He stifled the expletives he so desperately wanted to let out. So much for the shadow-goer. He stood and vaulted the final fence into the empty gap between the buildings and spun around, seeking his target.

Nothing. No one was there. Bill quickly looked around for footprints to show his man had been here. It was like he had disappeared into the night. Maybe Orson Welles was the real shadow-goer? Bill knew he hadn't imagined it. The unknown agent had come down the alleyway but was now gone. Bill walked over to it, but there was no sign of him. Was all this just some madness Bill had formed in his mind? An extension of the bizarre dreams, like some kind of thought-residue?

Then he heard it. The sound that he would never shake from his ears. The shots. The two sickening claps of noise sounded like someone banging two wooden boards together. He had heard many gunshots in his time. Some were a lot closer than others. These shots sounded dampened and came from about four buildings away, back the way he had come, deadened perhaps by closed glass windows.

Irene. He had left the front door to the building unlocked.

Bill sprinted up the alley with little care about who might be waiting at the other end. Rounding the corner onto the street, he made barely a cursory glance about him as he ran straight back towards the building. The few hundred yards seemed, at that moment, to be five miles. The faster he ran, the farther it seemed. He felt like he was running through custard. His feet grew heavy as he pushed through the rising lactic acid that had started to grip his muscles.

Adrenaline took over, and his heart raced it around his body. The world's oldest and most reliable wonder drug. He soon felt a renewed lightness. Now he was moving like a greased weasel. Then, finally, he arrived at the doorway of the end. The glass door was wide open. He ran towards the stairwell and up the stairs, his feet barely touching them. He emerged into the hallway with his arm outstretched, holding up his gun. He could smell the cordite from the gunshots.

Shuffling and muffled voices emanated from behind the doors of the other apartments. Bill had to move quickly. He could only hope it had been Irene who had fired the shots. He dared not call out in case the agent was still there. Instead, he approached Irene's open door and peered inside. He couldn't see anything except his own shadow, cast long into the room from the hall's ornate wall lights. He reached around and flipped the light switch.

Across the empty sitting area, through the archway, Irene was sprawled on her side on the bed. Her hand was outstretched, touching the small table on the far side of the bed. The back of her head was wet with blood, which was now seeping into the sheets and blankets on the unmade bed. The windows at the back were open, and the open curtains fluttered gently in the light breeze.

"What's happened?" came a French voice from out in the hallway as the other residents started to bravely leave the sanctuary of their apartments and the wooden doors they thought might have somehow protected them from a crazed killer.

Bill darted across the room. He forced himself to switch off his emotions and concentrate on the facts. He probably had twenty seconds before one of the nosey busybodies poked his head around the open doorway. Irene had been shot nearer the foot of the bed, but the blood trail indicated she had reached for the drawer in her last moments.

"Someone call the police!" the next voice called out in German this time.

Bill looked around for clues. He didn't notice anything particular but hoped his near-photographic memory might help him later. Checking the drawer she was reaching for in those dying moments, he found only a key. It had been carefully polished at the ring end, and only a few letters were barely visible from the original stamping. Attached was a small brass disc with the number ninety-four cheaply stamped. Bill avoided looking at her face but caught a glimpse of her expression. For a moment, Bill just wanted to lie next to her and wait for the police to show up. But he knew that was foolhardy. It could only end in a prison cell. British, Russian, who knows, but he would struggle to prove his innocence from behind bars.

A head appeared around the doorway, and a young woman looked shocked, then disappeared. Bill looked up and noticed a discarded Luger on the floor. The killer's weapon? He did not want to further tamper with the scene, but he briefly smelled it and confirmed it had been recently fired. From his knees, he glanced around and spotted the single brass case it had ejected under the bed. That accounted for one shot. But what of the other? The Luger could have been Irene's. No other case was present. Did the killer use a revolver?

Bill looked down at the revolver in his hand. A fairly standard American-issued Colt Detective Special that fired a common .38 bullet. Looking at the exit hole in Irene's head, it could have been about that size. With its far heavier bullet, a British service revolver would have caused more damage. He noticed, too, his pipe tobacco strewn across the floor, trodden into the carpet by the killer. Too much of this circumstantial evidence pointed to Bill.

A small crowd gathered in the hallway. Witnesses that could identify him. It was time to leave. Rapidly.

26

Run

Berlin, 27th February 1947

Bill risked a glance back. He had lost them, for now. He couldn't risk heading home, as he had no idea who he was running from and whether they might head there.

As he reemerged and headed along Bernauer Strasse, he stopped to check his watch. It was one o'clock in the morning. The familiar city took on a menacing appearance. The large sash windows in the once-grand facades eyed him warily. Bill paused in a doorway and backed into the darkness.

He checked his pipe pouch, then the tin, and found he had run out of tobacco. Remembering the spilt flakes on the floor of Irene's apartment filled him with dread. It wouldn't take a particularly experienced British agent to recognise the tobacco. There were few pipe smokers among the British agents and even fewer who smoked St. Bruno. Most preferred a more expensive blend, like Dunhill. None of the French or Americans would even know where to obtain it, and the stuff the Russians smoked could hardly be described as tobacco at all. St. Bruno was made with a small amount of vinegar as a preservative, making it smell distinctly unique. The conclusion was obvious that it could only have come from Bill.

They were already looking for a Soviet double agent, and now that one of their own had wound up dead, Bill would be the most obvious suspect.

He looked up and spotted a small group of French soldiers walking his way—five or six of them, shining torches illuminating the various alleyways and doorways. Bill waited until they were distracted, then slipped out of his hiding spot and made the long walk, cautiously, down towards Unter den Linden. An hour later, he crossed to the city's southside and worked his way through the back streets into the American sector.

He felt safer already. The alert had evidently not gone out here, as there were no patrols. Only the usual lax attitude to security Bill had grown to rely upon. Heading home in the early hours of the morning, you could always count on the Americans to not be particularly observant. The cold was biting, but Bill kept moving to keep warm.

He began to wonder if he should ditch his gun. Police and patrols always checked permits with a call to the relevant sector's office. He might be able to survive a random stop with his identity papers, but a call to the British to check his gun permit would be a definite compromise. Ultimately, he decided he'd rather have it in case his life depended on it.

As he arrived at the large house on Dorfstrasse, he briefly

checked the street behind him and then knocked on the solid door. A light was on inside, and Bill knew that Chester was usually still awake until daybreak anyway. He had stayed up late drinking with the old man more than once. Bill heard footsteps approach the door, a rattle of bolts, and the door opened a few inches. He was then greeted by Chester's wrinkled face, which appeared in the gap, along with the business end of a Colt 1911 pistol.

"What the hell you doin' here?" he exclaimed as he de-cocked the gun and placed it back on the table by the door, opening it to allow Bill to enter.

"Chester, I need somewhere to lay low for a few hours."

"Well, get in here, and quit letting the heat out."

The old musty hallway had bare plank floorboards covered with a long runner-style patterned rug. It was almost threadbare from the constant footfall up the centre. The ceiling was high, with an ornate plaster rose from which a bare lightbulb dangled. The bracket remained from the long-gone chandelier.

Chester shuffled ahead down the hall. In front was the kitchen, with its door propped open with an old ammo tin, but instead, he turned left through the panelled door into the sitting room that doubled up for dining too. Chester cursed as his trouser pocket caught on the bakelite doorknob, then continued through and offered Bill a chair at the large dining table.

Much like most of the houses in Berlin, the decor was minimal, the possessions almost non-existent. It was a home which even a Trappist monk would call bare. The closest thing to possessions Chester owned was an extensive collection of empty wine bottles he kept against the back wall, too lazy to dispose of them properly. The only thing of worth the old man owned was his 1911 and a battered trumpet.

"What's happening, Billy-boy?"

"I had a bit of a problem with the police and can't go home."

"Gotcha, say no more. Wine?"

"Sure, thanks."

Chester grabbed a chipped china mug and then filled it to the top from his open bottle.

"Well, you are welcome to crash here, my friend. I don't normally sleep until about six myself. Too many years of touring with the bands."

"It's just nice to get in the warm."

"Listen, I've been hoping to see you. Our boy, James? Ain't no one seen him since he spoke to you that night. Even his guys said his locker is cleared out, and he hasn't been back. What did you talk to him about anyways?"

Bill told Chester all about the Jeep crash and the passenger's identity.

Chester listened intently, then asked, "So, why are they moving Nazis around in secret?"

"I don't know, but I guess he was a prisoner."

"Sounds like Sergeant Pheonix might be in trouble for talking to the press."

"Certainly the most obvious scenario."

"Well, I'll keep asking around. Most of the boys come to the club. They look after me down here, too. They are good boys, looking after this old drunk."

"I don't think you are quite as helpless as you like everyone to think."

"Well, if they like to help, who am I to refuse? I like it here. That's why I never went back to the States. I played most of the bases after the war, but Tempelhof feels like home."

"I can't wait to get out. The history and the hypocrisy stick in my throat."

"Ain't no getting away from the hypocrisy wherever you go, and you tell me any place that ain't got history."

"True enough," Bill replied in exasperation as he took a gulp of the cheap white wine. It was awful and sweet-tasting. "How do you drink this stuff?"

"Boy, I'll drink anything. Got this locally, you know how it is." He winked. "Cheap if you buy in bulk."

"If you don't drink it, you could probably clean the drains with it. What is it called?"

"Damned if I can pronounce it. I just call it *leaping frog's milk.*"

Bill picked up the bottle and looked at the label. It rather hopefully called itself quality wine. It was Liebfraumilch, although Bill couldn't help but think frog's milk probably tasted nicer.

* * *

It was only a short walk to the dull grey house. It looked remarkably like every other dull grey house on the street. This early in the morning, the area was also full of dull, grey people.

Bill walked up to the front of the plain, nondescript building and, after checking around for possible witnesses, pulled out his pistol and knocked on the door. There was no answer at first. Banging on the door once more finally disturbed the occupant, who could be heard tramping down the stairs, cursing audibly.

As the door was finally swung open, an American voice said, "What the hell sort of time do …"

"Make another sound, and I'll blow your head off," Bill said through gritted teeth as he stuck the Colt under Malone's chin. "Now step back inside and keep your hands where I can see them. Where's your piece?" The American agent gestured towards the coat hanging on a hook from the wall by the front door. "Good, leave it there. Do you have anything else around you could hurt me with?"

"I could call you nasty names."

"Yes, very clever," replied Bill, closing the door behind them with his foot.

Bill dropped his gun down but kept it pointed at Malone, who, in turn, let his arms drop to his side.

"How'd you find me?"

"I checked your ID while you were out cold. I have an excellent memory."

"Well, it's just as well. It saves me looking for you. Coffee?"

"Looking for me? What?"

"I need to talk to you. That's why I was tailing you before. I had too many eyes on me, so I had to play along with orders, but I was hoping to get you alone. I had no idea you were so jumpy then. Some journalist you turned out to be!"

"I don't take kindly to being followed."

"I'm not keen on being pushed into my own house at gunpoint, so I guess we're even."

"But, you were tailing me to find out what I was up to?"

Malone laughed as he made his way under Bill's suspicious gaze. "*We* know exactly what you are up to. I wanted to help you, you stupid bastard!"

27

Uncle Sam's Secret

Berlin, 27th February 1947

Bill eyed Malone through the smoke from his pipe. He had managed to liberate a half-tin of Prince Albert from Chester. It burned too hot for Bill's full enjoyment, and the Burley tobacco had more than a hint of American cigarettes about it, but beggars can't be choosers.

The house could probably be best described as minimalist. The pale walls were decorated throughout with clean square patches of phantom paintings or picture frames, long since removed. The discoloured yellowing walls only emphasised their conspicuous absence.

After half an hour of clattering his way around the tiny kitchen, Malone finally sat down and presented Bill with an abominable-looking plate of food. It looked like an explosion in a pie factory. Somewhere under the meaty mess was a damp-looking bread roll, and above, what appeared to be luminous vomit. Malone picked up a handful of the disgusting-looking concoction and thrust it into his mouth.

Still chewing, he grinned and said, "Philly cheesesteak, my ma's recipe." His lips were smeared with grease.

"Has anyone ever survived it?" Bill asked, prodding the mound of molten cheese.

Malone laughed. "Everything the growing body needs."

Bill helped himself to a fork from the kitchen drawer and then returned to the table. He scooped up some of the steak pieces and tentatively put them in his mouth. To his surprise, it was delicious.

"Not bad. Although I hasten to add, I haven't eaten for almost twenty-four hours."

"We'll make an American out of you yet, Hoffmann."

Bill glared at him. "You can call me Bill, William, Mr Fuchs or just plain old sir, but do not assume to use my real name again."

"Sorry, Bill. You're right."

"Alright, forget it, we're clear. What do you need to tell me?"

"That Jeep crash you've been investigating? I assume you've worked out by now the occupant was an ex-Nazi, right?" Bill nodded, and then Malone continued, "Well, he was recruited as an agent by the State Department. I don't know all the details, but something very dirty is going on here, and I don't like it one bit. They are picking and choosing who to prosecute and parade in courtrooms for the world's cameras and who to recruit instead. It's like they've forgotten the horror of the past eight years. Have you ever seen one of those camps, Bill? Smelt the stink and seen the bodies? Do you think those Germans are just soldiers like you and me?"

"I have seen enough of it, yes. I don't think I could share

a uniform with them. I think there might be some that were almost normal, but quite where they misplaced their humanity since 1933 is beyond me. So why are you coming to me?"

"I was assigned to tail you. The department knows you are getting close to uncovering the truth, and to be honest, I want the truth to be known. I will not stay silent while my country gets into bed with the Nazis. They think a few classes where they tell them they were bad and show them some old newsreels filmed at the camps will somehow cure them."

"I see your point."

"Well, it seems the US government has no qualms about recruiting Nazis for the new secret war against the Russians. That wasn't the first one, either. I've been back in Germany for a year and have seen quite a few of these covert transfers going on. Sometimes they move them down and onto a train out of Wannsee, sometimes on a plane at Tempelhof. There is one, though, that they kept in Berlin."

"Klaus Barbie," Bill said out loud, under his breath.

"Exactly."

"You know they sprung him from British custody then?"

"I heard. It wasn't me, but I know the guys that had to go and collect him."

"So, what was his mission in the city, and where is he now?"

"He was meant to be reporting back the activities of some of his ex-colleagues who are working as Russian agents, but from what I hear, he hasn't given us a thing of any value to the Intelligence boys."

"Russian agents?"

"That's what I heard."

"Where is he now?"

"Since he has now been severely compromised in Berlin, the word is he has been shipped out to Bavaria somewhere."

"When?"

"The same day they liberated him from Spandau."

"Do you know why American agents have been operating in the French sector? They've been leaning on the police chief there. His name is Müller."

"No idea, I'm afraid. Maybe investigating the commie connections within the Berlin Police?"

"Our governments would have us believe there are Soviet spies everywhere. Perhaps a smokescreen while they secretly recruit some of our old enemies. So, with all they know about him, the US isn't even concerned Barbie's just committed murder?" Bill inquired.

"That bastard's always been a murderer. I doubt *that one* will make much difference."

* * *

It felt a lot like returning to the scene of the crime. It had been a cold, long few hours. Jack finally appeared at around eleven o'clock, just as Apolonia had promised. The chill of the morning had numbed Bill's face and toes, and he cursed himself for leaving so early. Old habits die hard.

The courtyard looked much larger in the daylight, and Bill had walked around enough times that he had to check to make sure he hadn't eroded the cobbles. The dark stain remained where the body had laid out. They needn't have bothered to remove it to take to the mortuary. The body would have remained frozen solid here anyway, like a giant human ice cube with a scarf and moustache.

"What are you doing here?"

"I'm in trouble. Or rather, we both probably are. They might try to find you, to get to me."

"Why? What's happened?"

"Let's head somewhere quiet, and I will fill you in on the details."

"Who's after us?"

"Our people, Misselwitz, the police, the Americans. Your guess is as good as mine."

"Great."

"I feel like we are under threat from all sides."

Jack smiled, jokingly tipped his hat forward, then said, "We're spies, brother. We're supposed to be surrounded."

* * *

"So, what next?" Jack asked as he mopped up the last of his egg yolk with a small piece of bread.

"I have no idea. I think I'd better go and see what's taking Albie so long. We need to know how the two victims fit into this picture. I don't think Malone is suspicious about the crash. I didn't mention Misselwitz to him. He seemed far more perturbed about the Americans recruiting Nazis in the first place."

A waiter was busy wiping up tables and smiled at them from across the room. The main morning rush over, all the staff were busying themselves with preparing for lunch.

"So, who do you think shot Irene?"

"There's the rub. Most obvious would be the spy with Orson Welles' face, whoever he is."

"Errington will know. But, if it was him, then Errington is

the one who ordered the hit."

"Why, though? Do you think I was the real target?"

"Probably, but then why would he have evaded you in the dark to head up to Irene? And who was in the car?"

"More questions. Let's stick to the trails we can follow for now. We'll go and see Albie at *The Post* and see if he has anything on our two dead Nazis. I feel like a trip to confession is in order, too, so we'll go and shake down Father Lardy after that."

"If it was Errington, we are in a very precarious position. Stuck in Berlin without funds, shelter or help."

"But, we can't risk it yet. What if he simply presses his little button? We'll be surrounded and under arrest before we could say, *traitor*. Even if we find out it *was* him, what do we do without evidence? We'd be up shit creek without a paddle."

The leggy blonde waitress returned with their two cups of coffee. As she picked up Jack's plate, she narrowed her eyes at him and pouted her lips into a seductive smile. Jack grinned back just before she spun around and marched the plate back to the kitchen. Jack watched her all the way.

"There's no time for that, either," Bill said through a chuckle, then mimicking his friend's usual pessimism, added, "Besides, she's probably more interested in the marks, not the man."

28

Albie's Papers

Berlin, 27th February 1947

Alighting the U-Bahn train near the eastern boundary of Wilmersdorf, they took the short walk towards the Bavarian quarter. It was quiet out—just another ordinary Thursday afternoon. An old man approached with a small mangy-looking, bearded grey dog on a length of frayed old rope.

"Have you seen my wife? She has short blonde hair. I have been looking for her."

"I'm afraid not," replied Jack. He looked quizzically at Bill, who just shrugged back.

"She has been out a long time. It's not like her at all. Do you have some spare money so that I may buy some bread and cheese? I need the energy to continue the search."

"Clever story, old man, here," said Jack with a smirk as he handed him a few marks.

The old man nodded in appreciation and shuffled off toward the tram stop they had passed, all the while talking and wittering away to his canine companion.

"I wouldn't be surprised if he really was looking for her, you know, Jack?"

"Perhaps. This is the city of missing people, after all."

Albie's office was just past yet another old, destroyed church building. The various houses of faith hadn't faired well in Berlin. Maybe even God dared not interfere with the self-proclaimed National Socialists' right to rule. The *Berlin Post*'s main office was located elsewhere, but Albie had his own right here in Wilmersdorf, conveniently located in the same building as their archives, which were kept safely in the basement.

They arrived at the main door, and Jack rang the bell. After a few moments, a great mountain of a man appeared at the glass door, completely blocking it like an apocalyptic eclipse. He opened the door and then shook hands with Bill, enclosing his hand with a giant fist.

"Good to see you, Bill," said Igor, "and you, Jack."

"Hello, Igor. How are you finding life as a bodyguard?"

"Very relaxing. I sit and read and drink coffee. I think a job as a journalist would suit me well. Josef has been helping me with my German. I think he is bored too."

"Well, it has certainly improved, pal," Jack added.

The three of them entered the building. Igor led the way upstairs, with Jack close behind. Bill locked the door behind them and followed them up. Climbing the stairs in height and size order, all dressed in suits and long coats, they looked like characters in a bizarre children's nursery rhyme. All they needed was their pantomime baddie, but Misselwitz still eluded them.

The wide, concrete stairs led up and around to the first floor. Through wooden double doors, the first room to the right had yet another door, with a frosted glass pane, ornately hand-painted in gold-and-black Germanic gothic lettering.

Albrecht Weber - Berlin Post - Editor of City Affairs.

While Igor returned to the open room next door and his newspaper, Bill opened the office door without knocking, and they stepped inside.

"Hello, gentlemen," said Albie enthusiastically, as he lifted his eyes from the document he was reading.

"Good afternoon, Albie," replied Bill.

"Are you keeping away from trouble?"

"I think that trouble is trying its best to prevent that. We are in it. Up to our ears. What do you have for us?"

"Doesn't sound good. I'm glad I have Igor with me now. Please wait while I go and fetch my notes from downstairs. I won't be a moment."

Jack wandered over and took a look at the various documents scattered across Albie's desk. He picked up and scan-read a few of them.

"Boring, boring, boring. They may as well be about cats stuck up trees."

"Anything interesting in this city never makes the papers. One of the governments will stick its beak into any nugget of decent news. So, it's all either boring or propaganda," Bill replied.

"Not much has changed here in Berlin, after all, then."

Bill turned and left Jack to his reading matter.

Entering the neighbouring office, he glanced around the filthy room and said, "I don't reckon much to your new office, Igor."

"It beats standing out in the cold at Anna's. This is warm, and I get better conversation than with that fathead, Fabian."

"Pleased to meet you, at last," said the slight man standing on the other side of the desk from Igor.

He was lean and wiry. He reminded Bill of his old, unarmed combat instructor, Fairburn. This man had the same mean eyes. Even his slender body matched. Bill had long since stopped judging a man's fighting ability by his build. He'd seen far smaller men turn out to be some of the most vicious fighters you'd never want to be on the wrong side of. This particular lean figure before him stuck out a hand to clasp Bill's.

"Hello, Josef. Albie has told me all about you."

"All good, I hope."

When Josef spoke he had the air of a soldier, with the accent of a man from the officer class but the curt direct manner of a combat leader. You can spot them immediately once you've been around those sorts of men long enough. Bill liked him already.

"Good enough, I suppose, considering you were on the wrong bloody side!" Bill responded and laughed.

"Yes, sorry about that. It couldn't be helped. Where did you serve, Bill?"

"All over, Europe mainly. I got around a fair bit. I believe you drove trucks?"

"Not to start with. I was in a combat unit but took some shrapnel from a tank shell during the invasion of Poland."

Igor looked up from his paper and shook his head. "Motherfuckers."

Josef nodded in agreement. "I didn't want to be there. The whole war was a bloody stupid waste of lives if you ask me. All it needed was one to be ended, as it turned out. That pale Charlie-Chaplin-looking bastard should have stuck a gun in his mouth years earlier and saved us the trouble."

"Yes, he should, although one of his equally psychotic friends would have taken over. Goebbels the cripple, or fat Hermann the cross-dresser. Timing is everything."

The three men sat silently for a few moments. Bill knew each of them was running the war through in their heads. It was like some twisted life-flashing-before-your-eyes moment, without even the liberating death at the end of it all.

Bill thought about Irene. The finality of her existence felt nothing at all like liberation. She died half-naked on a bed in an apartment she didn't own, in a city she didn't much care for, and even he wasn't there for her at the end when she needed him most. He felt so utterly deflated and guilty, too, that he now had to prioritise his own situation first.

"Are you a Berliner, Joe?"

"Yes. We grew up around here, Albie and I. Do you see that half-demolished building across the way?" he commented, pointing at the crumbling ruins out the window. "That's the old synagogue. We used to play outside it when we were young, before the Nazis. We used to play war and pretend the grand brick synagogue was a castle that needed besieging. We were just little kids, for Christ's sake. I didn't know what a Jew was until the Brownshirts turned up and kept telling everyone."

Jack had appeared in the doorway, having no doubt overhead the conversation. Igor sat and listened in solemn silence.

Josef gazed out the window at the ruined building. "We never spoke out when we should have. We all just laughed it off. Things like that don't happen in Germany, we'd tell each other. Then came *that night*."

"You couldn't have known how far they would go."

"I had spent the summer as an intern at one of the local papers here in Wilmersdorf. The tension was bubbling away. It was palpable in the street, among a certain section of society. What started as comments became violent. I was ashamed to be a German. That building, there, came down in one night. The firemen that attended just prevented the flames from spreading to the other buildings and allowed it to burn."

Bill waited for a moment, then changed the subject.

"I hear you know our dead friend from the Jeep?"

"Well, I met him a few times. He was an arrogant bastard. A captain in the SS. Some kind of hunting party. A police battalion, they called it. It would be funny if it wasn't so repugnant. Anyway, yes, that's your guy. Any idea how long we need to stay holed up in here?"

"Not much longer, I'll let you know. Maybe a few more days. Just until we know who we've pissed off."

Albie appeared in the doorway next to Jack.

"I've got some interesting news on your Jeep jockey," he said as he squeezed past Jack and put a small stack of papers down on the table, knocking Igor's cup aside. Igor shot Albie a look of displeasure while Jack stifled his laughter.

"Sorry, friend," Albie said, with a tremble in his voice. "Right, this is a lot of waffle," he said, pointing at the pile, "but here are the highlights," he added as he scanned through his page of notes. "First, let's address the crash victim. So, we already know our late Jeep jockey was a certain Captain Grüning. I found a mention of him in our archives. It has a photo, which is hard to distinguish." Albie found the articles and scan-read them. "Yadda, yadda … Here we are. Captain Grüning of the First SS Infantry Brigade awarded the War Merit Cross, Second Class, for exemplary leadership on the Eastern Front."

"So, he got a medal for mass murder," Bill said. "Sounds like a model National Socialist. Why would anyone want him dead?"

"I found something far more interesting," Albie added as he hunted through the pile of papers.

Jack pulled out a chair from a nearby desk. "Where are the other staff?"

Albie continued sifting through the articles and type-written documents. Without lifting his head, he said, "Most don't work out of this office anymore. The building needed renovation, even before the war started. It's just a document library in the basement these days. I prefer to be in the quiet, so I look after the place, along with my secretary and the bookkeeper, but I have sent them home for a few days, with pay. They were mostly happy with that arrangement if a little confused. Any reservations they had were quickly dissolved when Igor walked in." He looked up at Bill. "Thanks for sorting that, by the way."

"No problem. You're too useful to me alive, Albie, to let you come to harm. Igor wanted a second job anyway, and Anna let him take some leave."

"Here it is!" Albie exclaimed. "The *Stars and Stripes* ran an article about the recent trials." He again scanned down to the relevant parts. "Work continues gathering evidence for further trials, including hours of interviews from both leading Nazis and their subordinate network of officers and head of departments responsible for the mass murder of the Jews and other minorities in Europe. Blah, blah, blah ... Among the witnesses were several leading members of the SS, responsible for so-called *Einsatzgruppen* units, who carried out widespread executions in the occupied Slavic regions. One such officer, Erich Grüning, a junior officer seconded into the SS, has been assisting the US government. After painstaking research in recovered Gestapo archives, *Stars and Stripes* can reveal that the regime had investigated Grüning for having possible Jewish heritage. In addition, one of our reporters tracked down his grandparents, who emigrated to the USA in 1924. They are both practising Jews, living a comfortable life in Florida. They are said to be deeply saddened by events in Europe and offer their sympathies to all victims of the Holocaust."

Silence fell as Albie continued reading the rest to himself.

"Christ, who would have thought it?" Josef said, breaking the silence. "What a hypocrite!"

Bill looked at Jack. Neither man spoke.

Albie picked up the story further down the page. "Grüning later went on to work for the SD, the intelligence arm of the SS, in Lyon."

Bill glanced back at Jack, who now had his eyebrows raised. Was that the connection they had been looking for?

"Grüning must have worked with Barbie in Lyon," Jack muttered.

"Great work, Albie. What do you have on our other man with the moustache?"

"Only what you expected. Former Nazi Party member joined in thirty-three."

"A March violet," Josef interrupted. The others looked to

him for an explanation. "There was a rush in applications to join the NSDAP in March of 1933 when Hitler took power. So many wanted to jump on the bandwagon of power, in any way possible."

Albie nodded his confirmation. "I rang around a few of my contacts with the two sets of ID documents. Unfortunately, one of the identities had no matches at all. The other one matched the identity of a former SD officer from Berlin. He was based in Belgium and Holland during the war."

"So, he got himself a new identity to avoid arrest," Jack added.

"Not quite." Albie turned and frowned at him. He cleared his throat and handed Bill the two ID documents he had left with him, plus the recovered documents and newspaper articles.

Bill took a moment to look through the papers. He paused and looked up at Albie, then back to Jack. Bill sat in silence.

Josef broke the tension. "Let's go and make some coffee, eh, Igor?"

"Right you are."

The giant man rose from his seat, which groaned in relief. The two men made their way to the open doorway, with Josef turning back briefly to nod at them before disappearing around the corner.

"Listen, Bill. Now that we trust each other, you are welcome to stay here if you need to. It's only me using this whole building at the moment. There are a few rooms made up on the upper floors. It's not the Adlon, but it's comfortable enough."

"Is this correct?" Bill asked as he continued to read.

"I'm afraid so."

"What is it, brother?" Jack asked, leaning forward with concern across his face.

"The documents all check out, and ... our fairy's real identity ... is on the *new* ID card. Captain Dale Bierhals. He wasn't hiding his Nazi connections at all. He was already living in secret. He obtained this new ID to come *out* of hiding."

29

Original Sin

Berlin, 27th February 1947

The twilight crept across the sky like the ink cloud from an angry squid. Tonight, there were two wool-clad sharks on the hunt. Striding towards St. Bernhardt's church, they were silhouetted by the headlamps of a parked French army truck. Bill could only hope they did not have his photograph or description.

"What's the plan here, boss?"

"I have no idea. Misselwitz will know we are onto him by now, so we don't have much to lose. Fatty's armed, so don't take any chances. If he goes for his pockets, or whatever, we put him down, and to hell with the consequences."

As they moved out of sight of the main street, they saw a police patrol sauntering along the road on the opposite side. Jack tugged the brim of his hat at them. One of the surly-looking coppers nodded in reply, and the two of them carried on towards the main street, smoking as they went.

As they approached, the church seemed to stare back at them. Its smashed and boarded old stained-glass windows were pleading to them like a puppy's eyes. The door was shut, and a dull light from inside escaped around the edge.

"Why do I have a bad feeling about this?" asked Jack, his eyes fixed in the direction of the battered church.

"Because nothing good ever happened in a church, pal."

As Bill checked behind them, Jack pulled out his Walther P38 and quietly flicked off the safety catch. The pair of them approached the church and stopped near the door. There was no activity around. Mainly because even the decaying buildings still standing were long since vacated. One of the few usable ones contained Mrs Krause's shop, which was still open. The lights were on, and no doubt the fire too. The small store lit the road in front of it in a strange criss-cross pattern with its taped-up glass window like a glow-worm attracting a mate.

They moved to the door, and in a well-rehearsed manoeuvre, Jack carefully turned the handle, booted the door open, and then entered, simultaneously sweeping his outstretched gun in front of him and across to the right. Bill mirrored his motions to the left, and between them, they had assessed the danger in all directions. With the slightest of glances, Bill steered Jack around the opposite side of the open church as they silently stalked their prey. Finally, they navigated the outside walls and met at the little doorway to the back room.

Peering through, Bill saw the rotund priest was flat on his back, surrounded by a dark area of dried brown blood. Checking around them as they entered and seeing the room was otherwise empty, they put away their guns.

"Well, at least we know who killed this one," Jack said as he looked over the body.

"Yes. Talk about stating the obvious. Thanks, Dr Watson," Bill replied, rolling his eyes.

Bill pulled the surgeon's scalpel out of the fat man's chest. It was stuck there like a little flag pole, pinning the handwritten note. Bill looked more closely at the blood-stained message, then placed it in his pocket.

"Someone else must have happened across him by now. Why did no one report the body?" Bill said to himself out loud.

"We know the usual clientele of this place. They are hardly likely to want to get involved with the law."

"That would explain Mrs Krause's ramblings."

"How do you mean?"

"She mistook me for a Gestapo officer when I went in there. She said something about other Gestapo men frequenting her shop. I don't think she imagined it. She is clearly a little mad, but I think she was telling the truth. These Gestapo officers were clients of this strange operation they are running here. Maybe they weren't all Gestapo, but anyone sounding official in a long black coat is Gestapo in her mind. They probably go over to buy their cigarettes or some food. It's the only shop around, after all. Plus, we know it stays open late."

"Or, at least, she forgets to close at the end of the day."

"We'd better see if she knows anything else."

Bill dropped the scalpel down next to the body. Then, holding the chin, he flexed the head side to side, lifted an arm and dropped it back into the dried bloodstain.

"The muscles have relaxed. Rigor mortis has all but gone, but there is no leaking from the nose yet, and very little smell.

So, I'd peg him at about two days, although it's pretty cold here, so rigor mortis could have been prolonged, perhaps up to four days. Knife up into the brain, look."

Bill held the head to one side, showing the small diamond-shaped slot at the base of the skull.

"The commando's calling card," Jack said as he studied the wound.

"Or, at least, someone who was commando trained," Bill said. They both nodded.

Bill pulled out his own commando knife and checked it against the hole. "The size is a perfect match. I guess that confirms it. One more thing I want to check. Can you give me a hand here, brother?"

They wrestled off Father Lardy's pullover with Jack on the opposite side. The blood inside the body had pooled to the lowest point, making the corpse look bi-coloured. The lower half was a deep purple, transitioning to a kind of marbled grey colour on top. His face looked peaceful, but the strange black ghosting in his eyeballs gave him a demonic appearance. After they finally got his old jumper off, as Bill had suspected, there, clear as day, was a small letter *A* tattooed on his left inner bicep. In the back of his waistband was an old Broomhandle Mauser pistol.

Bill stood and glanced around the room. It was exactly as he remembered it. He placed the gun on the table and poked around but found nothing that would provide any new profound revelation. He opened the old shoebox again and flicked through the various currencies.

"Well, he won't be needing this anymore," he said as he pulled the wad of notes out and pocketed them.

The travel tickets fell like confetti onto the floor as he did so.

Bill knelt to gather them up. Then, as he sorted them face-up in his hand, he stopped.

"There is a disproportionate amount of tickets to Wannsee here."

"A trip to Wannsee is on the cards, then is it? They have some good restaurants down there. The kind where those green notes can secure you the best steak."

"Nothing else here, except ..."

"What is it?"

Bill scooped the rest of the tickets and travel permits up. In amongst the pile of tickets was a single photograph. He looked at it closely, then turned it around as Jack approached so he, too, could verify what Bill suspected.

"That's her again, isn't it? The one with the big tits, Anna's girl."

Bill nodded and frowned at Jack gravely.

"But that's not where the others were taken, is it?"

Bill shook his head.

"That shirt. Was that taken in a ..." Jack couldn't quite get the words out.

Bill nodded, swallowed, and then turned the photograph face down.

The two men said nothing more as they headed back into the main church. Bill reached into his pocket and placed the photograph carefully in the bottom as if it were made of some fragile parchment. As he did so, he removed the note recovered from the body.

Jack continued past him and bent down briefly to collect the white chiffon scarf they had spotted as they entered. It was lying in the middle of the central aisle.

Bill sighed and looked down again at the pierced and

bloodied note one last time before burning it. He didn't want that bastard cop, Müller, to have the satisfaction of having any useful evidence pointing to her. As Bill dropped the burning paper to the ground, the flames took hold and licked around.

It had only two handwritten words in a beautiful looping cursive script:

For Violette.

30

The Man From Before

Berlin, 27th February 1947

Fabian smiled and nodded to them as they arrived. Bill handed him a few marks and continued downstairs.

"I'll catch you up," said Jack, as he stopped to chat to Fabian in Polish.

"Look what the cat dragged in!" said Anna, uncharacteristically unsteady on her feet. "Get this handsome boy whatever he wants on the house!"

The barmaid smiled at Bill with her eyes and reached for the vodka bottle.

"I need to see Katya. Is she in?" Bill asked.

"You break my heart, Bill. So, you don't want to spend some time with me first?"

"It's all business, Anna. We'll talk when I'm done. Look, I don't want to frighten her. Do you mind if I stay here tonight? Do you have a spare room?"

"This is a business, Bill. I don't have the money to keep rooms empty. You could pay for Katya for the night if she'll have you, or one of the other girls if you'd prefer," she said with a wink.

"Just put me down for an hour with Katya for now, thanks."

"I'd like to head up and see Apolonia," Jack added as he wandered in. "Could you send up a bottle of vodka and two glasses, too, please?"

Anna chuckled to herself as she scribbled something in the giant diary. The barmaid placed two glasses of vodka down on the bar and a cigar, with matches, for Bill. Bill sank the vodka like it was water. The sweetest, coolest water he'd tasted in weeks. He nodded for another, cut his cigar, and then put it in his inside pocket. The barmaid just looked quizzically at him.

"For later. I think I might need it."

* * *

"You're back so soon? I thought you'd been arrested, for sure."

"It will take more than the Russian army and the Berlin Police to take me down," Bill joked.

"You still owe me for last time. I paid it out of my own money. Otherwise, Anna would have had your balls."

"I intend to settle up tonight with you. But, first, I need some answers."

Bill pulled out the photograph they had found at the church and gently placed it on the bed. Katya turned to look at it and tilted her head.

"Where ..." She picked up the photograph and stared at it. Tears started rolling down her cheek. She did not sob, just sat simply staring at the image.

"I found it in the possession of a fat Nazi masquerading as a priest. You'll probably be pleased to know he is also dead."

"Who was he?"

"I was hoping you could tell me."

"I have no idea. The tall, thin photographer will know. He …" She stopped to compose herself and swallowed, then stood and moved around the bed to get herself a tissue from the box on the little bedside table. She did nothing to hide her modesty, with her thin sheer robe half-open to the waist. "I tried to tell you when you were here last, before the murder outside. The tall man. I knew him from before."

"Before he visited you here and took the photos of you?"

"Yes. And, before that, before all of this. Do you remember you asked me why business is down? Well, after the tall man visited, it kind of broke me. I can't face this life anymore. Seeing him again, remembering the … I just don't bother hiding it any longer."

"Hide what?" Bill asked as tenderly as he could manage.

"Hide this," Katya replied, pulling her sleeve up to reveal a tattooed number on her forearm. "This photo is from my time there." She looked again at the photograph of the young girl with a shaved head on her back on top of a dirty mattress, her breasts on display, with her camp-issued, blue-and-white striped shirt held wide open. Her neck looked black from bruising, and her body was covered in scratches. "They weren't always gentle with me."

"Jesus. How did you end up there?"

"I was arrested outside my school by the Gestapo. We used to live in Alsace until the Nazis showed up. You see, my father was a well-known German communist, so we were living in the open under false papers. We ended up at the Dachau prison camp. After a few months of learning to survive, I was moved, without warning, along with some others a long train journey away. I never saw my parents again. It was Auschwitz. On arrival, the tall man picked me out. He was in an SS uniform and carrying a camera. He put me to work in the brothel. They would give prisoners from the men's camp special passes to visit us as a reward. You could say I was born for this line of work."

"Don't even think like that, Katya. Those men were evil. You did not deserve any of it."

"I don't know how long I was there, as it seemed futile to bother to count the weeks, but when they heard the Russians were coming, the SS got us out and marched us back towards Germany. We had it easy compared to those poor Jews. At least we had shoes. I had been a political prisoner, so the red triangle on our shirts seemed to save us from the worst treatment, and we were reasonably well fed. Those with the yellow stars had clogs or no shoes at all, and they were all painfully thin like walking skeletons. The guards shot so many who could not continue and left them on the side of the road. Eventually, they put us on a train in open cars, like the kind they use to move coal. We wound up at Ravensbrück camp, just north of here."

"What a terrible experience. I can't imagine how you survived anything like that."

"You have no choice," she said as she finally let her emotions take over.

Bill sat down beside her and put his arm around her. She laid her head on his shoulder and sobbed. Then, after several minutes, she started to compose herself.

"You know, you are the second person to ask me about this recently. First, the tall man shows up. Then a French girl came in asking about him a few days later. She spoke no German, so we conversed in French."

"French girl?"

"I speak French too. I don't know how she knew that, but she asked many questions. I can't recall it all, but the tall man, Ravensbrück, and some girl came up. She was kind, like you. Beautiful too, like a movie star. She said her name was …"

"Irene," Bill interrupted.

"That's right. Do you know her?"

"I did. She was murdered."

"My God. Sometimes it feels like the war is not over, doesn't it?"

"I'm not sure it will ever be over." Bill stared out of the window, which was still open, Katya having never replaced the blackout panel that Bill had torn off. "I have a favour to ask you, Katya. Would I be able to sleep here tonight?"

"Erm … I don't …"

"Alone, of course. I have nowhere else to go. You have your own bed in your apartment, don't you?"

"Well, yes. I understand. That will be fine. But, Anna …"

"I will pay, don't worry." Bill reached into his jacket and pulled out a large stack of bills in various currencies. He carefully separated the stack into two and put half back in his pocket. "There is a lot of money here, Katya. Enough to get you out of Germany and start a new life somewhere. Anna is talking about letting you go. You need to take this and leave for the American sector in the morning. Don't stop off anywhere. Get the first train out of Wannsee station and get yourself to France or somewhere. Don't tell anyone you have this money."

"Bill, you can't be serious. Are you sure?"

"I have never been more sure of anything in my life. This money got my friend killed. I want to use it to do something good. It's yours."

She started to cry again, grabbing Bill in a tight embrace and kissing him.

"You are my hero, Bill. Sent by angels."

"I wouldn't go that far."

"Are you hungry? I can heat up some soup, and I have fresh bread."

"That sounds great. I'll pop down and get us some wine."

"Sounds lovely. This week isn't turning out so bad after all," she said through a smile.

"I wish I could say the same," he replied as he lit his cigar.

31

Belomor Breakfast

Berlin, 28th February 1947

Bill checked his watch. His head felt heavy, and his eyes were refusing to cooperate. The morning sun was creeping through the cityscape and dust haze. It was seven o'clock, but after the wine, before he fell asleep, it felt to Bill more like four. Wine had never agreed with him. He should know better by now.

He dragged himself away from the window and got dressed. He took his gun from under his pillow and put it in his coat pocket. He picked up his hat and slipped out the door into the long hallway. As quietly as possible, he crept down the stairs and headed towards the back door. Before he could reach it, the last door on the right swung open with a squeal of angry hinges.

"You ought to get those hinges oiled, Anna."

Anna padded out into the hallway, barefoot and wearing a

dress with a pale-blue lightweight jacket thrown on over the top. Her hair looked like it had been styled, in some haste, by a blind weaver with a bad case of the shakes.

"Good morning, Bill," she cooed, "how was she?"

"It was strictly business."

"Sure it was. Make the most of her. She won't be around much longer."

"Yes, I know." Bill looked her up and down. She looked curiously feminine for a change.

"I wish you men would stop leaving at such strange hours. Especially your buddy. My room is right next to this back door, you know, and I am a very light sleeper. You can quit looking at me like that, too. You couldn't afford me, even if I *were* for sale."

"I just didn't know what you looked like without the army chinos and the gun on your hip."

"There's never one far away." She giggled as she let him have a peek of the little automatic she had in the pocket of her jacket. "I'd be naked without it," she added.

"Which buddy, Jack? Has he left already?"

"No, but he woke me on my night off. It was the night before last. When the bar is open during business hours, customers always leave through the front door. I was having an early night, and he came blundering out this door." She gestured over her shoulder. "Woke me up. I know it was him, as I looked out the window, ready to give him a piece of my mind!"

"The night of the twenty-sixth? What time was that?"

"I don't know." She shrugged. "I guess around eleven."

"Did he return?"

"I don't know. I slept through after that. He's been here

fairly regularly lately. She's a Red, you know? She fought with the Partisans in the war. Very communistic tendencies."

"Didn't you fight with the Partisans, too?"

"Yes, but I never caught it. Are you heading out to get some breakfast?"

"I thought I might take an early walk and see what's available."

"Give me ten minutes, and I'll join you. We can go to my regular place, but it ain't going to be cheap."

"It never is with you, Anna," Bill muttered to himself.

* * *

Bill nodded hello to the Soviet officer sitting alone at a neighbouring table, reading a newspaper covered in what may as well have been hieroglyphics.

While most of Berlin suffered from shortages and squalor, the upper classes and those with money continued to live relatively well. The neon lights still glowed, and there were enough black marketeers to keep the hotels' fridges well-stocked. Plus, wherever the various military forces frequented, the owners of those establishments always found a way around the lack of legitimate supply. It's who you know. Or, Bill imagined, in Anna's case, *who you blow.*

Bill had always had the benefit of the king's bank account while he had been here, and never one to look a gift horse in the mouth, had exploited it at every opportunity. It was rarely an operational necessity, but he always thought better with decent tobacco, a good whisky and a belly full of decent food. With the stroke of luck finding the fat priest's stash, he was able to continue this lifestyle. For now, at least.

"She had it hard, you know?" Anna said as she poked at a piece of sliced ham that was more fat than meat.

"Who?"

"Katya."

"So I hear."

"She arrived here pregnant. Most of the girls did. So I set up the bar at the end of 1945. I'm as disgusted as anyone at what the Russians did. I kept away from them as much as possible. My connections with the Polish Army kept me relatively safe. Not that I didn't have to protect myself a couple of times. Let's just say there were a few *missing in action*, telegrams sent to some Russian *babushkas* that weren't the result of enemy action."

"I hear they were not too pleasant to the locals around here."

"After what those *Szkop* did to us? The men had it coming. Those poor girls, though. The Russians went through the city like rutting hogs. They did the world a favour by clearing out the Nazis, but the average Russian soldier is no different really. The fucking pigs. The officers should have shot the lot of them once the city was liberated." Anna calmed her rage by stabbing a piece of cheese on her plate. It was so measly and thin that you could have used it as tracing paper. She continued, "One day, the river Spree will dry up, and do you know what they will find?"

Bill just stared at her, sipping at his pipe. There was no doubt that the Russian officers were complicit in mistreating the German women. He opened his mouth to speak, thought better of it, and then simply shook his head.

"Bombs, bullets ... and babies. Dozens of dead babies that met their watery end at the hands of young girls with eyes full of tears who had no idea what else they should do. Fucking men. It doesn't matter where you are from. They are all pigs."

Bill remained silent. This was not the time for some lame defence. Bill did not feel in the least bit offended by Anna's misandry. It just so happened Bill felt very similar. Strong women had brought him up, but the war had been a bigger eye-opener than he could ever have imagined. Now he generally found it easier to distrust almost everyone, regardless of gender.

"Your friend Jack is becoming close friends with Fabian lately. They stayed up after hours the other night, drinking. Thinking about it, that would have been the night he'd disturbed me."

"Yes, I've noticed the pair of them seem to like a chat. What night was that?" Bill asked, eager for proper confirmation.

"Must have been the day before yesterday. He had been with Apolonia all afternoon and into the evening and disturbed me as he headed out the back. Then, when you called to speak to her in the morning, she told me he had returned to her unannounced in the early hours, having been let in by Fabian. The pair of them had been drinking, apparently."

"I see. Does Fabian often hang around after hours to let customers in?" Bill asked, mulling over the revelations in his mind. That was the night that Irene was murdered.

"Not usually, but, as I say, they seem to be friends these days, and perhaps they'd made an arrangement. I don't really mind, as he paid the night in full and left a hefty tip." Anna shrugged and sipped her coffee. "I guess I feel sorry for Jack, as he seems a bit lonely. Apolonia is good for him, I think. Sometimes they just talk. Is a girl waiting for you back home, Bill?"

"No. There was someone ... but no."

"You surprise me. A handsome, polite man like you. Your heart is too big for this dump. What are you hanging around Berlin for anyway?"

"Just a sucker for punishment, I suppose." He blew out a cloud of blue smoke and tried to glance surreptitiously over at the Russian reading the paper. He seemed too engrossed in his gibberish to be paying them much attention.

"I don't mind it here. Maybe I'm doing some good, too. The girls are better off with me and a roof over their heads."

"As long as they keep the money rolling in."

"It's not a charity, Bill. If word got out I was running some kind of a refuge, I'd have girls queuing around the block. The street is the only place for most of them. A few marks for a knee-trembler with one of the Ivans is all they are likely to get. I only take the best-looking ones. Besides, I have to keep the Russians happy. I'm in their sector, and they keep the cops looking the other way. What I run is not exactly … legal." She ate the last morsel from her plate and turned and waved her empty coffee cup at the waitress. Turning back around, she smiled as Bill emptied his own cup and said, "The coffee is good here, right?"

"Not bad at all," Bill replied, placing the cup on the table between them.

Anna smiled and pulled out a pack of Belomors. She removed one of the sticks, balanced it between her pink lips and leaned forward for Bill to offer her a light. That odd lipstick shade never did look right on her.

"You aren't seriously going to smoke that thing, are you? Here in polite company?"

"Where?" she asked, emphasising a mocking look around the room.

"I think I'll die of asphyxiation the moment that thing catches a flame."

"Ha ha," she feigned, "just hurry up and light me, you prat."

Bill ignited the foul-smelling cigarette. It almost crackled as it came to life. It had a smell of damp dung. Russian smokes were notoriously strong and were usually too dry or too moist to burn consistently. Even the black market had no real desire for them. Cigarettes were often the most valued currency on the bombed streets and among the city's refugees. But you'd be lucky to swap a single American cigarette for a whole pack of Belomors. Bill winced as the smell engulfed him.

"I'm used to them. You take whatever you can get out in the field. I think I would have died without a steady supply of these things."

"Death seems rather more appealing, to be honest." Bill chuckled, tamped down the contents of the bowl, and relit his dying pipe. "Did you get much grief from the bulls over our dead friend?"

Anna inhaled deeply on the appalling stick in her mouth. "They came in, of course, and asked a few questions, but a few complimentary vodkas, and date each with the girls, and they soon went on their way with a smile on their faces."

She checked the cigarette in her hand, sucked the smoke from the last of the tobacco, and then dropped the flattened empty tube end into the ashtray. Those things were only good for about five drags.

"The bulls have enough on their hands. They have no desire to look too deeply into a street killing, as they never know who they might piss off. Who was he? You came looking for him. Who wanted him dead?"

"He was just someone I wanted to question about some

black market dealings," he lied.

"I see. Well, whatever it was he was into, other than young boys, I guess he won't be into anymore."

"Quite."

Anna checked her watch. "Fabian usually picks me up on his way through to the bar. Do you need a lift back?"

"I think I'll take a slow walk back." Then he added, "Fabian drives? That's pretty rare these days."

"Yes. He has a motorcar that he liberated from somewhere. You know how it is."

"Yes. A swap here, a bullet there, and suddenly you have a vehicle. Where is he getting fuel for it?"

"Who knows? I never ask." She stood up and pulled out some marks.

Bill rose too. "Don't worry about that. I've got this."

"Ah! The perfect gentleman. Take care of yourself, Bill, whatever it is you are mixed up with. There are precious few real gentlemen left in this shithole of a city."

Bill paid up as Anna shimmied out of the front door. He collected his hat and coat and made his way out into the cold, amber-lit morning. He adjusted his hat and tied his scarf as he walked back in the direction of the bar. Suddenly he caught sight of something that made him halt in his tracks. He moved into the nearest doorway as casually as possible and pretended to search for something in his pockets.

He squinted into the near distance at Anna climbing into Fabian's motorcar. A motorcar he had seen before. A couple of nights back. The night he could not shake. It was *that* night.

On the street side of the car, Anna greeted Fabian through the glass, then clambered into a pristine, dark red, pre-war BMW roadster. The driver's door was painted black, the same colour as the canvas roof.

32

Books

Berlin, 28th February 1947

"I hear you've been seeing a lot of Apolonia lately?"

"It's not a secret." Jack shrugged. "She's a good listener."

"I hope you aren't telling her things you shouldn't be?"

"Of course not, what do you take me for? We have things in common. The war, family, missing home."

"I get it, mate, just be wary, okay?"

"I know. You can trust me."

Bill wondered to himself if that were true. He sucked on his pipe as they strode up the street. They were heading, yet again, into the French sector. The Spree gently lapped behind them as they headed north, away from both it and relative safety. The French might well be on the lookout for them.

"I was just thinking that perhaps someone went after you the same night as they came for me? It's just a theory."

"Well, I was with Apolonia that night."

"All night?"

"You found me there in the morning, didn't you?"

Bill nodded. He seemed to dodge that question, he thought. "I guess we won't know then. It's too dangerous for you to go home and check. If they want us, they are bound to be watching there."

Jack agreed, and the two men continued on their way. Bill glanced across at Jack, and wondered just how well *did* he know his friend?

They continued the rest of their walk, in relative silence.

* * *

The shop was closed. Bill looked down the fancy street. It was a Friday morning, but it was still quiet. Pretty much the only people who could shop around here were soldiers and diplomats. The gleaming storefronts were too expensive for the average Berliner to even look into. They mostly had bigger concerns than a new hat or getting a book re-bound.

"It's locked," Jack muttered as he rattled the door. "Luckily, I brought my own key." He grinned, pulling out the half-brick he'd gathered up from a bombed-out building on their way to the bookshop. He carefully wrapped a handkerchief around it.

"What's that all about?" Bill shook his head and sniggered. "Just chuck it through the glass."

"To deaden the sound." Then in one movement, he punched it forwards, through the thin glass door, which shattered into four or five large pieces and smashed loudly onto the ground, narrowly missing Jack. "*O kurwa!*" he exclaimed and jumped back.

"Well, that went well," Bill added, checking to see if they had, as he suspected, now woken the dead, as well as the rest of the neighbourhood. "Let's just get this done."

They knew exactly where they were going. They moved swiftly into the store, drawing their guns as they did so. The broken glass crackled under their feet as they walked. They rounded the last bookshelf behind the counter and headed immediately to the rear area where the thin man had his workshop. Bill approached the bookshelf at the back, half filled with books, all neatly aligned, which was slightly out of place in the otherwise disordered workshop, and picked up a large leather-bound book at random.

Without warning, the backroom door swung open, spilling the dark back area in a dull-crimson light. The tall, thin man was silhouetted like some strange lanky creature from outer space. He looked almost surprised as Jack, who was nearly knocked off his feet as the door was flung open. Bill instinctively moved to use the bookcase as a kind of half-cover. That caused the heavy book to fall to the floor with a thud, making the thin man flinch and wince, as if Bill had pulled the trigger of the snub-nose Colt revolver pointed his way.

"What the ... where the hell did you two come from?" he spluttered, as he looked at Jack regaining his balance.

"Sit down, before I knock you down," replied Jack, visibly agitated from having been quite literally wrong-footed.

"Look, I don't know what ..."

Jack cut short his protestations by grabbing him tightly by his throat. The defiant skeleton just stared indignantly back at him. Jack pointed at him with his free hand, then placed his finger on his lips and released his grip on the man's throat.

"What's your name?" Bill demanded, his gun still trained on the man. "Your real name, I mean."

The tall stick-man looked past Bill, at the now-open book on the floor and, realising the game was up, replied, simply, "Klein."

"Mr Small. How ironic," sniggered Jack.

"Gerd Klein. I guess you don't work with Müller after all, then."

"We'll get back to that, Klein," Bill said as he struggled to gather up the large book from the floor with his left hand. "I assume these books are all like this one?"

The book was open on another image of a nude woman. Bill didn't care to look at it too closely. He only saw the dead-eyed stare and the overwhelming sadness in her eyes.

"Are these all full of such filth?"

"I cater for a very specific clientele."

"Yes, those sick in the head, but you'd know all about that, wouldn't you?" Jack held up the photograph of Katya taken in the Auschwitz brothel.

"Katya was different. She was special. Look, whatever you think of me, I did everything I could for that girl. She would never have survived if I hadn't got her assigned there."

"We know what happened in that place. You think being raped daily, month after month, was helping her?"

"She's alive, isn't she?" he grunted back.

Jack thrust his gloved fist square into Klein's face. The pathetic man's head whipped back like his slender neck was made of rubber. He looked up at Jack, and tears welled in his eyes.

"Please, you don't have to hurt me. I'm no soldier, really, I'm barely a man. I know I did wrong, but you don't understand what it was like then. I love Katya, and it was the only way I could keep her safe. She was only there due to bad luck. Please, I was only part of the administration there."

"Did this administrative role involve many visits to the camp brothel?" Bill interrupted, placing down the book onto the workbench and flicking through various photographs of different women in the same drab room as Katya, all in various states of undress. "Part of your job there, or more of a hobby, would you say?"

"I admit, I did take photos in the brothel there, but a great many of the books are filled with more willing models from before the war. I still get girls who knew me before the war coming to have the photographs taken. That red bound copy, there, is full of my latest work," he stated proudly, like it was the final dissertation for his PhD or something.

"So, you got this job in the SS, as you already had a questionable reputation?"

"I was a well-known photographer here in Berlin, yes. Before the Nazis, the city was full of cheap bars, flophouses and good-time girls. They loved making some extra cash on the side, and I was always on the lookout for models for my particular style of photography. I had a very large client list, including politicians. I couldn't get enough new material." He noticed Bill was grimacing. "What, you don't like looking at naked girls?"

"There is a difference between taking pictures of a paid prostitute and the kind of photos you took in Auschwitz, Klein."

"How? They earned the right to a better life. Better food, even alcohol. They were willing participants."

"They were forced to do whatever they had to, to survive."

"No different to most of the people of this city under the Weimar Republic then. Money was fast becoming worthless, no jobs, crippled economy and a government unwilling to sort out the problems. The whole country going to the wall."

"You and I both know there is a difference. How does this all fit into what you are doing here now for the fat priest?"

"Hasi? The useless fat shit."

"*Hasi*?" Bill repeated, surprised. Jack looked quizzically at him. "It's a pet name, like what you'd call your girl," Bill added, by way of explanation.

"That's just his nickname. It's sarcastic, as he's so repugnant."

"So, you are helping this Hasi with this ID business."

"I just take the photos and make the IDs, but you already know this. He pays well and I use the money to fund my other activities. He's working for some guy who runs the show and has the money and contacts apparently. Quite why this mystery businessman chose Hasi to work with, I'm sure, I have no idea."

"He's not really a priest then?"

"Ha! That fat prick would need some praying to balance out his past, I can tell you. I was unfortunate enough to meet him when I arrived at Ravensbrück in January of forty-five. We fled there just before the Russians arrived in April. Most of the others were captured, but I let Hasi hide with me at my parents' house on Lake Wannsee until it had died down a bit. I lost touch with him for a few months until he showed up one day with a proposition."

"And, what was that?"

"He had some deal with this mystery man who he said was protected by the cops. He said I could come back and run my father's print shop, in return for producing the ID documents they needed, and that I could do whatever work I wanted on the side with protection from the cops."

"So, Müller knows you and Hasi are ex-SS?"

"Of course, he knows."

"This ID racket, it's not to enable ex-Nazis to flee, is it? We know the new documents are genuine, and that the details are correct."

"There are a dozen forgers in this city who will produce fake ID for you to get to Spain. No, we are giving them their identities back."

"To prove they were Nazis?"

"Times change. Evidently, it's not the crime it used to be."

"What do they use these IDs for?"

"No idea. Get jobs as cops?" he ventured, sarcastically.

"Are they being recruited by the Americans?"

"Maybe. I never ask."

The sound of crackling glass broke the hanging silence as Bill was wondering what he ought to ask next. Jack moved quickly and silently to the edge of the bookcase. Bill peered out as best he could into the dark shop and could see a shadowy figure looking around the doorway and inspecting the wrapped rock that had done the damage.

He glanced back at Klein, just as the spindly pornographer pressed the little Walther under his own chin and pulled the trigger.

33

International Relations

Berlin, 28th February 1947

As Müller rounded the corner, Jack, well-hidden to the side of him, pressed his automatic into his temple.

"Jack, meet my acquaintance, Chief Müller," Bill announced.

"Ah, the bent copper," Jack replied.

"They don't come much more bent than this one."

Müller said nothing as he made his Luger safe, opened his creased cheap suit-jacket and placed it back into his expensive-looking handmade shoulder holster. He then shoved his large glasses back up towards the bridge of his nose and sat down, uninvited. He casually looked at the body of Klein, then followed the invisible path of the bullet up and into the splattered ceiling. No stranger to the aftermath of violent death, much like the other men in the room, the cop in him took over as he looked around the edge of the table and scanned for the spent cartridge on the floor.

"I have cops on their way down here now," he calmly stated, uncharacteristically.

"Sure, you do," Jack snorted and returned his gun to his jacket pocket.

"Until we can establish the facts, you will be under suspicion of murder. I don't like dead bodies appearing in my sector, and they keep showing up, thanks to you two clowns," he said, looking over at the lifeless body of Klein. There seemed to be very little blood, despite the hole in the top of his skull and the brain matter on the ceiling.

"Keep showing up? What are you implying? Had a busy week, have you?" Jack sarcastically replied.

"Yes, it's all very regrettable. I had other plans for your friend here," Bill said, half grinning. "Were you a fan of his ... work?"

"He was no friend of mine. Not my thing. If you ask me, he was a sick pervert, but I take my orders, and he was supposed to be allowed to carry on."

"He also gave us a potted history of his war service." Bill had a glint in his eye and started to feel like he was finally getting somewhere. He also knew he had one up on Müller and wasn't about to forego the chance to stick the boot in. "So, you were a camp guard too?"

"I guess the scrawny fuck talked, then, huh? Of course, he did." He nonchalantly shrugged, looking contemptuously at the slumped body. "A lowly camp guard?" he scoffed. "No. I was a fighting man. Spent my years on the Eastern Front. It was my second war. When I got evacuated back with frostbite, I returned to my role as a detective with the police, right here in Berlin."

"And, so they let you keep your job," Jack added, speaking to himself.

"The allies couldn't run a bath, let alone a city like Berlin. They have too much else to deal with. Mainly squabbling amongst themselves. They *need* men like me to keep order. Besides, an Iron Cross, First Class, and a *frozen meat medal* open doors in Germany, even after the Nazis."

"Men like *you,*" Bill repeated. The words sat like ash in his mouth.

"Mind if I smoke?" Müller asked and pulled out a pack of French cigarettes without waiting for a response. He carefully drew out a stick from the pack and offered them around. Both men shook their heads. Then, lighting up with a small silver lighter from his jacket pocket, he drew on it, expelled a stream of bluish smoke, and said, "I'm afraid to say you are both under arrest. There is no point in fighting this. You may think you have one up on me, but I can assure you that my employers know all about my past. You have no bartering chips here, gentlemen."

"You mean your sworn enemy, the Russians?"

"I don't have enemies anymore. Haven't you heard? The war's over."

"Maybe we'll just add you to the city's recent body count and chalk it up to bad luck in a bad neighbourhood," Jack suggested.

"Bad neighbourhood? Around here? We are surrounded by shops frequented by the cream of the French military, civil servants and diplomatic delegates. You won't last a day out there having killed the French sector's chief of police."

Müller suddenly stopped speaking, and the three men turned to watch a black-suited figure appear from around the bookcase. He had a loose-fitting baggy newsboy cap pulled down to the bridge of his nose. His face was cast in shadow, revealing only his wide, rounded jaw. Above his mouth was a thin, neat moustache. Between his lips sat a glowing half-smoked cigarette, surrounding him in a misty spectral aurora.

The tall, well-built, shadowy figure made his way towards Müller, who, to his credit, didn't so much as widen his gaze. He sat and smoked with barely a hint of concern. The shadow said nothing as he slowly paced the twelve feet to the workbench. His thumb carefully pulled back on the hammer of the old, police-issue, short, four-inch barrelled Webley revolver. He slightly raised his arm and pointed the gun at Müller, looking up as he did so to peer from below his floppy peaked cap.

The dull light of the room caught his features. They were the distinct features of a man with the face of Orson Welles.

"I don't think I will let you arrest anyone today, Müller."

34

The Lake House

Berlin, 9th March 1947

The lake shimmered in the morning sun like a cloak made of rose gold thread. Somewhere in the distance, a truck rattled by, and the sound of children's laughter broke the tranquil peace of the lapping water. Bill peered through the binoculars at the house. The lake-side property sat nestled in the raised, grassy bank. It was surrounded by birch trees that dotted in and around a large lawned area that led down to the water's edge. From there, long, spindly wooden jetties jutted out into the rippling surface of lake Wannsee, where small sailing boats bobbed gently in the slight swell.

"Is this the right place then?" Ronnie said, still on his back, his hat perched over his face.

"Well, it matches the description and location. It looks to me like Albie was spot on. It's a serious house."

"Mr Klein Senior obviously did well out of books."

"Among a lot of other things."

Bill continued to peer through the binoculars, pausing briefly to watch two young girls holding hands and paddling at the edge of the lake just to the side of them. The youngest of the two, who was perhaps twenty, smiled at Bill when she noticed him, and he smiled and nodded back, then resumed the stakeout.

Bill sighed and placed the binoculars gently onto the grass and pulled out his pipe. The weather had quite suddenly turned unseasonably mild. The light drizzle of the previous day had been some kind of signal to Mother Nature to turn up the thermostat. It was still chilly in the shade, but the clear sky and the warmth of the sun were a welcome relief from the cold front that had been hammering in from the east.

As he sipped on his pipe and cupped the warm briar bowl, a small sailing dingy came skipping along close to the coastline, sending out a little triangular wake behind as it went. The two girls giggled as the spotty youth waved at them from his little vessel. They then embraced each other in a kiss as if to taunt him. The young man almost capsized the boat in excitement, leaning back and fighting the tiller as the boom swung by his head.

Bill chuckled to himself and then picked up the binoculars to check again on the house.

"Anything happening?" asked Ronnie, now sounding half-asleep.

"Plenty, but nothing at the house."

The small mansion had an orange roof, with a large gable-ended dormer protruding from the centre. The central glass back door again had two smaller counterparts leading onto an outside patio area. The whole place looked like someone had placed a mirror down the centre. The obsession for accuracy and precision was so typically German. Bill hated it.

"Where's Jack today?"

"He has a prior engagement."

Jack was spending as much time as possible with Apolonia. His friendship with Fabian was also concerning to Bill. It seemed beyond usual networking. Perhaps it was their shared language. There wasn't much Polish spoken in Berlin, so maybe it was simple as that? Bill had kept back the description of the car he'd seen on the night of Irene's murder, though. Who had been the passenger that night? Anna had placed Jack with Fabian on the night in question. Jack was even seen leaving a short time before ... before. Bill couldn't make himself consider it. He shook the thought, and the image. The image that seemed seared onto his retinas.

Returning his gaze to the real world, the two girls slowly sauntered off along the coastline in the direction of the beach and lido to the north. Both had their arm around the other, hands resting on hips. Both girls were carrying their shoes and chatting. Young love. A small glimpse of carefree happiness, Bill thought. He smiled as he imagined how much the Nazis would hate to know that this soon after the war, the city was moving on, eager to forget their tyranny. Leaving the dark shadow of both oppression and war behind them. The next generations, he hoped, might just be a little more accepting than the last.

He took another peek at the mansion. "They're leaving," he said, nudging Ronnie, as he stood up and placed his hat back on his head.

* * *

The Officers Boat Club on Koenigstrasse was beginning to get busy. Numerous large German and American motorcars decorated the parking area at perfect angles like the lions in Trafalgar square. Ronnie stopped and admired a particular Ford with high-shined navy-blue paint and a ridiculous chrome bumper.

"I heard about these, but it's the first one I've seen."

"What? A blue Ford? They are all over the city. You want to keep your eyes open more."

"Not like this," he said, heading around the back for a 360-degree view. "It's one of those new Super Deluxes. Only came out last year."

"Looks exactly the same to me," Bill replied, gesturing at a nearby matt army-green Ford, complete with white star ID marking, "except it's got a stupid-looking giant chrome grille on it."

"You are such a philistine. For a man so in love with American hardware, I can't believe you don't recognise beauty when you see it."

"Does nothing for me." Bill shrugged. "Let's get on."

Ronnie nodded a final act of appreciation, then circled back around the car and rejoined Bill, who had walked away without him.

"Anything?" Bill asked him, as he drew level.

"No one. The man with the limp has disappeared again. I don't think he was following us after all. Just a coincidence."

"Do you believe in coincidences?"

Ronnie didn't bother to reply as they arrived at the main door. There was no security there at all, as promised. They could see through the doors and out the other side, where all the various attendees were busying themselves with ropes and various other boating equipment. Bill had no idea what any of it was called, how it was used or, indeed, where it went.

"How are your sea legs?" came a voice behind them.

Ronnie spun on his heels and blurted, "Where the hell did you appear from?"

"I'm a master in the art of surprise. It must be the *Cheyenne* in me."

"Ronnie, this is Deschamps. Deschamps, this is our friend, Ronnie." The two men shook hands.

Ronnie peered at Deschamps carefully. "When you said he looked like Orsen Welles, I thought you were pulling my leg."

"So, are you ready for this little expedition?" Bill asked.

Deschamps grinned at Ronnie's wonder and then turned to Bill and replied, "All set, they've gone. I've been watching the house already."

"You're sure there's no chance of American or police patrols?"

"They are all too busy preparing for the big handover. US Command is finally releasing its grip on Germany to the new European command structure. The Berlin office is coming under a lot of scrutiny. It's carnage over there with all the paperwork they have lost since the war."

* * *

"I thought you said we only have three hours."

"We do, let's save the pleasantries for afterwards," Bill replied.

Deschamps glanced nervously around, then said, "I'll head

back and make my way around to watch the house from the front. If there is any danger, I'll blow the horn and then try to distract, to give you enough time to get out. Head north up the lake's edge and I'll collect you later."

"Why don't we just threaten to shoot the old bastards and make them open it?" said Ronnie, bluntly.

"Always the subtle approach with you, isn't it?" Bill shook his head as they headed into the open rear door.

The large room was lavishly decorated with all manner of dead things. Taxidermy animal head trophies adorned every wall and stared at them in a kind of lifeless panic. Bill wondered if they were more worried about the intrusion into the property or just the mere fact they were dead.

The largest wall was covered in photographs of Mr Klein Senior posing with various people at glamorous events. Bill had a quick look but didn't recognise anyone. A few of the photographs were just landscape images taken around locations of the lake outside. One was even of the house from approximately where they had been observing a short while earlier.

The house was tidy, and the floors were immaculately swept. The wooden parquet flooring led them through to an immense entranceway. The hall was decorated with drinking horns, a couple of mounted shotguns and a large, ten-foot long, flintlock punt gun.

The grand sturdy oak door contained stained-glass panels, through which Deschamp's black car was just visible. The mottled panels either side of the door were made up by an ornated patchwork of lead. The obscured privacy glass flooded the hallway with light, helped by the triangular glass panels in the vaulted elevation. The whole room had the feel of a miniature cathedral.

They knew where they were heading as they climbed the stairs, entered the master bedroom and approached the giant wardrobe.

"We aren't going to get disturbed by the charlady or anything, are we?" asked Ronnie, having opened the doors of the wardrobe.

The giant green box within had a large golden brass cast crest featuring a British coat of arms, with the lettering proudly declaring it to be a Milners 212 thief-resisting safe.

"No, the Kleins insist on having all the help accompany them to church every Sunday. They won't be home until thirteen hundred hours."

Bill leaned in for a closer look, as Ronnie clanked down his canvas bag and started to rummage through it, extracting various tools.

"Did I get any change?" he asked.

"This stuff is expensive and hard to get in Berlin in only a few days."

"I guess that's a no then. How long will it take you to open it?"

"There are probably only a handful of people in this city that could open that safe. Most safe breakers would have that open in around three hours."

"That's going to cut it too tight."

"But I'm not most safe breakers," Ronnie proudly proclaimed. "I should have it open in two."

"You are wasted as a doorman at the Castle Club, Ronnie," said Bill, peering out onto the empty street below through the large window.

35

The Ledger

Berlin, 9th March 1947

The leather-bound book from the safe looked to be of the same type they had found on the bookshelves at the back of Klein's shop. Bill sipped his whisky as Deschamps scanned his way through it.

"I can't believe you managed to find seemingly the only bar in Berlin that has proper malt whisky," Bill said, swirling his glass and admiring the golden liquid.

"You aren't the only one with contacts, Bill."

Bill smiled and looked across the room, where Ronnie was now laughing heartily with his two female companions, and clinking glasses.

"I thought they had us for sure. You should have seen the way Ronnie managed to swan dive into the bushes at the last moment, carrying his tool bag under his arm."

"Do you trust him?" asked Deschamps, as he looked up

from the ledger, peering over his reading glasses.

Bill watched on as Ronnie lit up his giant cigar sticking out of his Cheshire cat grin as he held one of the girls around the waist and shared a joke with her.

"I don't have to. He doesn't know anything. Besides, I don't trust anyone. I have plenty of friends and acquaintances, but they all know what they need to know. No more," Bill answered as he tamped down the embers in his pipe bowl.

"And Jack?"

"He's my partner."

"So, you trust him?"

"If you'd asked me a few weeks ago, I'd say yes, he would be the only exception."

Deschamps thinned his lips and nodded slightly, then returned to the book. It amused Bill that his lips moved when he read. He wondered if he did the same when reading in his native French, too.

"This is the evidence we needed. We can't all share it, though."

"Well, quite," Bill replied. "We can't really use it to much effect either. That book could bring down governments. If nothing else, having that book is a death warrant."

Deschamps continued to read and, without looking up, nodded again. "We will have to treat this delicately. The payments and messages are all by dead drop, no face-to-face at all. They were definitely recruiting Nazis for the allies and getting rewarded handsomely for it. There are regular payments here from the Americans in return for information and men. Here is your Erich Grüning listed. Handed over to the US government in February. There are various other names I don't recognise, too. No direct fee is associated. Just the normal weekly payments, which are ticked off as collected from the dead drop on each occasion."

"So, like a retainer for services. And, we can assume the fat priest, Hasi, was the courier and bookkeeper?"

"I would say it's a fair guess. It's all in the same handwriting."

"The same handwriting as the notepad in the church," Bill added, talking to himself out loud.

"Notepad?"

"I found a handwritten note sending the other victim to a brothel by the Spree."

Deschamps nodded thoughtfully. "This is interesting though," he said as he spun the book around on the table between them. "Here," he pointed at the page. "Grüning has a black cross by his name, and the initials E.W."

"Ernst Witzer. Our man Misselwitz must have made the hit."

"He took him out. Tampered with the brakes, or whatever, because ..."

"He was known to be a Jew," Bill finished the sentence. "It figures it was him, he was at the scene of the crash. He was caught by the photographer, but it was the Americans who shut it down and blocked the publication. Why would they do that if they wanted to recruit him?"

"Misselwitz has the Yanks in his pocket?"

"We know he was working with Barbie, and the Americans protected him. Snatched him away out of our custody. Misselwitz could be a US agent, too. Maybe we need to go back to headquarters with all this, but I don't know if I can straighten out Irene's death yet. I haven't found her killer."

"I wouldn't hurry back to headquarters just yet," Deschamps added as he reached over and flipped a few more pages.

Bill looked down the page, and saw week-after-week of payments, stretching back to the previous summer, all ticked as *delivered* to the dead drop. The next was due the following day. In amongst the payments were a few sporadic entries of names, with handover dates, and into whose custody they were delivered. The last three deliveries were all names Bill didn't recognise, then he scanned the delivered-to column and saw a name that he definitely *did*.

"There's more," Deschamps interrupted, flipping a few more pages. "The Russians are in on it too. In fact, according to the ledger, the only people not involved seem to be the French."

As Bill scanned down the list, he saw the evidence in their hands was damning. He looked up at Deschamps. He realised he had been reading the lists upside down, too. The two of them just looked at each other for a few moments.

"Jesus," Bill said before flipping back to the British lists and double-checking he hadn't just imagined it all.

"So Misselwitz is delivering ex-Nazis into allied hands. For what purpose?"

"Scientists, police officials, intelligence, anything they need in this new Germany, I guess. Most of the top people from the old Germany were Party members."

Deschamps pondered a moment. He picked up his drink and inspected it up to the light, before slumping back more comfortably in his chair. "If only we knew where the dead drops were."

Bill nodded as nonchalantly as he could. He knew. He realised at that moment that he knew exactly where to find one.

There was a clatter of chairs and smashing glasses as Ronnie fell back on his chair. The other patrons all spun to look at the commotion. Bill quickly pulled some marks from his pocket and thrust them into the nearby waiter's hand.

"He's with us. That's to pay for the damages."

The waiter nodded and made his way to the bar.

As he watched him walk away, Deschamps added, "What are you going to tell Jack?"

"About all this? Jack knows everything he needs to know."

Deschamps nodded, somewhat solemnly, then continued, "Former soldiers can make good spies, too. Who better to report back all your secrets to your enemies than your best friend?"

Bill glanced across to watch as the waiter spoke to Ronnie, then back at Deschamps, who just stared blankly back at him and raised his eyebrows. He then looked back over at the shower of glass, blood and swearing.

Deschamps watched the subdued commotion. "Foreign Legion, wasn't he? They really will take anyone, won't they?"

"He's one hell of a fighter. Ex-crook, boxer, and much more besides."

"What did you have to pay him to open that safe, anyway?"

"Nothing. I just promised him tickets for the cup final in April. His team are in the semis in a couple of weeks." Then, changing the subject, Bill said, "I'm sorry for all that's happened. I think it may have been my fault. She must have tailed me and done her own investigating. I think Hasi was the man who killed Violette at Ravensbrück, and I believe she bribed Klein to tell her."

Bill pulled out the newly-developed image that they had found on one of the film plates in Klein's studio. It was a nude photograph of Irene, taken in the rear of the bookstore.

"She just couldn't let it go." Deschamps tried his best to

conceal his emotions, but there was a quiver in his voice. He stared down at the last photograph of Irene alive, then sharply and shakily, involuntarily inhaled.

"I think it was her way of doing right by her friend. It was a reckoning."

"Where the offence is, let the great axe fall."

Bill nodded and looked down at the photograph. "For what it's worth, I'm sorry. Not just for her death, but, well, you know."

Deschamps looked up, and in the clearest, calmest voice he could manage in the circumstances, said, "There was only ever one, Bill. We may have been married, but she only ever loved you."

36

New Ownership

Berlin, 10th March 1947

There was a certain chill in the air that the morning sun was struggling to extinguish.

An ugly-looking, olive-green staff car rumbled up to the gates opposite and waited as a US Army soldier came out and passed through a little personnel gate to check the occupant's ID papers. The white band painted around his helmet signified to Bill that the M1 Carbine he let haphazardly swing around his side was more for posing than firing.

The semi-brutalist structure of the barracks on Finckensteinallee was quintessential Nazi architecture. The twin red brick buildings of the entrance framed a larger two-story structure beyond, with mock-roman pillars that looked more like poured concrete than hand-finished stone. The glut of red brick, for some reason, reminded Bill of the grander, prettier, facades of Chiltern Street in Marylebone, London, but with none of the charm. As he gazed at this testament to National Socialism, he reminded himself how much he hated most of the buildings in Berlin.

The Military Police pretend-soldier finally handed back the ID documents and waved them through, as his two colleagues swung the gates open to allow the awkward-looking, drab-green Buick into the compound. The ghosted remnants of the imperial eagles on either entrance post betrayed the barracks' past as one of the main training bases for Hitler's elite bodyguard, the SS-Leibstandarte. The new signs declaring the base to be *Andrews Barracks* couldn't have looked more misplaced if they had hastily painted over the old iron swastikas with blue paint and added the new name with a child's chalk stick.

There was a second giant structure just round to the right, out of sight, they had observed on their way past on foot that was even bigger. That was the attraction to the various staff cars and uniforms headed to this part of the city. The famous swimming pool here was one of the largest in Europe. Built for training the Nazis' Aryan supermen. Oh, how he really hated it.

A small group of soldiers came striding down the street as a bus hissed to a stop at the intersection. Aboard was a group of student-aged girls who waved and grinned at them. The soldiers waved back as they continued their determined way towards the barracks.

Bill swilled the last of his coffee in the cup and threw it down his throat.

"At least the coffee is still good, even if the whisky seems in short supply."

"Whisky, tobacco and caffeine. Everything the growing

body needs."

"What about the mind?" Bill pondered aloud as he stared into the compound.

Jack sniffed dramatically. "Hate ... hate, and an enemy worth shooting at."

"I'll drink to that," Bill said, lifting his empty coffee cup and nodding.

The slim middle-aged waitress brought them two more cups of the strongest, blackest, coffee in Berlin. She smiled politely as she collected the chipped empty cups and then disappeared just as quickly. She had probably lost at least a husband, if not a son or two in the past few years, aside from whatever the Russians had put her through more recently.

"It's funny how life just goes on, isn't it? Whatever else happens, whatever the turmoil. Life goes on," Jack pondered.

"You have to get yourself right with the world first."

"That's the plan. An eye for an eye."

The two men nodded as they got lost in their own thoughts. Bill thought about Misselwitz. That day in Paris from his cell window as he watched him shoot what he thought was Jack. The way he smirked up at him, then coldly pulled the trigger. Bill didn't believe in demons and monsters, but this man was as close as it might be possible to get. He still didn't know for sure who killed Irene, but he had a pretty good idea.

He turned and looked at Jack. His partner. The man that on and off over the past six years he had trusted with his life. He recalled the gut-punch he felt as he watched the body drop to the ground and the crimson flood across the paved pathway on Avenue Foch, and the grey-uniformed monster that had put it there.

Bill turned back to the barracks as another staff car pulled up and squeaked to a halt at the entrance. Irene's face flashed across his mind. The smell of cordite had been drifting in the air of the apartment. The smell of violent death. The guilt he felt for leaving her alone. He wondered if she deserved such a fate. Perhaps they all did really.

"Remember that evening in St. James's?" Jack interrupted.

"I can hardly forget, can I?"

"The last time we were all together."

"Happier times," Bill said as he checked his watch.

Bill leaned back in his seat and tapped his coffee cup in a gentle rhythm with his fingers. The sky was bubbling up a storm. The short period of clement weather was now giving way to what looked like rain. The chill in the air had, mercifully, not returned.

"Do you think *they* are trying to find us?" Jack asked, looking up the street.

"Probably. It might surprise them to find us sitting outside one of the Amis' main barracks. This is the last place they'd think to find us."

Jack just nodded and sipped his coffee.

Bill's mind flashed through the past few weeks. He scanned his memory frantically, searching a series of snapshots like so many photographs in a flick book.

"The last place they would look," Bill said quietly to himself as he frowned and stared into the middle distance. "If you were Misselwitz, where would you be?"

"Somewhere no one would find me, I guess."

"Or, somewhere no one would look."

Jack stared blankly at him, puzzled.

There. He had found him. He could kick himself.

"Somewhere the cops don't go. Somewhere the cops

wouldn't go," Bill said as he stood and pulled out some coins and donned his fedora. "Keep a look out while I make a phone call. I know where Misselwitz is."

37

A Nice Day For It

Berlin, 12th March 1947

Bill stopped people-watching and looked quizzically at Jack.

"Photographs of the lake."

"What?"

"The photographs on the wall at the lake house."

"What about them?"

"There was a selection of various meet-and-greet-type photos, right? Pretty standard, I'd say."

"And?"

"Some of the others were of the lake outside. The same lake you can literally see out the glass doors behind you when looking at the wall."

"People are strange." Jack shrugged.

"I think they have been swapped out. Some particular meet-and-greets are less favourable now the war is over. The Kleins are known to entertain officers from the boat club at their regular candlelit suppers, and I think they are none too keen to let the Yanks know they rubbed shoulders with club-foot Joey and his friends, every chance they had."

"Goebbels?"

"So Albie said, anyway. Good friends, apparently. Klein was a party member in the early days, back when Hitler was just a beer hall rabble-rouser, by all accounts. Some even say he was at the *putsch* that got Hitler his jail time."

"I bet a lot of party badges got flung into Lake Wannsee in April forty-five before the Russians arrived."

Bill checked his wristwatch and then peered across at Ronnie. He was still sitting in the chair, pretending to browse the paper. From their angle, Bill had no clear view. He just hoped Ronnie was paying proper attention.

"I wish we had someone more reliable."

"He's a great bloke but he wasn't in the Legion for his crossword solving skills, that's for sure," Jack said with a chuckle.

A small group of people alighted the tram and spread in various directions. A well-dressed woman in her forties smiled provocatively at them as she passed in the direction of the train station. As she turned away, her large jaunty hat obscured her face. That didn't bother Bill, as it wasn't her face he was watching anyway. She clutched a little designer handbag and her hips swayed when she strutted. Bill watched her stalk her way out of view along the avenue.

"Nice day for it," Jack interrupted.

"I only wish it were, Jack," he sighed and took a large draw from his pipe. Returning his gaze to the window, he saw Albie carefully fold his newspaper and stand up.

"It's on." Jack leaned against the wall and narrowed his eyes like a hawk observing its prey.

Bill looked away and continued smoking. "What's happening?"

"Ronnie is heading to the exit … Our target is heading to the wall of boxes … Glancing around … Checking his pockets … Found the key, opening it now."

"Stay on it," Bill replied and, leaving Jack, walked off down the avenue.

Bill looked down into his hand at the little key he had taken from Irene's bedside drawer as he walked. The key to box ninety-four. In her last moments, as the life drained from her body, she had given him a clue. It was all she could do to help him. Killing Hasi and securing revenge for Violette had been her aim, and she had done her duty by their friend. Ensuring Bill could nail her killer appeared to be her last request. Bill knew this now. He still couldn't say for sure, even to himself, that he loved her, but his heart longed to see her again.

He risked a quick look through the glass as he saw Errington pocket the envelope and hurry back through the door he had emerged from, past the giant front desk. Ronnie walked casually out the main doors, barely even looking up, then made his way into a throng of pedestrians, busy in their own world.

"Hook, line …" Bill said to himself as he crossed the busy road.

As he headed north, the tram drew up to the stop, and he hopped aboard. It lurched forwards, fighting its half-seized brakes as it shook back into life. Looking back towards Jack as the tram passed, he watched a car pull up. Jack nodded and jumped into the impressive pre-war BMW roadster. In the last moments, before they were out of view, he saw Jack shake hands with Fabian, as the red car with the mismatched driver's door purred back into life and screeched a risky U-turn across traffic and made its way back towards the east of the city.

"... and sinker."

* * *

Bill puffed his pipe nervously, whilst Igor twittered away about nothing in particular as they walked. Bill wasn't listening as he attempted to play out the final act in his head. No matter how many times he had attempted one of Violette's infernal spidergrams, it had ended in him tearing it up. Like he ever needed a reason to turn to drink.

"Did you hear me, Bill?"

"What?" he snapped back.

"Sorry, I just wondered if you are sure about all this?"

"No, to be honest, Igor. I don't know if this will go down how I plan at all. I can't even promise you we'll all be getting out alive. Did you bring a gun, as I asked?"

As if to answer him, Igor pulled out a giant Broomhandle Mauser, complete with wooden shoulder stock from under his long coat.

"I said to bring a gun, not an artillery piece!" Bill shook his head. "And put it away for God's sake!"

"It's all I have." Igor shrugged and hid the cannon back under his armpit.

As they entered Anna's bar, Bill flipped the sign to closed, and they made their way down the stairs. He saw that they were the first to arrive.

The regular brunette barmaid beamed a smile as they entered and instinctively reached for two glasses, placing them on the bar. Although, there was nothing *regular* about her. She disappeared from view as she squatted behind the bar.

"Good to see you, Igor, how's the new job?" she enquired as she bobbed, pleasingly, back up.

"Better paid than the last one," he quipped as he grabbed at one of the glasses with a giant fist.

"Your German has certainly improved," she teased. "Even if the company you keep hasn't."

Bill raised an eyebrow at her, and she winked in reply. Bill remained transfixed by her green eyes if only to avoid staring at her half-open shirt. "I think it would be remiss of me not to ask if you would like to go out for dinner?"

"What makes you think I eat dinner, Casanova?"

"I know a nice place. They have the best food in Berlin. It's on me, of course."

"Well, it's been a while since I ate a decent piece of veal. Do you think they could manage that? Oh, and you'd better know that I only drink champagne."

"I bet you do. I'll see what I can do. Look, I am expecting someone for an important meeting, but I have a car waiting for you out back. A black Mercedes to take you shopping. I'll square it with Anna, don't worry. This should be enough for a new outfit." Bill passed her over a fold of US dollars.

"Wow, you *are* keen. I'm not a whore, you know. I'll not be kissing on a first date, and I want to be home by eleven."

"Of course. I expect nothing but your company for the evening."

She smiled and pushed the money down her shirt. "I'll leave

you the bottle," she said as she walked around the bar and leaned in close to plant a kiss on Bill's cheek.

Igor chuckled as he helped himself to the open bottle. Bill grinned his inane smile and watched her walk away. Her black stockinged legs crossed slightly as she walked. She paused a moment to look back at him, smiling with only her eyes, before heading through the rear door.

"So far, so good," Igor sniggered, with his glass at his lips. "She's dangerous that one, Bill."

"So I gather."

"She worked with the resistance in Austria. Killed a man with her bare hands, they say. She must have a hell of a grip."

"I hope so, Igor. I hope so." Bill laughed and slapped the colossal man's meaty shoulder.

As Bill knocked back his drink, in the large mirror behind the bar he spotted Errington appear in the doorway.

"Bill?"

"Take a seat, sir."

He looked hesitant.

Bill drew his revolver. "Please, I insist."

Errington's eyes widened as he quietly sat at the nearest table and placed his palms down on the top.

"So, I guess you think you know what is going on then?" Errington remarked.

"You have been paying Misselwitz and his gang of thugs and murderers to recruit former Nazis."

"It's government policy now, I'm afraid, Bill. Telephone Whitehall and they'll confirm. You are in way over your head. Your career with the government is over, you'll be in the shit for this."

"So, what's new? I'm always in the shit. It's only the depth that varies." Bill pulled out a pack of smokes and threw them onto the table, as Igor moved around and took Errington's small Walther out from inside his jacket. "I'm sorry it has to be this way, sir."

"Look, Bill, the order for this operation has come directly from Atlee."

"I know. I have already called London."

"So, what is this all about? You can't think I had anything to do with Irene's death? Remember it was me who set you two up together here," he reasoned as he lit up a cigarette between trembling fingers.

Bill watched him quiver and tremble like a worm in a science beaker. "I know you are not a soldier, Errington. You are quite safe from me."

"I was just following orders."

"Just following orders," Bill repeated. "The go-to excuse for an entire nation, and look where that got them." Bill snorted in disgust, as he poured himself and Igor another ice-cold vodka. "I think you know me well enough to know I don't make my move until I have all the facts. I have an interesting dossier of evidence in my possession. It confirms you have been recruiting former Nazis, under orders from the War Office, for British Intelligence. You were right about one thing though. There is a Soviet spy in our midst. You have also been collecting agents from Misselwitz on behalf of the Russians."

"They'll never believe you. You are making a big mistake if you share what you know. And, we both know that you aren't going to just shoot me, or I'd be dead already."

"Maybe I'm the one making the mistake here. Maybe not. With your connections, a call here, a favour there, you might well squirm your way out of this. They are unlikely to believe a mere agent accusing his commander of treason. So that's why I won't be the one bringing you in. When did you meet the Klein family?"

"The Kleins? How do you know about them?"

"I paid them a visit. More specifically, I paid a visit to their safe. A green Milners one. Identical to the one in your office. Not exactly common here in the Fatherland, are they? It's not the safe that nailed you, Errington. It was the ledger inside."

"Fucking German efficiency," he spat.

"I assume you know about their odious past?"

"Everyone in Germany has a past, Bill. Most of them are odious."

"The Kleins were at the pinnacle of Berlin society. Personal friends of Goebbels, early party members. I did a little digging. Mr Klein Senior had a gold party badge. You know what that means, right? One of the originals. Nazi through and through. How could you work with these people?"

"If you want to pick mushrooms, you have to crawl through the dirt."

The distinctive smell of Senior Service cigarettes entered the basement bar as the door carefully swept open. Bill hadn't seen Vera since the last time he left for France the month before D-Day in June of forty-four. She was wearing an immaculately tailored blue-grey tweed skirt suit with American-style black patent leather shoes. She plucked the cigarette from her lips as she entered and smiled at Bill.

"Sorry, I'm late."

"Bang on time, Vera. Drink?"

She shook her head and fixed Errington with her characteristic piercing stare. Errington turned and looked at her, then simply returned to face Bill and smoked his cigarette.

"Well, as you can see. I can also call in favours. Your place in the peerage may protect you, Errington, but Vera has the ear of the king himself."

"This is Igor, Vera. He is a good man and a valuable asset. He is at your disposal while you are in Berlin."

The giant Igor did the best impression of an agreeable human he could manage and smiled at Vera.

"Bill has told me all about you, Igor. We may have some work for you after this if you are interested?"

"Thank you, ma'am, I would like that."

"Very well. Take this prisoner upstairs and into the waiting car. I'll be back out presently, and we will travel to the Gatow aerodrome together. We'll sort you out with a decent meal and a bed for the night and do the proper introductions."

Igor turned to Bill and grabbed his hand in a vice-like clasp. "Thanks, Bill."

"I told you I'd pay you back. Stay lucky, Igor."

Errington looked at Bill as Igor grabbed him roughly under his armpit, said nothing, and then looked down as he was spun around and out the door. Vera walked across to Bill and leaned back at the bar next to him.

"I was quite enjoying my final few weeks at headquarters until you interrupted," she said, pouring herself a drink from the cold bottle, using Igor's glass. "Life's been pretty boring now it's all over. I traced all my girls, but there isn't a day that goes by that I don't blame myself."

"You can't think that way, Vera. It is what it is."

"I'd give anything to have them back home to their families, you know?"

"Thanks for everything you did for Violette. She'd be proud

of all you did for her, and to know the king himself has honoured her service."

"The things I've read and heard, Bill. I just … it's all just so …"

"I know. There is nothing to explain. You were an excellent agent, Vera. Not to mention the best detective I've ever known. Thanks to you, we know what happened to them."

Vera sipped carefully at her vodka, then pulled out another smoke and lit it with the table lighter on the bar.

"What about Irene? You think Errington could have done it?"

Bill put down his glass and turned to her. "No, but I know who did."

38

Early

Berlin, 12th March 1947

Jack came wandering down the alleyway around five minutes earlier than agreed and walked past the house with the red door, right over to the place where Barbie had killed the man with the moustache, Dale Bierhals. It was rare for Jack to arrive early. He was notorious for being late. Bill checked his watch again.

Jack sauntered casually into the little enclosed garden square and then spun around towards the alleyway, almost with his back towards Bill.

Bill drew his revolver and took shallow breaths as quietly as he could.

* * *

A few minutes had passed. Jack was standing as still as a statue.

Bill wondered if this was the reason that most men choose to smoke. It gives your hands something to do while you wait around for people. Bill suddenly wished he could have his pipe out and lit. He could, at least, feel the vodka coursing through his veins. He had considered asking Igor for his help but decided against it; it was bad enough he was risking too many lives already, especially as he only really needed to end one.

Bill carefully slid out of the doorway into the open. As he did so, he looked around the square at the overlooking windows. He couldn't see any movement or prying eyes. In Berlin, people tended to look the other way, anyway. The far side of the square, beyond Jack, was maybe two hundred yards away. With the little alleyway entering in the middle of the left side, that made it approximately one hundred yards Bill needed to cover, remaining largely out of sight.

Bill could hear footsteps coming along the alleyway. He had run out of time. He squatted and half-ran until he was about fifteen yards from Jack. He carefully pulled back the hammer of his revolver and winced to a click that sounded louder than if he had just closed the breech of a fifteen-inch naval gun.

Jack remained still. Bill raised his arm and aimed the little snub-nosed Colt, then gently rested his fingertip onto the front inside of the trigger guard.

39

The Final Act

Berlin, 12th March 1947

"Deschamps! What the hell are you doing back here? You are supposed to be watching the front!" Bill exclaimed as he pointed his gun at the ground and carefully de-cocked the hammer.

"There's a problem," he replied. "Müller must have tailed you. He's snooping around on the street, maybe a block away. I don't think he knows where exactly you went."

Jack turned to Bill and shook his head.

Bill rolled his eyes in response, then called out to Descamps, "He probably followed you. Now, get out of here before they show up!"

"Or perhaps he followed Vera?" Jack added.

"She can handle herself. Let's focus on the task at hand."

Deschamps didn't wait to be told twice and backed out of the alleyway and out of sight.

Jack looked up. "Is it me, or has it just got darker? It looks like rain."

"Quite fitting. Even the gods are angry."

"Contact, front," Jack muttered, returning to his previous forced-nonchalant demeanour.

Bill squatted back behind the small wall as Fabian's car pulled up to the curb at the end of the alley. Anna stepped out and walked around the back before the car purred away out of sight. She smoothed down her long red raincoat and then headed down the alleyway towards Jack.

"Have you been waiting long?" she called out to Jack as she approached.

"No, not long."

Bill stood behind Jack and moved forward, keeping his gun trained on her chest.

"Don't make any sudden moves, Anna."

"O *kurwa*!" she muttered to herself.

"Yes. *Kurwa* is about right," Jack replied to his fellow Pole.

Her eyes darted in every direction as she looked for an opening or some escape from the fate she knew awaited her. She was the fox, cornered in a hunt. Bill was conscious of the fact that Anna knew what she was doing. Service with the partisans during the war. She would not hesitate to kill him, given a chance. Unlike Errington, Anna *was* a soldier.

"Please, Anna, don't give me an excuse to shoot you," Bill pleaded. "I won't be taking any chances here."

The sky crackled with lightning, followed by an ominous rumbling as the heavens finally prepared to give way to the rain it had threatened over the last couple of days. The rumble echoed through the courtyard. Bill could feel it in his stomach as he moved close to Anna. Jack pulled out his own gun and moved around behind her.

"Just do it. Let's get on with it if you are here to kill me. I'm living on borrowed time, anyway."

"I should have put it all together sooner," Bill explained. "Misselwitz had to have help in the city. Somewhere to hide out like a rat in its nest while he sent out people to coordinate everything. He couldn't meet with everyone, of course. He needed a go-between. That's where you came in. Errington informed you of my presence in the city and helped you hide him away."

Anna narrowed her eyes and pouted, defiantly, like a toddler caught with her hand in the biscuit tin. Bill shook his head. At himself as much as Anna.

"I had assumed it was me you were trying to kill that night," he continued. "It wasn't, was it? It was Irene. She had gotten too close. You thought she was unpicking the threads to get to Misselwitz and his operation. It was a logical conclusion. I mean, she had already visited Katya right here and was hot on the trail of Klein, the pornographer. She was flying too close to the sun. So, you started to plot her murder. When she killed Hasi at the church, you made your move. You had Fabian drive you to her apartment."

Bill glanced over Anna's shoulder at Jack, who had his gun pointed at her back, then placed his own gun away and pulled out his pre-packed pipe. He charred the packed bowl and tamped the tobacco before a second light got the embers glowing.

"It took me a while to recall the ashtray in Errington's office. On one of my visits, there were lipstick-marked cigarette butts. Not particularly unusual. We have female agents too. But the pink colour, *that* pink colour," he said as he gently brushed her lips with his gloved hand, "is not at all that common."

"You are going to kill me over my pink lipstick?"

"It was the butts, too. It may not surprise you that British agents don't smoke Belomors. Then there is the ledger," Bill smirked. "You forgot how efficient the Germans are. Hasi recorded every transaction in a leather-bound book inside a safe supplied to the Klein family by Errington. The evidence against Errington was damning. It was clear how he worked to secure agents for the Russians. You may be relieved that your name was not even mentioned. The ledger, however, was bound recently. In a book-binding shop in Berlin. The only one that remains trading, to the best of my knowledge. The very same place that bound the elaborate visitors' book in your fine establishment, Anna. Bound for you at the hands of the skinny photographer with the penchant for naked ladies, Mr Klein Junior, the late SS officer of Auschwitz and Ravensbrück."

Bill nodded at Jack, then looked back at Anna and continued, "Despite you trying to plant the seed that it had been Jack all along, your biggest mistake was using your own gun to kill Irene. My contact in the newspapers obtained the coroner's report. I bet you didn't know there was a functioning forensic ballistics department in the British sector in Berlin, but they recovered a hundred grain, 7.62 mm pistol round, the type and calibre fired only from a Nagant revolver ... This one," Bill said as he held up the pistol he had recovered from Anna's room. "I also found this."

Bill held up the business card:

You have a friend at St.Bernhardt Church. All sins

cleansed. Escape in the arms of our Lord.

A clap of thunder sounded as large droplets of rain began to fall all around. They hit the ground with a force that sent the water back up as if it were trying to rain from both above and below simultaneously.

"You really think Misselwitz is hiding out in my place? Check all the rooms."

"I don't have to. I know he is not in your place, Anna. That was the most curious part for me. I couldn't fathom why you had helped me. The man with the moustache. The one you called the fairy. He wasn't, was he? A fairy, I mean." Bill puffed his pipe, pulled up the collar of his coat, and tipped his hat forward to keep the rain from his face.

"You knew that I had the note that directed him to you," Bill went on. "After speaking to an old friend, I finally identified our friend with the moustache. Dale Bierhals. An ex-SD officer and spy for the British government. He had been feeding intelligence back to the British since before the war. In thirty-three, he even joined the party. When war broke out, he joined the SS and worked in counter-intelligence with Klaus Barbie in Holland. That was his downfall. Barbie had been quite resourceful after the war and, whilst working as Misselwitz's patsy, unearthed Bierhals' credentials. Barbie killed him for attempting to infiltrate their sordid little operation here, along with a lot of other things."

The rain began to thin out into a steady fall. The sky lit up white like a photographer's flash, and there was now a delay in the steady rumbling as the lightning moved away from the city. Bill felt as if the beanpole, Klein, was watching from somewhere. An iniquitous voyeur from the grave.

"That was the final piece of the puzzle in the search for Misselwitz. That night. The night Bierhals was murdered. I was so shocked to spot Barbie in the crowd that adrenaline took over, and I chased him. I failed to notice the faces of the other men. The men in the doorway. The house with the red door. You assisted me when I enquired, for much the same reason that Errington and Misselwitz selected this place as the hideout. You knew the police were in your pocket already, or at least they took their direction from the Russians. You also knew I wouldn't have much appetite to go into a homosexual brothel in the Russian sector. Getting caught in there would take an awful lot of explaining."

Bill placed his pipe away and pulled out Anna's revolver again. Anna visibly flinched.

"I saw him. The night of Bierhals' murder. Misselwitz was among the men in the doorway. Right there," Bill pointed. "It's just the way my mind works sometimes. I collect snapshots of what I have seen but don't always notice the details until later. How am I doing?" he asked Anna. He smiled and held the revolver, pointing without aiming. She answered by closing her eyes, sending a single tear down her cheek. "One more thing you should know. Irene was not coming for you or Misselwitz. So, despite what Jack believes, coincidences do happen. Hasi killed her best friend at Ravensbrück. She was only trying to get to him. I'm pleased to say that, in that at least, she succeeded. She did not deserve to die. Not yet, and not like that."

The red door slammed open like another thunderclap and out walked Misselwitz. The pretty boy still had the chiselled glass jaw, but it was newly decorated with bruises. One eyelid was closed, and blood seeped down his face from the ruptured eyeball. He was followed out with Deschamps holding a gun pressed into his lower back.

"Thank you for joining us," Bill said. "Now, perhaps we might get some proper answers."

Misselwitz grinned, then exclaimed, "Heil Hitler," earning him a crack across the back of his head with the butt of Deschamps' pistol.

He was battered and bruised but not broken. The darkness of his soul was palpable.

Bill just laughed and moved past Anna towards him. "The shoe is on the other foot this time, Ernst. You are coming with me. You can expect to be in prison for a very long time. Think yourself lucky I'm not turning you over to one of the Jewish hunting parties operating in the North. Don't think it hadn't crossed my mind."

"I'll not be in custody long. They'll spring me out within days, just like they did for Klaus. You British are laughable," he spat.

Bill ignored him, then continued. "Why did you risk killing Grüning?"

The rain made the blood run down Misselwitz's face onto his white shirt, staining it in a cerise wash.

"He had it coming. He came to us for help, but we don't help fucking *Yids*. We took the money from the Amis and then made it look like an accident. Win-win."

"Who else were you working with? How did you square it with yourself and your vile politics?"

"It's just business. A means to an end."

"You'd better start being straight with me, Misselwitz. You have much explaining to do, and many questions need answering."

A single shot rang out as the bullet burst through Misselwitz's chest, sending bright red blood spraying across the wet ground. Bill almost jumped out of his skin. Misselwitz's dead body slumped onto the pavement. Bill looked in shock at Deschamps' still-smoking gun.

At the very same moment, he heard a commotion behind him.

Taking advantage of the sound and confusion, Anna had swivelled around, drawing a little Makarov pistol from somewhere on her person. Just as Bill turned to aim, she fired at Jack, who grimaced as he tried to dodge it. Bill fired but missed. The bullet ricocheted harmlessly into the courtyard behind. Anna now turned her gun towards Bill, who, despite still not having a good aim, began to squeeze the trigger again. His second shot hit her in the leg and passed straight through. She didn't flinch. They both reached the point of proper aim at the same moment. Their eyes locked for a split second as Jack fumbled for the Walther he had dropped.

Time seemed to stop. The futility of life and the certainty of death washed over Bill.

"Look after my girls, please, Bill," were her final words as a sharp, sickening crack sounded.

The bullet passed behind her eyes and buried into the wall. A chunk of bloodied skull span through the air in the following moment it took for the sound of the gunshot to reach them. Bill did all he could do at that moment. He winced and waited for the bullet from Anna's gun.

It never came. She had not killed them, though she'd had the chance. Jack shouted out in pain as he laid down on the wet ground. Anna collapsed down next to him.

"Where are you hit?" Bill called out with a voice that

wasn't his. The adrenaline had grasped him by the throat and crushed his oesophagus.

"In the arm. It missed the bone. Just a flesh wound, but Christ, it hurts. I'm sorry, Bill, I messed up."

"We're still alive, aren't we? Mission accomplished, I'd say."

Bill looked up at the far side of the quadrant, to the half-open window where he could now see Ronnie standing up with the scoped rifle still in his hands, and gave him a thumbs-up gesture.

"What was that all about, Deschamps?"

"Sorry, Bill. I couldn't tell you before, but Misselwitz was our guy. He had gone to ground, and we have been searching for him for the past few weeks. You weren't the only one looking for him, I'm afraid. He was only meant to be an informant. But unfortunately, once he had contacts in the French sector and the police, he went rogue and started his racket of recruiting his old friends. First for the Ivans, then the Brits and Amis."

"So, he was a French agent? No wonder there was no mention of *your lot* in the journal." Bill frowned and then said to himself, "Why didn't I realise that? The Yanks must have only been protecting Barbie. That's why they were putting pressure on Müller."

"We couldn't risk the journal getting out. We have it. It would look bad for everyone, especially back at the *Piscine.* Paris would have a lot of explaining to do, and this soon after the war. It could make relations turn sour. Things are on edge enough as it is. The last thing we need is for the Soviets to isolate themselves entirely. We'd lose the tactical advantage, and it would hinder the flow of intel. I'm sorry to say you've lost this one, pal. No one will ever know about Misselwitz or what went on here. Feel free to claim the kill for yourself. Or just let it go. The Berlin Police will probably do their usual hatchet job, and he'll go down as another unidentified *John* killed outside a brothel. We only wanted the journal, and to be sure Misselwitz didn't do any more talking to anyone. Least of all, the independent enquiry that's being planned to investigate him for war crimes. No one could know we had recruited him, then lost him for so long while he helped the Russians."

"So, Vera is dead too?" Bill pleaded.

"She's safe, Bill. Igor, not so much, I'm afraid. He took a bullet to the back in the confusion. An ambulance rushed him to the hospital, but he'll probably live. We didn't want to hurt them, Bill. We just needed the ledger back."

"What about Errington?"

"He was allowed to leave with Vera and her driver. That will have to be settled between your government, your king, your agency and your God. I'm sorry I couldn't tell you. It had to be this way. At least we got Irene's killer."

"So, you lied to me? You were not her husband?"

Deschamps shrugged. "Sorry, friend. I needed you to help us."

Bill placed his gun back in his pocket and tried to think of something clever to say. But, in the end, he settled simply for, "Fuck you."

He turned away from Deschamps before he got the sudden urge to put a bullet between his eyes. Instead, he carefully checked over Jack's wound.

"Barely a scratch. It's missed the artery. It looks clean. You'll be alright. Let's get you back to the British hospital before the Reds or Müller show up."

"Thanks, brother."

Bill removed his coat, emptied the pockets, and carefully placed it over Anna's body. He paused for a moment and sighed. The rain was still spreading a flood of watery, bright crimson blood.

"We'll leave all this for Deschamps to explain away." Then, Bill added, "Let's hurry up. I need to change. I might still be able to make this hot date in a couple of hours."

Jack shot him a look, snorted a laugh through the pain, and then said, "Forget the hospital. I need a drink. Take me to the bar."

40

Happier Times

London, 2nd June 1944

The week prior to their departure to France

Bill stopped and leaned on the bench by the lake in St. James's Park. The place looked like a hobbit's village, with seldom-used air-raid shelters dug into the landscape here and there. The sun was setting, and the sky was painted in a rainbow of subdued hues. Buckingham Palace was silhouetted against the cornucopia of colours that hung in the air. Somewhere, a nightingale chirped its happy song to the rhythmic sway of the trees in the gentle breeze.

He looked back to where Jack and Violette were giggling and attempting to balance on a line painted on the road surface of The Mall. Violette wobbled and almost fell. Jack saved her, holding her at her waist for the final few yards.

Violette had a mischievous laugh that seemed to grab you

and pull you into the joke, however you were feeling. Her quick cockney wit and endless stories of growing up on a farm in Northern France from an early age and then in South London were always popular among the agents at Baker Street.

Bill smiled as he watched them, knowing the three of them would soon be separated from her. He didn't know how he was going to break it to Lena that her best friend would be going to France with a different team.

"They are getting on well," Lena said, smiling as she watched them.

"So are we," Bill replied, putting his arm around her shoulders.

She turned and smiled warmly at him. "Whatever happens, you'll protect me, won't you, Bill?"

"Always."

Lena smiled and then rested her head on his shoulder as Jack and Violette trotted down the slope to join them in the park, both still laughing and holding hands.

At that moment, the war seemed to be a million miles away.

The life that I have
Is all that I have
And the life that I have
Is yours

The love that I have
Of the life that I have
Is yours and yours and yours

A sleep I shall have
A rest I shall have
Yet death will be but a pause

For the peace of my years
In the long green grass
Will be yours and yours and yours

* * *

Violette Szabó's memorised code poem.
Written for her by Leo Marks, one of SOE's code masters.

Thank You for Reading

I'd really appreciate it if you could leave an honest review wherever you bought this novel or via the links listed at **CraigWFisher.com/review**.

Any feedback will help the development of future releases.

In addition, please join my mailing list at **CraigWFisher.com** and follow me on Twitter @craigwfisher.

Acknowledgements

Thanks to Gerald Shaw for copy editing. Any remaining errors are my fault, not his. Thanks also go to my good friends Damian and Lizard for their contributions, plus everyone who read and reviewed early previews.

Special thanks to my mother, Tracey, for patiently reading endless sneak previews throughout the writing process and giving me helpful guidance and support.

Finally, thanks to you, reader. Without you, the characters have no voice, nor the work a purpose.

Historical Notes

The following section contains spoilers and should therefore be avoided until you have finished reading the story.

I have taken many liberties with the portrayal of the British Intelligence services and SOE for the purposes of narrative interest. For example, the entire operation involved code names for all operatives, teams, circuits, commanders, bases and locations. However, I mostly used only conventional names rather than bore the reader and overly complicate the plot with such things.

Coding and deciphering were a large part of operations in France but are only briefly referenced in the story. I recommend the book, *They Fought Alone,* by Maurice Buckmaster, for insight into the actual workings of SOE.

It is unlikely many agents knew much of each other or interacted at any length with the commanders.

SOE and its F Section were based at other locations during the war, not only at 64 Baker Street. The weapons, combat, escape, and evasion and commando training were carried out in various areas in Scotland, including Arisaig.

SOE finishing school was, indeed, based on the Beaulieu

Estate, Hampshire. The grounds of Beaulieu House are now home to the National Motor Museum, which includes an exhibition about the SOE training that took place there.

The Café de Paris was based on Coventry Street, Piccadilly, London, and opened in 1924. It was one of the busiest theatre bars that hosted jazz in England. Sadly, it permanently closed in December 2020, partly due to the Covid-19 pandemic.

The world famous La Coupole Brasserie on the Boulevard de Montparnasse, Paris, was opened in 1927. Its American-style bar and roaring twenties art deco decoration attracted the glitterati from far and wide. Famous patrons have included Pablo Picasso and Jean-Paul Sartre. It is still trading today.

The location at 84 Avenue Foch, Paris, was commandeered by the German occupation forces for use as the SD and Gestapo headquarters. Prisoners were frequently brought from Fresnes Prison, on the city's outskirts, for interrogation and torture. In addition, the SD often used captured radios and passwords to play what they called the *radio game* to flush out other agents in France.

The concentration camps (KZ - *Konzentrationslager*) of Ravensbrück, Dachau and Bergen-Belsen all existed in Germany, and their notorious and sad history would require an entire book of their own. Anywhere up to 190,000 people died at these three camps alone, including resistance fighters, SOE agents, political prisoners, and POWs, on top of the almost unimaginable amount of civilians.

Drancy internment camp in the suburbs of Paris was designed to hold around seven hundred people. Instead, at any one time, it housed more than seven thousand, including lone children whose parents had been sent directly to extermination camps. Between June 1942 and July 1944, more than 67,700 people passed through the camp and onto their deaths in places like Auschwitz and Sobibor. The site of the camp now houses a museum and memorials to what happened there.

French police carried out the Vel' d'Hiv' Roundup at the behest of the German authorities. As a result, 13,152 Jews were arrested. Around four thousand of them were children. They were held at the Vélodrome d'Hiver in cramped conditions with little food or water before being taken to Drancy, then in rail cattle cars to Auschwitz for their mass murder. After many years of denial of any responsibility by the French Government, an apology was issued in 1995. They finally admitted responsibility in 2017.

Despite the widespread knowledge of the practice today, only a comparatively small percentage of Nazi prisoners were tattooed in various places on their bodies. Mostly those used as slave labour in the Auschwitz sub-camps of Birkenau and Monowitz throughout 1941-43. The serial numbers used indicate around four hundred thousand people were forcefully tattooed to aid identification.

Many books have been made on the history of the camps of Auschwitz and the dehumanising, suffering, torture and death that happened there. More than a million people perished. It was organised killing on an industrial scale, and one of the true lasting legacies of the Holocaust, all of which must never be forgotten.

The Battle of Berlin lasted a little over two weeks at the end of April 1945. The Soviet forces totalled at least two million, plus around two hundred thousand Polish troops. They outnumbered the Germans by more than 2:1. The dead, casualties and prisoners taken were massive. No one knows the exact number, as in the mayhem, very little was documented, but it was possibly eight hundred thousand killed, wounded or captured. Most of the German prisoners would ultimately die in captivity under the brutal communist regime, some of them, many years later.

The Red Army carried out a reign of terror on the civilian population in retaliation for the invasion and years of war. Around 130,000 women were raped in Berlin alone, often multiple times by numerous assailants. The suicide rate among them was more than ten per cent. Almost no one was spared. The Soviet soldiers violated all in their path, not just young women, but very young girls and even old women in their seventies and eighties.

Across the Russian campaign in Germany in 1945, at least two million women were violated. Sexually transmitted diseases reached pandemic levels throughout the Soviet-occupied areas, including Poland, Czechoslovakia and Germany.

The Castle Club existed at 19 Kaiser-Augusta-Strasse. The Victory Club was a short distance away, on Dorfstrasse, and was a bar classified by the US military as being for *Colored Troops*. The nearby main route of Berliner Strasse was renamed in 1949 and is now known as Tempelhoffer Damm.

The US Officer's Boat Club on Koenigstrasse was later called the Wannsee Yacht Club for soldiers and diplomats to relax off-duty and enjoy the waters of the Grosser Wannsee. Today it is called the Potsdamer Yacht Club, and a short history is on its website (in German only).

St. Hedwig's Cathedral was rebuilt in the 1950s and still stands near the State Opera House in what is now called Bebelplatz.

The swimming pool on Finckensteinallee was originally constructed for the training of SS recruits, particularly the SS-Leibstandarte, the personal guard regiment of Adolf Hitler, and later used by the US military. This fine example of National Socialist architecture received listed protection in 2001 and, after extensive renovations, was opened to the public in 2014.

Following the end of World War II, the trees of the famous Tiergarten were felled for fuel, and some statues were secretly buried to protect them from destruction. They were only rediscovered in 1993.

The 7800th Infantry Platoon was an honour guard consisting only of black soldiers based at Tempelhof Airport, Berlin. They were handpicked and often used for propaganda purposes to impress visiting dignitaries. Whilst Berlin officially had no segregation laws, the US military was keen to keep the so-called *Colored Troops* contained within their own drinking establishments, regardless of rank, even listing the permitted bars and clubs in the official city guides for their forces. Black servicemen found in other premises, whilst allowed under German and US Sector law, were often forcefully and violently removed by Military Police.

The US military capped black troops at ten percent after the end of hostilities to ensure their ranks stayed overwhelmingly white and was not officially integrated until 1954. But it was not until 1965 that the US government finally abolished the Jim Crow segregation laws back home in the USA. In reality, though, black servicemen faced a much longer fight to be assigned much more than menial labour and driving roles until well into the Vietnam War.

I recommend the New York Times article, *When Jim Crow Reigned Amid the Rubble of Nazi Germany*, by Alexis Clark (19th February 2020), for further insight on the topic.

On top of my own first-hand knowledge of Berlin, I frequently consulted a copy of the *1945 US Sector of Berlin - Information for New Arrivals* pamphlet, which, along with others covering a period up to 1958, have been painstakingly compiled and are available in the book *Berlin - in Early Cold-War Army Booklets* by T.H.E. Hill.

* * *

Violette Reine Elizabeth Szabó GC was born in Paris, the daughter of a British Army driver and a French dressmaker. Shortly after the First World War, the family moved to England. Whilst serving in the Women's Land Army in 1940, she met her future husband, the Hungarian Étienne Szabó, a decorated NCO serving with the French Foreign Legion. He was killed in October 1942 at the Second Battle of El Alamein, having never met their four-month-old daughter. Violette Szabó was later recruited into the SOE.

Her first mission in April 1944 was to assess the damage to the network after arrests in France. Having parachuted into Cherbourg, she went undercover as a commercial secretary and travelled to Paris for a final briefing after visiting Rouen and Dieppe. Her intelligence reports on German manufacturing were vital for identifying targets for allied bombing sorties.

Her second mission on the night before D-Day resulted in compromise a few days later. At a German roadblock, she and a resistance fighter named Jacques Dufour jumped from their Citroën car, and a gun battle ensued. Jumping a gate and crossing a field, they ran up a hill where Szabó fell and twisted her ankle. Urging Dufour to continue without her to safety, she took cover behind a tree and gave covering fire with her Sten submachine gun. With eight full magazines, she managed to hold off the Germans for thirty minutes until her ammunition ran out. She killed at least one and wounded several others.

Upon capture, she was imprisoned at Fresnes Prison and subsequently tortured by the SD at the Gestapo HQ at 84 Avenue Foch, Paris. In August 1944, she was moved to Germany with other prisoners, including other SOE agents. After a terrible eighteen-day-long journey with no hygiene facilities and very little food, Szabó arrived at Ravensbrück concentration camp.

Her time there is worth further reading, but suffice to say, she was put to work, like the other women there doing hard labour. Her time was spent planning escape and comforting other inmates. She even saved the life of a fellow prisoner, a Belgian resistance courier called Hortense Daman. Wearing only summer clothing, sleeping with no blankets, and suffering awful physical and psychological abuse, her time at Ravensbrück was brutal.

On or before 5th February 1945, she was executed by

an unknown guard, with a bullet to the back of the head while kneeling. Her body was disposed of in the camp's crematorium along with two other SOE agents, Denise Bloch and Lilian Rolfe. Violette Szabó was murdered when she was only twenty-three years old.

On 17th December 1946, her five-year-old daughter collected her posthumous George Cross, Britain's joint highest award for gallantry, from King George VI on her behalf. In 2015, she arranged the sale of her mother's medals and other memorabilia to secure their future custodianship. With buyer's commission, the sale price totalled £312,000—a record for any George Cross. Violette's medals are now on public display in London's Imperial War Museum.

A blue plaque honours Violette Szabó's service and marks her former home at 18 Burnley Road, Stockwell, London, SW9 0SJ.

Colonel Maurice James Buckmaster OBE was head of F (France) Section of SOE and instrumental in building Churchill's desire for a *ministry of ungentlemanly warfare* in France. A graduate of Eton and Oxford, he commanded F Section for most of its history. He worked undercover in France in the autumn of 1944, giving speeches and lectures as an opportunity to wrap up F Section's operations personally.

After the war, he worked in PR for the Ford Motor Company. He also assisted in movies and wrote various articles and two memoirs of his time with military intelligence and the resistance movement. General Dwight D. "Ike" Eisenhower credited him and his work for helping to shorten the war by six months. He died, aged ninety, in Forest Row, East Sussex, on 17th April 1992.

Vera Atkins CBE went to great lengths to conceal her Jewish heritage while at SOE. Despite almost single-handedly managing the thirty-seven female SOE agents, she was generally treated with mistrust at Baker Street, except by Colonel Buckmaster.

After the war, she went to great lengths to find out what had happened to her *girls*, as she lovingly referred to them. As well as tracing almost all the 118 missing F Section agents, Atkins uncovered the circumstances of the deaths of all fourteen of the missing women, twelve of whom had perished in concentration camps. Due to Atkins' efforts to record their bravery before capture, almost all the dead women received posthumous official recognition from the British government, including a George Cross, the nation's joint highest award for bravery, for both Violette Szabó and Noor Inayat Khan. There would also be a GC for Odette Sansom, who survived the horrors of Ravensbrück concentration camp. However, despite official recognition by foreign governments, it wasn't until 1997 that the British finally awarded her a CBE. She is rumoured to be former intelligence officer-turned-author Ian Fleming's inspiration for the character of 'Moneypenny' in his James Bond books.

After a life of service with the UNESCO Central Bureau for Educational Visits and Exchanges, the Romanian-born Vera Atkins died in Hastings, Kent, on 24th June 2000, aged ninety-two.

William Ewart Fairbairn and **Eric Anthony Sykes** served in the Shanghai Municipal Police, with Fairbairn having previously served in the Royal Marines Light Infantry. Fairbairn and Sykes' names became synonymous with the commando dagger they designed. The men were recruited to train commandos and special forces in early 1940. Their Close Quarters Combat System was based on a mix of jujitsu and boxing. Fairbairn published the methods in the book *Defendu* in 1926.

Together the men taught their form of gutter fighting using hands, feet, bayonets and pistols, with Sykes' trademark addition, *and then kick him in the testicles,* at the end of every lecture throughout the early part of World War II. It has been speculated that Fairbairn may be the inspiration for the James Bond character, Q. Their F-S knife is not only still in use today, but it has also become the iconic insignia of British commandos.

Nicole Minet was the *nom de guerre* of Simone Segouin. Aged seventeen, she joined and served in the *Francs-Tireurs et Partisans* group, participating in numerous perilous missions, often alongside **Roland Boursier**, whom she called 'Lieutenant Roland'. She was featured in *Time* magazine at the liberation of Paris in an article called "The Girl Partisan of Chartres". Her photographs with an MP-40 became among the most famous of the liberation. After the war, she worked as a paediatric nurse, and she and Boursier went on to have six children together.

Klaus Barbie played a pivotal role in the Holocaust, arranging the capture, transportation and murder of Jews, Freemasons and other peoples considered undesirable by the Nazi regime. After a leading role under Adolf Eichmann in Holland, he set up and ran the Gestapo in Lyon, France. Among others, Jean Moulin was captured in Lyon by Barbie and delivered to Ernst Misselwitz in Paris, whom he knew well and often worked alongside. In addition, he frequently arranged transportations of prisoners to death camps, most notably the Rue Sainte-Catherine Roundup, and carried out so-called *anti-partisan police actions.*

After the war, he was recruited into the United States Counter Intelligence Corps. He worked in anti-Marxist operations and as a spy to identify fellow Nazis among other allied intelligence services. Then, in 1951, the Americans helped him escape to Bolivia after the French sentenced him to death for war crimes.

Whilst in Bolivia, he collaborated with the totalitarian nationalist government, instructing and assisting the president's paramilitary forces in the arrest, torture and murder of their opponents. He worked with various dictators throughout his time in South America, assisting with coups and anti-communist activities and even assisted Pablo Escobar's drug activities.

In 1965 the West German intelligence service, the BND, also recruited him as an agent. Eventually identified by Nazi hunters in Bolivia in 1971, it wasn't until 1983 that he was finally extradited to France to stand trial.

Although he had been previously sentenced to death in absentia twice, capital punishment had been abolished in France in 1981. Barbie died of cancer in prison in 1991 after serving only four years behind bars. *The Butcher of Lyon* remained a staunch anti-Semite and fanatic believer in Nazi ideology to the end. Historians estimate he was directly responsible for the deaths of up to fourteen thousand people.

Ernst Misselwitz was running Section IV E (the anti-spy

bureau) by the time of the liberation of Paris, having taken over from the previous commander, Josef Kieffer. He was involved in the torture of prisoners there, including Pierre Brossolette and the then head of the Resistance in France, Jean Moulin, whom he tortured alongside Klaus Barbie. In early 1946, after turning himself in to the French in Northwest Berlin, he was interrogated but ultimately recruited into the French secret intelligence services. This was unknown to the French courts in Paris, who later sentenced him to five years imprisonment for the torture of Brossolette. His whereabouts, or place of death, remain unknown.

Glossary of Terms

- **Allied Occupation Marks** - Also known as the AM (Allied Military) Mark - The only legal tender in Berlin from 1944 until the Soviet blockade of mid-1948.
- **Ami** - German Slang - An American. A shortened version of *Amerikaner.*
- **Au contraire** - French - On the contrary.
- **Babushka** - Russian - Old woman or grandmother.
- **Baker Street Irregulars** - Nickname of the Special Operations Executive (see also SOE), after the fictional gang in Arthur Conan Doyle's *Sherlock Holmes* novels.
- **Baton** - A type of club-type truncheon weapon. From the French, *bâton,* meaning stick.
- **Beer Hall Putsch** - Failed coup d'état by the Nazi Party against Germany's Weimar Republic government in 1923.
- **Belomors / Belomorkanal** -Brand of cheap Soviet-era Russian cigarettes, still in production today.
- **Bent** - British slang - Morally crooked and corrupt.
- **Bloke** - English slang - A man.
- **Boche** - Slang - A derogatory term for a German.
- **Bon Chance** - French - Good Luck.
- **Bordelle/s** - French brothels.
- **Bratwurst** - A popular type of German sausage.
- **Broomhandle Mauser** (See Mauser)

- **Bull** - Slang - Policeman.
- **Cheyenne** - Indigenous people of the Great Plains in what is now the USA.
- **Coffin Nail** - Slang - Cigarette.
- **Colt** - American firearms manufacturer.
- **Cognac** - French luxury brandy from the wine-growing commune of Cognac.
- **Copper** - British slang - Policeman.
- **Croix De Guerre** - French military decoration, most often awarded for heroism in combat.
- **D-Day** - 6th June 1944 - The allied invasion of Normandy.
- **Derrière** - French - Behind.
- **Deutscher Volkssturm Wehrmacht** (See Volkssturm)
- **Dunkel** - A type of German dark beer.
- **Eau- de-vie** - French clear fruit spirit. Similar to German schnapps.
- **Ersatz** - Product used as a substitute, typically an inferior one, for something else.
- **F (France) Section** - SOE's Operational command for missions in France.
- **Fairy** - A homosexual man. Derogatory slang, but in common use in colloquial parlance at the time of the story. In German, the word *schwul* is used similarly.
- **Feldgendarmerie** - German military police.
- **Fritz** - Slang - Derogatory term for a German man.
- **Frozen Meat Medal** - German Winter Battle in the East Medal - Awarded for service on the Eastern Front between 15 November 1941 to 15 April 1942.
- **Führer** - German - The NSDAP Leader, Adolf Hitler. Literally means leader.

- **Gendarmes** - French paramilitary police.
- **George Cross (GC)** - Britain's highest decoration for acts of gallantry and conspicuous courage in circumstances of extreme danger, not in the presence of an enemy. Equal in stature to the Victoria Cross.
- **Gestapo** - Nazi secret state police.
- **Gulag** - Russian labour camp where most prisoners were starved or worked to death.
- **Hasi** - German - Informal name between lovers, akin to *darling* or *honey bunny*. From the German words for hare or wild rabbit.
- **Hoi polloi** - Proletariat. The masses, the common people.
- **HQ** - Headquarters.
- **Ike** - General Dwight D. Eisenhower, Supreme Commander of the Allied Expeditionary Force in Europe.
- **Intel** - Intelligence.
- **Iron Cross** - Eisernes Kreuz (EK) - German military decoration with Prussian origins, awarded mostly for bravery in battle. Only holders of the standard second class award were eligible for the first class variant.
- **Ivan** - Slang - A Russian.
- **John** - Slang - Client of prostitutes.
- **Kubelwagon** - Small engined German light military vehicle, similar to an armoured Jeep.
- **Kraut** - Slang - A German. Due to their penchant for eating sauerkraut.
- **Kurwa** - Polish - Used colloquially as *fuck* is in English. Literally, though, means whore.
- **Luckies / Lucky Strike** - Brand of American cigarettes.
- **Luger** - German toggle-action semi-automatic pistol.
- **Marks** (See Allied Occupation Marks)

- **Mauser** - German firearm manufacturer, including the C96 known as the broomhandle, due to its ribbed cylindrical wooden hand grip.
- **Military Cross (MC)** - A decoration for bravery in the face of the enemy. At the time of the story was for officers only (with other ranks being eligible for the Military Medal). Second only to the Victoria or George Cross in order of precedence and stature.
- **MP-40** - German sub-machine gun.
- **Nagant** - Russian firearms manufacturer.
- **Nail** (See Coffin Nail)
- **NCO** - Non-commissioned Officers, such as corporals and sergeants.
- **Nom de Guerre** - French - An assumed name under which a person engages in combat.
- **NSDAP** - Nationalsozialistische Deutsche Arbeiterparte - (National Socialist German Workers Party) - The Nazis.
- **Occupation Marks** (See Allied Occupation Marks)
- **Pan-Pan / Panhard 178** - A four man French reconnaissance 4x4 armoured car.
- **Panzerfaust** - Single-use anti-tank rocket launcher.
- **Pied-à-Terre** - French - Property for occasional use. Literally *foot on the ground.*
- **(La) Piscine** - French - The Swimming pool - nickname of the French Intelligence (SDECE) agency's headquarters in Paris.
- **Pips** - The term used for the insignia of officer ranks in the British Army.
- **Pomme De Terre** - French - Potato.
- **POW** - Prisoner of War.
- **Prefect** - An older, senior boy at a school, given extra

responsibilities, including discipline among younger pupils.

- **Putsch** - (see Beer Hall Putsch)
- **Queer** (see Fairy)
- **Rendezvous / RV** - French - A meeting at an agreed time and place.
- **RSHA** - Reichssicherheitshauptamt - The Reich Security Main Office.
- **S-Bahn** - Rapid railway transport system around Berlin (see also U-Bahn).
- **Schmeisser** (see MP-40)
- **Schnapps** (See Eau- de-vie)
- **Schnitzel** - Dish of fried, breaded, thin meat cutlet.
- **SD** - The Sicherheitsdienst des Reichsführers-SS was the intelligence agency of the Nazi Party. A sub-division of the SS.
- **SHAEF** - Supreme Headquarters Allied Expeditionary Force - The command group of the allied advance.
- **Szkop** - Polish Slang - Contemptuous term for a German, especially a soldier.
- **SMG** - Sub-Machine Gun.
- **SOE** - Special Operations Executive. Churchill's WW2 Secret Ministry of Ungentlemanly Warfare. He famously ordered them to *set Europe ablaze!*
- **Sortie** - Mission carried out by military troops or aircraft.
- **SS** - Schutzstaffel - was a major paramilitary organization under Adolf Hitler and the Nazi Party.
- **Sten** - A very basic select-fire blowback British submachine gun.
- **Stogie** - Slang - Cigar.
- **Strasse** - German - Street.

- **Swan Vesta** (See Vesta)
- **Tail / Tricks** - Euphemism for prostitution. Offering sex in return for payment. Referred to as *selling tail* or *turning tricks.*
- **They** - Euphemism used by the military and security services to refer to faceless or mysterious operatives. In this novel, refers to the commanders at headquarters.
- **Trench Coat** - Long coat, often made of waterproofed cotton. Originally worn by the military, but later developed into a fashionable civilian garment.
- **Truncheon** (See Baton)
- **U-Bahn** - Berlin rapid underground transport system (see also S-Bahn).
- **Uncle Joe** - Joseph Stalin.
- **Ushanka** - Traditional Russian fur hat.
- **USAAF** - United States Army Air Force.
- **Vesta** - Type of strike-anywhere match, most commonly produced under the Swan brand.
- **Volkssturm** - A national militia established by Nazi Germany during the last months of World War II.
- **Walther** - German firearms manufacturer.
- **Webley** - British firearms manufacturer.
- **Wehrmacht** - German regular forces.
- **Weimar Republic** - Germany's government 1919-33.
- **Weissbier** - Popular German cloudy wheat beer.
- **Woodbine** - Popular English cigarette.
- **Yalta Conference** - February 1945 - Meeting of the heads of government of the United States, the United Kingdom, and the Soviet Union to discuss the postwar reorganization of Germany and Europe.
- **Yank** - British Slang - An American.

- **Yid** - Slang - Derogatory term for a Jew. Short for Yiddish.

Made in United States
North Haven, CT
07 November 2023

43725671R00217